To the love of my life!
Thank you for making all this possible, for the
support and the love,
for being the best husband and father.

Thank you most for being my
happily ever after!

Trigger Warning

** Attempted sexual assault, violence off screen, aggression, violence, graphic language, sexual content

I wouldn't consider any of these strong, except open door, 5 pepper romance scenes. However, being a mafia romance, there are obviously certain levels of violence and language.

I hope you enjoy Kris, our villain of circumstance, fighting for love. ♥

Prologue

Kris

"You sniveling little weasel!" Jon's knuckles snap across Doc's cheek, not caring about leaving a visible bruise. If the damn doc would just do what's good for him!

Shit! I'm fed up with my life! I must be if I'm freaking bored to death watching Jon give it to the doc. So much of my life in the inner circle… Is this worth it? All year, I've been out of sorts. But I can't put my finger on why.

Discontent boils in my blood… constantly.

It's affecting everything. My efforts have hit rock bottom. My damn conscience is pissing me off. But what else can I do? I've played the damn role for so long. And I do it well.

Intimidating badass is who I am. The personality is so engrained that I can literally warm the wall—like right now—and still scare the shit out of people.

At least, I have since puberty.

In one year, I grew a foot in height and added four inches to my biceps. Even that defensive sixteen-year-old would run if he could see me now. He witnessed the battle for hierarchy and accepted it as my life. My only option, after losing my parents.

Now I'm the bully I hated growing up, the angry brute.

Conditioning at that early age proved my worth against other low-lives in the organization. Only, in my head, I never included myself in the cattle-call of corruption. I survived.

Except, after Dixon split ranks, I realized how divided gang loyalties were. Rougher men went with the Georgia boys. Others stayed in Tennessee under Dixon's leadership, including me. With no other path to follow, I bulked up, winning beating after beating until my reputation solidified as one hell of a brawler.

Another slap of skin jerks me back to reality. Is that my problem? Has my reputation worked me out of a job?

Like here with the doc... I cross my arms, scowl, and my muscles do the rest.

He's the sort I scare without lifting a finger. Growl with just enough dragon temper seeping through and the weaker ones always wet their pants. A smart target will spill the intel long before I need stain remover to get their blood out of my clothes.

That's standard M.O. for the doc. He's a snitch.

Now, eyeing the doc, I hold my stance against the wall, lowering my voice so Doc feels the threat. "Look... The only reason I won't let Jon-Boy beat your ass is because I owe you one. But Doc... Fuck man, I'm losing patience."

He's skating on thin ice, the shit.

Worse... That weaselly voice scratches my eardrums with every half-assed excuse falling from that smarmy mouth. I'm so far past giving a shit. I'm ready to get home!

It's a rat-hole. My dragon's complaint irritates my headache, stacking on top of Jon's skinny ass hording in on my shift.

Shut up! It is what it is.

My little apartment is all the peace I get. It doesn't matter though, because Dixon ordered us not to leave until Doc ups his quota. And since Jon-Boy's getting all heavy-handed, without my level of smooth intimidation, we're going to be here all night.

Hell, watching him work over the doc is damn near excruciating. My blood pressure skyrockets the longer his adolescent ignorance delays my head hitting the pillow. Doc's crying more than he's talking now. That's goddamn useless. Rookie!

Why the hell is this runt my underling?

I've learned to shut my mouth over the years, let people dig their own graves. JB's done the opposite. That kid works those new nineteen-year-old muscles to bully his way up the ranks. He hasn't figured out his recent promotion from collections is thanks to him being the boss's nephew, not any actual skill. I've gritted my teeth for weeks now, dealing with his shit. So far, I'm not impressed. JB's rage has no finesse. At least not by my standards, nor Dixon, who trained me.

My main concern now is preventing this goof from getting us exposed... or killed.

"That's enough!"

Finally, I shove off the wall and stalk to where Jon holds the doc by his shirt collar. My heavy boots echo, elevating the tension in the room as I take him in. "Should I take over for the kid, Doc? He's half my size and half my piss and vinegar."

Jon scoffs, and it's hard not to laugh at them both. Doc's knees trembling, and Jon's rage almost making him drop the doctor on his butt. I manage... barely.

"Look, Doc. I owe you a solid for the bullet you pulled out of me. For that, I'll give you another week. But Dixon won't wait long. You get that?"

His head bobs, but JB has other ideas. The idiot interrupts my threat to slam the doctor against the door. His head ricochets off the flimsy wood, his eyes dazed with confusion... again. "Listen here, old man. Ya either clean more dough through this sham of an office, or our next visit's gonna end a little diff'rent. Got it?" His fist lands under Doc's jaw, drawing a cry of pain that bugs me more than it should.

What the hell is happening to me?

Jon chuckles when the broken man wobbles to the floor like a medical rag doll. "Knock it off!" I bark, eyeing the bastard. My conscience is pissing me off. Still, I fist the vet's scrubs and lift his slouched body, depositing it behind his desk with all the care of discarded trash. It's all part of the game. "Let's get out of here," I say to Jon, ignoring his confused expression.

You don't like my tone. Get over it. It's like the boy can't fathom why I don't share his sick enjoyment over pounding the doc. Jon knows better than question rank, though.

He stomps for the door. "People always mess with my fun. If I were—" His voice cuts off the second he yanks Michaels' door open. In one breath, I know. JB's temper is the least of my worries.

An agitated heartbeat weakens down the hallway, retreating. The scuffle of feet in the next room, coupled with the lingering fear souring the hallway, and... shit! JB's out the door, pursuing the sound before I catch his intentions.

My reflexes snap and I dart after the kid, catching him right before he turns the corner for Doc's back room. I rip the back of his shirt, easily jerking that lanky body behind the cover of the wall before the terrified female stands up from gathering her supplies. Dread sinks in my gut like a stone. I watch the girl, considering how big of a problem she'll be. The moment her eyes connect with mine, I know. The sheer terror in them, the way they widen into giant saucers, tells me everything.

And when she frantically squeezes herself, and a giant whining cage, through the rear exit like her ass is on fire, her fate is set. Her finagling that dog crate might be entertaining if I didn't know the girl just eavesdropped her way into a death sentence by the boss. And if Dixon doesn't, Earl will... if he gets wind of it.

JB jerks, trying to free himself from my grip. His curses fall on deaf ears. My sole focus fixates on the panicked brown eyes climbing into a red SUV.

"What the fuck, man?"

JB growls and shoves my much wider shoulder, blocking the doorway. Nothing happens, except the kid experiencing the effect of my elbow hitting his ribcage and my 'don't fuck with me' glare.

"Come on, Baldy. We gotta go after her." He wisely backs off from laying his hands on me again, but the punk is pouting like I took away his goddamn ice cream sundae.

Idiot!

I pull out my phone to update Dixon, the guilt and regret tanking my already sour mood.

A tobacco roughened voice picks up on the first ring. "Done?"

"In a manner, Boss. Got a situation." I know before I finish what his instructions will be... get the girl. And that's exactly what gets snarled in my ear. "Fuck!" The call ends abruptly, and I groan, wishing I could erase this entire night and start over.

When I turn around, Jon's at my back, his eyes lit with excitement. This boy enjoys what we do way too much. Goddamn psychopath! I know he overheard my side of the conversation. What he'll do about it is the question.

Watch your back, my dragon snarls.

"Let's go," I snap, hoping the kid doesn't cause anymore problems before I deal with this one.

Chapter One

Abigail

THE SCENT OF MELTED cheese is heaven.

My dinner warms on the stainless-steel cooktop I picked when Dad remodeled the kitchen. Even if I'm not a stellar cook yet, I intend to fix that eventually. Especially with more time on my hands since graduation. Since my current dinner is a pot of children's food, that cooking class might need to move up my list.

"Mmm, mac 'n cheese heaven," I moan to the room.

After a day like today, I'm going to give myself a break on the junk food, and thank my dinner for its comfort. I've got no significant other to curl up with, no one to vent to. The few girlfriends I had, I left back at college. I didn't mean to, but somehow, under Dad's roof, I sank right back into that crappy loneliness.

Maybe not being allowed to invite friends over growing up just stuck with me. Dad's constant need for secrecy and the bodyguards 24/7 doesn't make it easy. Not to mention, most parents in town frowned on their kids fraternizing with me. I always wanted to scream at them... *I am not my dad's reputation!*

Why couldn't they see that?

Any time I found a small bond with someone, Dad would get paranoid about our secret and eventually ban me from seeing that person.

By the time I got to middle school, no kids would talk to me, either out of fear of my dad or hating the weirdo girl.

It's hard coming back now with that same feeling. "I'm a freaking adult!" Huffing, I stir my pasta, pissed to still feel like a lone ladybug in a hive of bees. My skin feels too tight here... daily.

Now, food is my only friend, but that's okay. Mac 'n' cheese never let me down. Hopefully, the junk calories will stick somewhere on my body too, so one day I can stop looking like a perpetual teen. Boost my breasts. Bless my butt. I don't care. I wouldn't argue if my skinny jeans looked sexy, instead of starving artsy.

"Maybe parents would take me seriously if I didn't look so young," I murmur to myself. Most bulldoze right over my opinion or treat me like I can't teach their kids.

It's why I'm so pissed today. I called a conference for the parents of a bully and the kid he abuses. The bully's parents refuse to admit he's violent. And the bullied kid's weren't any better. The father, Clint, or Red, as the guys call him, works for my dad. That man's temper is truly cringeworthy. My stomach knots thinking about it. If I look at the wife's skittish behavior in our meeting, I'd bet my master's degree that Red's temper doesn't discriminate against those who love him. Their relationship was pitiful to watch.

It was all I could do to hold composure when the woman shrank into the metal accent chair in the principal's office. She never said a word. Worse, she startled like a spooked kitten every time one of the dad's voices boomed too loud. I can't imagine what she and her son deal with at home if this is how she acts in public. The bullied kid, Max, wasn't as bad, but I hated the guilt in his eyes. He looked almost ashamed in front of his father.

The second I walked out of that meeting, I felt horrible about myself. I failed Max as his teacher, at school with the bully and at home for whatever he's dealing with that gives me the jitters. For the rest of the afternoon, every thought went to Max, until I had chewed almost all the skin off my lip and it hurt like hell.

I'm biting it again when a shout below lifts the hairs on my arm. *Dad, of course.* I bet that vein in his forehead is bulging, considering the volume. I'd hate to be the person who ticked him off. Why do I have to be so paranoid in my own house? The raucousness sets me on edge, every time.

With no other option, I go back to prepping dinner as a distraction. As usual, I keep my head down when the basement door creaks in the hall. Dad's volume gets louder, but thankfully, the door slams shut before more curses float this way. A heavy clomp of boots head for the back door—in the kitchen. My spine straightens with a shiver of fear. *Who's heading my way?* It could be any of them.

Half the time, I think they live here. The consistent rotation of terrifying soldiers—and I use that term loosely—never leave our house. Someone is always on guard. But these footsteps freeze outside the kitchen. The moment they do, I know exactly which pair of sea-green eyes I'll find when I turn around. The tingles on the back of my neck tell me. It's not Red, or one of Dad's other leery men. No, only one sexy hulk of a man produces enough electricity to fry my brain cells.

Immediately, a wave of excitement crashes over me.

To prepare for the inevitable, I take my noodles off the stove. I'd like to survive the encounter with my fantasy man with my dinner intact. I move slowly, buying time to cool my racing heart. Not that it matters. The worst thing about living with shifters is knowing Kris already hears my crazy heart rate when he's near.

How can I hide a crush I've harbored for ten years from a dragon shifter? Especially if I'm back in my childhood bedroom, constantly hiding my reactions from those heightened senses.

"How are you, Abi?"

Kristopher Wright knocks me out with that sexy rumble of his. My eyes flit to where he stands, unable to resist or ignore my long-time—unrequited—puppy love. A man I'm drawn to, despite my drastic inferiority, despite knowing he works for my father or how ill-equipped I am to handle that massive expanse of muscle.

"Hey, Kris." Nerves lodge in my throat, coming out garbled. *Ugh! Why does my voice abandon me? I need to prove I'm not that same shy little girl.*

You're not ten-years-old anymore... chill out.

With my mind working overtime, I grab two forks, offering one to Kris. "I made some comfort food if you want to share."

Kris's eyebrows crease with a sexy V, softening his appearance as he debates my offer. Until my father's screaming voice carries into the kitchen from downstairs, and he tenses. Immediately, worry tightens my shoulders for whoever's in trouble. Nonetheless, after a few torturous seconds of waiting out on the cliff, Kris steps forward. He grabs the fork, his thick fingers brushing mine. A shot of electricity races up my arm, sending shocking heat straight to my core. Only the slight tick at the corner of Kris's mouth shows I'm not alone.

Please... please don't notice me acting like a dork, Kris.

The safest way to avoid that is by keeping my head down, so I do. My elbows drop to the counter, focusing on lifting a forkful of pasta straight from the pot instead of the hunk of man beside me. An involuntary moan of satisfaction slips out at the first bite of cheesy goodness.

"Oh, my God! I needed this today." I swallow the mouthful, still not looking at Kris's handsome face, so my fair skin doesn't give away my nerves.

"I can tell." Kris chuckles low, scratchy, like the sound doesn't happen often. Who knows... maybe it doesn't. Heck, I've only seen Kris smile a few times since high school. He's always so serious.

I risk meeting his eye, despite my cheeks burning. "Are you laughing at me?" I hate how the heat firing between us rattles my common sense. No other man has ever had this effect on me. Of course, no other one has watched me with such intensity, either. *Is he going to kiss me?*

Am I misinterpreting that look?

Because I could really get behind that game plan.

Just in case, I lick my lower lip and send a silent prayer that there's no cheese stuck to my face, especially when Kris's eyes linger on the path of my tongue. Except, instead of leaning in—like I wish—Kris straightens his back and puts a few extra, very pointed, inches between us. Instantly, reality slaps me with a hefty dose of disappointment.

Come on, Abi. Kris can't wrap you in his arms and make all your teenage dreams come true in your dad's kitchen.

Frustrated with myself, I turn back to the pot of mac 'n cheese. Should I grab a bowl? Does it matter if I'm classless at this point? *Gah!* Why is Kris standing there, anyway? We're not buddies anymore, if we ever were, beyond him protecting me. He didn't know about my ogling teenage hormones.

I don't think.

His sigh hits my ears, heavy and stressed. I tense, waiting for the letdown. Instead, Kris steps in, scooping a bite of my dinner right over my shoulder. His body presses close, until I need to angle sideways just for him to share. My pouty side wants to cover the pot. Then Kris will leave me to my moping. Especially when his sharp jaw is way too fascinating. The way the muscle twitches as he works the mushy noodles longer than necessary... a foot away and close enough to lick, close enough for his intriguing scent to circle around me.

"You home for good now?" His question breaks my focus.

Obviously, the man is unaware that watching him eat drives me ten-levels of crazy. I look away, scooping another bite. My brain needs time to process. It seems I'm not over the blushing adolescent phase around Kris. *Gah! The man leans over my shoulder and suddenly I can't talk.* I have this overwhelming urge to wallow in his scent any time we're in the same room. It's made life difficult since moving home.

At least Kris doesn't seem in a hurry to leave. That makes chatting with him slightly less awkward. "I am... I guess. I'm teaching fourth grade in town. Dad insisted I live here until I get on my feet." I stop, suddenly feeling childish.

"Hmph." One lone, distracted grunt. That's it. Except his grip on our stone countertop tells me I said something wrong.

Why does his disapproval mean so much? *It just does.*

Kris's stormy eyes twist my mind for anything to fill the silence suffocating the room. I should scrap the entire conversation and take my college-level dinner upstairs, eat alone. Hell, Kris interrupted *my* dinner, not the other way around.

"You just going to stand there and brood?" He could at least make polite conversation. In fact, if he's going to eat my dinner, Mr. Rude could say thank you.

Fine! If he's going to stay quiet, he can just leave. I ditch my fork in the pot and turn to tell him just that, except the confined space of his body traps me in his heat. I glance up, only to find Kris's eyes flitting across my face, his pained indecision obvious. My blood sizzles under his scrutiny, but I give it right back to him. Trying to figure out how to bring the smile back I used to love so much.

"Kris, are you ok?"

His chest deflates like a balloon leaking air as he moves to the side and rests his elbows on the counter beside me. He buries his head in his hands, fingers tugging at the tight buzz on top. Bent over, Kris is closer to my five and a half feet, less menacing. That's my only excuse for the hand I place on his shoulder's muscular curve.

The only one you'll admit, a snarky voice comments in my head.

The instant my hand touches Kris, I know it was a bad idea. He jolts upright, his eyes firing a warning, and I cringe. *Am I not supposed to touch him?* My heart plummets. I drop my hand from his arm, fighting the urge to scratch my palm and the tingles left behind. It's a battle. I struggle to keep a straight face, hiding the tears from his rejection.

Immediately, that too-handsome-for-his-own-good face softens. He tucks a loose strand of hair behind my ear. "Abigail, I'm fine..." He stops, sucking in a breath and moving his hand away. "Just... I have some research to do. And I can't make myself leave."

My skin flushes. A quiet hope resurfacing that Kris might look at me as more than his boss's daughter. I know my dad told them all I was off limits. But I've never had a boyfriend, and I'm tired of being the little princess. The one time I admitted a crush to Dad—in middle school—the guy showed up with a black eye the next day and avoided me in the hallways for the rest of the year.

"What's going on in here?" My dad's voice thunders from the doorway, startling Kris and I apart. His back is ramrod straight, his hand falling to his side like it was never there, before we turn and face my dad on high alert. Kris angles his large body in front of mine, and my eyes jerk to his profile, my curiosity burning at the protectiveness.

It's my dad, for Christ's sake.

"Nothing's going on, Dad. I made dinner and offered some to Kris. You want a bowl?"

"Hmph." His eyes fixate on Kris, the gold from his dragon beaming. An obvious threat. "Don't you have somewhere to be, Baldy?" Kris flinches at the nickname, but it's the menace in Dad's glare that shakes me. Oddly, it doesn't have the same effect on the beast of a man blocking me.

"I do, sir. I was just leaving." Kris's head dips to my dad before he turns. I can't look away from the regret in his eyes, but neither of us speaks. Only the light brush of his pinky on the way out lets me know I didn't imagine the last twenty minutes.

I bite back a groan as I turn to soak my empty pot in the sink. "Night, Dad."

Without meeting his eye, I drop the expected kiss to his cheek as I pass, not wanting my father to see the yearning there. The roller coaster of emotions clogging up my head would just set off a truckload of drama for his men and a long lecture for me. Neither sound appealing. I just want to close out this crap-storm of a day.

For the rest of the night, I calculate how long it'll take to pay down my student loans and save up for an apartment. Dad hasn't offered to help on that one. He knows—other than the heaping amount of guilt and Mom's memories—the low starting salary as a first-year teacher is my biggest obstacle that keeps me home.

Chapter Two

Kris

"Wʜᴀᴛ ᴅ'ʏᴀ ᴛʜɪɴᴋ, ᴍᴀɴ?" I look over at Jon bouncing around the shadows like a prizefighter.

"Think about what?" *Why the fuck am I on recon with the newb again?*

"That hit, dude. Did you hear the doc squeal?" I scowl at his obnoxious bark of laughter. It doesn't stop the kid's antics, nor the racket he's making.

We're supposed to be stealth, you little prick.

I ignore the question. This is a goddamn stake-out, not a social club.

When I don't play along, the bony shit stops that ridiculous clap-dance thing to look at me. "Weren't you listening, Baldy?"

"Not really, dumb ass," I grumble under my breath.

Thank God, he quiets down once our nosy little target leaves her apartment. The little dog she wrestled through the clinic earlier is taking a bathroom break, but I'm surprised she bothers. There's a considerable stench of fear in the air, strong enough to waft this far away.

"Let's grab her," Jon says, way too excited.

Maybe it's hanging with this piece-of-crap kid that's getting to me, the reason I feel worse and worse with every mission. "Shh!" I don't even try to hide the anger in my voice, but my eye never leaves our girl. She'd be cute if she didn't give off such a goody-goody vibe, but it's been a long time since I've found any woman attractive.

Just one. My dragon points out the obvious anytime I try to look at another female, so I've given up.

Still, my shifter senses make out every detail about the girl in the dark. The way she scans the dark parking lot, the quickness in her step as she follows the little mutt on his business. Even the frozen fear in her eyes when she stops under the streetlamp for the yappy dog to sniff. *Smart girl.*

"What are we waiting for?"

"We're not here for a snatching. We do recon, like the boss said. See if the girl acts weird or calls the cops."

Jon groans. "That's bullshit! Of course, she saw something. She hauled ass, man." He releases his talons to scratch the tree acting as our cover.

Damn! This bored eight-year-old routine grates my ears. And I find it ridiculous that I have to remind this kid of our orders... again. He was in the same room I was in earlier. He heard the boss's warning. *Don't draw attention to yourselves.*

"Don't you think a public attack is gonna draw a lot of attention?" To our species and the organization. That's the last thing we need when our ranks have already divided in two. The little twat mumbles something I can't hear, sharpening his nails even faster along the bark.

"*Quiet!*"

I watch the female's agitation grow. I bet she hears the kid fidgeting in the dark, even without shifter genes. She's pure human. If we aren't careful and she finds us stalking, there'll be no saving her then. Our instructions are *stealth or death*; always have been in the dragon community. This girl could out us and that's dangerous.

I hold my breath until our target and her little dog return to her apartment before I lash out, my frustrations getting the better of me. One swipe knocks Jon's wrist off the mutilated tree. I jerk quickly, catching him off guard and bending it behind his back... hard. I keep the kid's exposed talons away from my skin, so he doesn't get any stupid ideas about topping from the bottom. When he's secure, I lean close, dropping to the lowest register that usually makes lesser morons piss their pants. "Listen, you grunt. If you wanna follow me around, there's a few rules you're gonna learn." I twist his wrist harder and wait to make sure he's listening.

"What! What, man?" His squeak makes me laugh, the satisfaction from hearing his panic relieving some of my agitation over the events of our night. For good measure, I twist again, staying mindful of our surroundings to curb my humor. "What, man... *Fuck!*" That whine irritates my ears, but I don't let up, even as he wiggles against my hold.

"Number one, you stay quiet. No noise, no bullshit... nothing. Number two... I make the calls. You follow rules. Got it?" He grunts, pain laboring his breath until it sounds like the boy's about to cry. I still don't release his arm until Jon's head gives me what I want... a nod. Simple. "I can't hear you, dumb ass."

"Yeah, okay. Fine... fine." The idiot's pout is hilarious, except I hate every part of this night. I hate the orders. I hate having my time with Abi cut short. And worse, I hate the guilt eating me up inside. I hate the disappointment in her eyes that I was just another of her dad's goons, that she knew I was leaving for something illegal, or at the very least, immoral.

When did I start caring about that? The woman has been gone five years. Now, she's home and my life isn't good enough. *Bullshit!*

Why does that bother me?

Growling, I step away from Jon. The temptation to lose my temper is too easy, my emotions too volatile. I can't be around the kid's adolescent bloodlust like this. The irritating tingles under my skin show exactly how close I am to losing control. I'm barely hanging on to my dragon. But I'll be damned if I succumb to an involuntary shift. I'm not a goddamn teenager popping a boner! Even if Abigail makes me feel like one.

"Baldy." Jon's obvious disgust drips in just his growl of my name.

Is this moron dumb enough to stand up to an elder?

Lucky for him, he holds back. Sad for the little office girl, we're still watching, catching the worst sign of guilt... her car full of luggage. That she hurriedly ran out and packed the car with constant glances over her shoulder doesn't help.

"Dammit, she knows." Immediately, my head rolls through our options. But when JB turns toward me, his eager eyes glowing yellow, I know for a fact he won't be a part of any. When he moves to strip and shift, I grab the nape of his neck, dousing his excitement before it gets off the ground. "Get the car, JB. Report to the boss." I toss him the keys, barking orders. It's a test. Can Jon control himself well enough to follow command? Not to mention, honor rank.

I bite my cheek against the burn and let my wings tear through my shirt. Fast shifts suck, but the girl's already pulling onto the road. I don't have time for precautions.

"But—" The kid looks like I stole his lollipop. *The prick.*

"No, buts, JB. Get the fuckin' car. Report to the boss. That's it. I'll track our target and radio in." With that, I leap like my legs have springs and spread my wings, letting the momentum take me high in the night sky.

Flying brings me a momentary peace, the higher the better.

All dragons fly high to stay out of sight. Humans fear our kind since our fire-breathing ancestors and every magical movie gives us a bad name. Although I can't help laughing as I pump my wings, riding a chilly current in my chase for a frightened human.

Damn, if I'm not fulfilling the stereotype.

Five days later, and exhausted from recon, I land at Dixon's home base.

My feet vibrate the earth, louder than I intend. But *goddammit*, I'm dead in the air. "Dixon can ignore a little rattle to his back deck," I grumble to the night sky.

Thank heavens for the soaring pine trees all over eastern Tennessee. The natural seclusion offers privacy, but still our crew heeds the repeated warnings by the boss about dropping too close to the house. To help, he cleared a landing space out back for his men, out of the way but open enough for easy take-offs and landings.

Keeping us in our place. Right, boss?

A crack of thunder in the distance signals the perfect end to this godforsaken trip. There's no way my wings would hold up in an electrical storm. I haven't done that since my young and dumb teenage years. Now my body's paying for so much time in the air. Hell, a powerful gust could knock my ass down at this point.

My dragon cackles. *Bitch much?*

Shut it. This trip was rough.

Thank God my feet are finally on solid ground. I can retract my wings now and take a *goddamn* break. I bite the inside of my cheek not to whine out loud, but it doesn't stop the painful groan while I rub my screaming shoulder blades. For the third time tonight, I think about how much I hate my life.

Chasing a girl to the boonies of some tiny ass mountain town means a lot of cold that my leathery hide can't buffer. Mountain valleys are too risky to fly by daylight. I had to hoof it to avoid prying eyes. At night, I could hunt in the clouds, but that's cold as fuck! Tennessee isn't tropical by any means, but the mountain elevations strained my wings something fierce, even in full transition. My dragon complained about it the entire week, as if I didn't already know he likes warm weather. *Me too, dumbass.*

"Baldy... my man." I recognize that callous voice immediately. It's not one to let sneak up behind me.

When I turn, Red's trotting up Dixon's steps two at a time. He drops a brotherly slap on my sore shoulder that triggers a growl from my dragon. He's never liked Red, but usually I can keep it under wraps. Technically, Red's a superior and insanely ruthless to boot. One you don't take lightly as an enemy.

Back the fuck off! My dragon's snarl ignites fire in my blood. He has no qualms about fighting our second in command.

Calm down!

Somehow, I hold my outward composure, despite the inner turmoil. My back straightens and I bite back a smug grin when I tower a solid half foot over Dixon's right-hand man. The victory is short-lived. Red's dark chuckle when he waves for me to follow him shows his complete lack of fear... or lack of awareness. I follow behind because I was heading there, anyway. But also, keeping this mercurial man where I can watch his movements is just smart business. This slimeball will stab you in the back as quick as he'll say, 'good morning'.

Watch this one, my dragon warns.

No shit.

Red and I enter Dixon's office, the same way we've done for ten years, him taking the lead, and me following orders. Tonight, unease in my gut makes it hard to sit still. Red does most of the talking, getting his business out of the way while I zone out for the first time since Dixon brought me into the upper ranks. The two of them hash out the night's run, Red updating the boss on loans and clients who've fallen behind. I shift on my feet, thinking of the unsavory things I've done on Dixon's orders to collect those loans. All this time, I never questioned the boss's choices, but lately my subconscious is making my life difficult and I don't know what to do about it.

Still, I owe the man my life. It's why I do what I do. He saved me from the streets, and possibly worse, as a child. I can't forget that.

Saturday mornings are freaking awesome!

I love staying in my pajamas and playing Nintendo all day. Nobody has woken up and said to get ready yet, so I'm going to play until Mom makes us leave the house to run errands. Saturday mornings are never this quiet. And Mom rarely sleeps in. Usually, she has something yummy on the table that's better than our weekday cereal breakfast.

She always does that... plans our Saturdays with a bunch of family time with Dad. I'm ten, Mom. I don't like dumb places like the zoo, or hanging with my parents. They're not back, but I'm always stuck beside toddlers in strollers and screaming kindergarteners at these things. Mom gets a kick out of it, though. And if it makes Mom happy, Dad will do it. He tells me to put on a smile and pretend I like it. Most of the time, I do.

It's not all bad. Mom is pretty cool. But I am happy we don't have anything planned today. At least, nothing they told me about.

School sucked so bad this week. Mom and Dad don't know I got in-school suspension, yet either. I almost wish I forged their signature, so I wouldn't get grounded, but I'm not sure I'd get away with it. Getting caught would make my punishment worse, but the thought of telling them makes my stomach hurt. The Fruit Loops I ate for breakfast aren't feeling too good in there.

I hit pause on my game and toss my head back on the couch. I close my eyes, wishing I didn't hate disappointing them. I will not cry. I will not cry. My fist slams into the couch.

Toughen up! I'm a big dragon... like Dad. Not a cry baby. I have to be brave, not annoyed at myself.

Before I chicken out, I hop off the couch and head for my parents' bedroom. I like the extra gaming time, but they're sleeping really late this morning. Automatically my bare feet tiptoe so I don't make a peep. It just feels like I shouldn't. The hallways have a creepy vibe. It's weirding me out.

Maybe they're sick.

As quietly as I can, I turn my parents' bedroom knob, in case they're asleep. The door cracks open just enough to poke my head through. I'm not all the way in when the metallic tang of copper hits my sensitive nose. It's gotten stronger as I get older and right now, Mom and Dad's room smells nasty, like dirt and sour cigarettes... My parents don't smoke.

Something's wrong.

Panicked, I shove their door wide and sprint with the first hint of shifter speed I've ever experienced. The sight in that bed hits my gag reflex, sending my Fruit Loops to join the other obnoxious smells in the air. I scream.

Mom and Dad lay still as rocks under their soft yellow blanket, the one I climb under when I have bad dreams. Like right now... this has to be a bad dream. Mom lets me invade their space for comfort and never says I'm too big for bad dreams, either. Now, their comfortable blanket has dark red streaked and splattered like a creepy tie-dyed nightmare. There's so much red soaked under my dad; it's pooling. This is bad!

"Dad!" It just looks like he's sleeping. Except for that slash across his neck, the one fracturing my dazed, ten-year-old heart into a million pieces.

My eyes dart to Mom. Her body reaches for Dad like she tried to save him in her sleep. Blood paints her hands and arms, but I don't see any wounds. "Mom," I cry. "Please wake up." I keep as quiet as possible, afraid that if I talk too loud something horrible will happen. Mom's head is at an awful angle, her eyes frozen open in a blank stare. My throat closes. I know she's not going to answer me. The pain in my chests feels like I'm going to die.

Who did this?

"Mooooommmm," I wail, dropping to the ground by her side. Oh my God, I can't catch my air. My legs give up and I sink, my fists balling into the edge of their ruined bedspread. I bury my face in the wrecked material and sob, my snot and saliva covering as much fabric as the tears.

This isn't happening. This cannot happen!

I can't look at their bodies anymore. Not with that ghostly color of their skin seared in my head. My stomach heaves, trying to empty itself again, but nothing's left.

Suddenly, the thought that whoever killed my parents might still be here freezes my sobs. I hiccup. How long ago did this happen? Was I asleep?

There's been no sound since I woke up.

The crushing guilt of how happy I was about Mom and Dad sleeping chokes me. "I promise I'll never play video games again, Mom." My heart breaks that I couldn't save them.

I have to get out of here.

Using the blanket, I wipe my face and nose and stumble to my feet. All my focus is on the door. I can't look behind me. Tears already blur my vision as it is. I can barely walk a straight line. My shoulder knocks my baby photo to the floor in the hallway. I freeze. Please don't let whoever broke in still be here! When the house stays quiet, I convince my feet to move for the door.

Where should I go? Ms. Chatham will let me call the cops from her house. But what after that? Without my parents, I have no one. I guess I can crash at Deacon's. His family is never home. They won't notice if I hide out there.

One thing I'm sure of, I'm never going back to that house.

Outside, a surreal numbness takes over my body. I rush the stairs, my lungs taking their fill of city exhaust—a big improvement over my parents' blood burned into my senses. My mind recognizes the pain in my chest, but I don't want to feel it. The sadness already threatens to take me under any minute. I blink away the tears that won't stop, and take off for the street toward the sanctuary of Ms. Chatham's house. Maybe if I don't look where I'm going, a car will take me out. Then I won't have to feel anything.

Before I fly into open traffic, a forceful hand wraps my upper arm and flings me backwards. "Oh, my God!" They got me!

My feet struggle, reaching for the ground to gain speed. I struggle, summoning all my strength to get away from my captor. To my surprise, the hand lets go of my arm and instead smothers my face into a giant barrel of a chest that smells like cigars and... mint. It strokes the back of my head with a comforting pressure.

"Shh, son. It's gonna be okay." I don't know the voice, but the words weave a spell over my shattered heart. The voice continues to shush until I wipe my eyes.

"What am I going to do?" I ask, searching for some kind of reassurance. My voice muffles into this guy's hug when he holds me in place, comforting me, so I don't feel so alone after what I just witnessed.

That day, Dixon was a hero to my childish mind. I leaned on a complete stranger to hold me upright, scared to death of my life changing. He let me cry into his chest, knowing I was too broken to do anything else.

With no other family, I would have ended up on the streets, but Dixon took care of everything. To get me into school with his daughter, he claimed he was my long-lost uncle. I never asked questions about the cops or anything official because Dixon said I could end up in the system, and his wife had gone through foster care and barely survived.

For years after he took me in, I learned a lot about how to color outside of the lines. Dixon was the only person I had, so I trusted everything he said or did for me. I had a roof, food, clothes... mandatory schooling, although I could have done without that. He even got a tutor when my grades tanked, and I acted out as a pissed off adolescent.

Why am I questioning everything now? Call it a rut, or a conscience. Call it a growing dissatisfaction with my life. But it's getting worse. With every job, I take less and less responsibility. I waffle between the guilt of not performing and guilt over the activities I perform.

"Debrief, Kris." Dixon's barked command breaks me out of memory lane. Red flops on the couch against the wall, waiting with an obnoxious superiority.

Great! Dixon caught me daydreaming, and now Red expects fireworks. His face falls when none come. I ignore him and roll right into the shortest recap of my week that I can get away with. The situation leaves Dixon puzzled.

"I think we can use the girl. The doc's getting sloppy." Dixon glances at the frame on the corner of his desk and it dawns on me why he doesn't issue a kill order on the girl. His wife. Red's feet hit the floor in front of the couch, obviously pissed at Dixon's plan of action. "Follow her first, though. Rotate your asses through her village until we know if she told anyone and if she can be trusted. If she didn't, bring her in. I don't want this blowing up in our faces if the whole damn mountain finds you guys lurking.

I nod, but Red has other ideas. "That's too many eyes on us. Too risky."

Dixon's eyes ice over before he turns to Red. He ignores the challenge to his authority, but the warning in his voice is crystal clear. "Red, start with the vet. Figure out what he knows about the girl."

"What should I do?" I already dread chasing down an innocent girl to ruin her life.

"We need phone records, addresses, next of kin." He slams a fist to the desk, dropping his weight in the chair. "No more fuckups, Kristopher. This peon overhearing your meeting is a giant problem. I just hope we can work it to our advantage." He levels me with those blue eyes ringed red at the center. "I've already dealt with Jon... you, I'll give the benefit of the doubt." The dark threat resonates. I know what's coming. "This time."

There it is.

"Got it." I try to hide my agitation, but it hits me hard. Taking a scolding in front of Red, like a misbehaving child. *It's shit!* I bite my tongue and make for the door before those inner thoughts slip out. "Anything else, Boss?"

"Not now." He waves a hand like I'm a *goddamn* gnat bugging his ear.

Fine.

I don't miss Red's shit-eating grin. His happiness over my failure is clear as glass. I might close the door with a heavier force than absolutely necessary, but considering the slam is less than what I want to do with Red's face, he should count the win.

Chapter Three

Abigail

Wednesday afternoons, I man the carpool line. Every teacher hates it, so we rotate. Otherwise, there'd be a lot more grade school riots on the nightly news. I suspect the job sucks worse for teachers with families, or any sort of life outside of the classroom.

For me, staying late isn't a big deal. I'd rather be here, around normal people, than at home in my stonewalled prison. The only noises there are shouts and slamming doors, or Dad's classic rock station he listens to in his office... which I hate. At school, there's life... kids laughing, tennis shoes screeching down the hall... even the breakroom gossips are entertaining.

God! Dramatic much? Mentally, I chastise myself for being so hard on Dad.

I close the last kid into a car and promise myself to shake off the funk I'm in. Determination fires me up and I shake my hands, trying to pump a little energy into my body so my gloom doesn't match the overcast sky quite as well. I don't care who says they love winter and snow... it's not for me. It's only fall and the gray clouds already depress me.

"What would it be like to move somewhere warm?" I mumble, turning back to our ancient school building for cover. It's a complete fantasy, of course, but a girl can dream. As soon as the thought pops in my head, a gale force wind mocks the ridiculousness, tossing my hair like a tornado having a field day. I wrangle the blonde mess with an elastic from my wrist, but it's pure chaos.

That'll be hell to brush out later.

With hair tamed, I zip my coat and duck against the stiff wind. There's not a damn thing out here that protects us—or the kids—from the weather. Either we freeze, we sweat, or we get soaked... no way around it. That part ticks me off that the school isn't providing better, but as I reach the door, I catch sight of a dark-haired kid trudging down the sidewalk, looking about as miserable as I was. His head bends low, bracing for each blast of wind that is way too strong for his tiny body.

"Is that Max?" No one's around, so I have no idea who I'm asking. I'm fairly sure he avoided his bully today, but Max should have been picked up twenty minutes ago.

Immediately, my brain jumps to the worst scenario. This is Red's son we're talking about. I jog over, needing to make sure the kid's okay. His house is only a fifteen-minute walk, but that threadbare coat won't give a lick of protection with this wind chill.

"Max! Max... wait." I wince when he startles, his tiny body bracing for attack, but I catch up before he's out of the parking lot.

"Oh," he sighs. "Hi, teach." Max's signature shy smile is one of those things that makes him such a sweetheart. I soften my approach, not wanting to scare him away.

"You walking home today, kiddo?"

His gaze drops to his shoes, hiding those pink cheeks. But he recovers fast, just like I'd expect from this tough little kid. When his head lifts—a touch higher than before—his jaw is granite. "Yes, Miss Dixon, I am. My dad must've gotten busy." His smile is almost convincing. It just doesn't meet his eyes.

Been there, kid. My heart clenches for the little man. I am not a fan of Red and this kind of crap doesn't help.

"How about if I drop you off on my way home? Just let me get my things from class and we'll scoot. Okay?" Max hesitates, worrying his bottom lip between his teeth. I laugh when he glances around the vacant lot. "Million-dollar question, huh? What's worse... riding with a teacher or walking home in the cold?"

He laughs and I know I hit the nail on the head. Still, I'll take the mocking to hear Max's giggle as my reward. This kid doesn't have near enough happiness. I give myself a mental fist bump for giving him that, and when Max follows me back to the school. It helps that I wrap his bony shoulder in a side hug and don't give him much choice. I want to get this little guy home quickly. If I were his mom, I'd be worried sick.

By the time we get to my car, Max's nerves are rattling mine. He picks his nails, fidgets in his seat. The entire drive, he stares out the window, only facing me when I park in front of his house. His eyes are clouded. "Thanks for the ride, Miss Dixon." That kid's quiet politeness breaks my heart. Like someone doing him a favor is such a hardship. *How could any parent forget such a sweet little boy?*

As I watch Max walk up his front walk, I vow that no matter who his father is, from here on out, I'll make damn sure this kid has better care than he's currently getting. He deserves that.

When I grow up, I want to be a hero-man. I don't care which one, but I would like to fight fires, get the bad guys, or be a soldier.

My head falls back in my favorite reading chair when Max's words sink in.

Normally, grading papers in my mother's parlor relaxes me. I love surrounding myself with her fine china and homemade curtains, all the softness she put in my world. Usually, it brings me peace. It's not working at all tonight. I miss her. It's adding to the sadness of the forgotten little boy who watches his dad do so much evil that all he wants in life is to do good. That he doesn't care how shows me he'll find a way.

It takes zero thought to mark a red 'A+' on the top of his paper. I circle it with a smiley face, showing way more bias than a teacher should. I don't care. There's not a bone in my body that wants to criticize this kid. It's been a full week since his parents forgot to pick him up after school, and every day has been one thing after another for Max.

His beanie was used for keep-away in the lunchroom. Kids tripped him in the hallway, on the playground. I fumed one morning, watching Red scream at the kid during drop off. It was so loud in front of school that teachers—and I'm sure students—heard it outside their car. Remembering the defeat on Max's face when he got out makes me want to kidnap him and run away. Every moment of pain and embarrassment he endures is one too many.

I may have responded by sticking to the kid like white on rice this week, but I wanted to be there in case he needed me. And I was close enough to sneak Max three dollars when I realized he had no packed lunch and no money to buy one. I was discreet, but I could tell Max waffled on the edge of mortification. He tried to pass the money back, claiming he wasn't hungry, but his rumbling stomach said otherwise. He didn't give in until I threatened to walk him through the lunch line myself. Being the mature kid he is, he pocketed the money with a smile and a 'thank you' and went on with his day.

I just wish there was more I could do.

The saving grace for Max is, nothing has pushed to an abusive point... yet. His problems fall in the realm of a shitty childhood and unfortunately, as his teacher, I can't do anything about the quality of parents a kid is born with. *I wish I could!*

Sighing, I wrap my blanket tighter around myself and snuggle into my chair.

My body is on edge even knowing Red's in my house tonight. The obscenities shouting from our basement are a lot rougher than the ones he used on Max. I guess it's a blessing that Red shows a smidge of control around his kid. Hell, my ears having to listen to this crap negates my arguments against Dad banning me from there. I shouldn't want to go down there. As a child, I felt left out, but didn't argue because... hello, basements are dark and scary. *I saw Home Alone.*

Since returning home, though, I resent being in exile from part of my home. I'm bitter... sue me. But it's impossible to relax when I fear what I'll overhear daily. I tip-toe around noises, ignore outbursts and nasty looking men coming and going all hours of the night. To say I'm walking on eggshells is the understatement of the century.

I think Dad only insisted I move home to have control again. He's forever paranoid about species discovery and drawing attention to ourselves. I just assumed the paranoia didn't involve me, since I can't shift. My lack of abilities didn't prevent a huge argument when I chose a college a few states over. I waited for him to forbid me to go. Then, when I put my foot down to pay for it, I expected another screaming match. I was willing to risk it knowing where Dad's money comes from. I don't want it.

Turns out, he sent checks to campus behind my back under the guise of a scholarship. The letter the university gave me said I received an honor of academic excellence grant—the magical answer to my prayers. I was ecstatic!

When Dad tried to send money for living expenses, I tore up the checks, counting myself independent. With loans and tutoring jobs, RA assignments, taking basically any job on campus I could get, I stayed free of Dad's pockets. However, after graduation, my grand idea backfired. Dad used my student loans as ammo to get me home.

"Pay off those loans, Abigail. It's so quiet in this house without you and your mom," he said. *Bull!* He pulled out the big gun.

I don't doubt he missed me, and without Mom here, he is all by himself in this giant house. But his men are always around. Dad's twisted motto has always been, 'Keep your enemies close and your dragons closer.' Not sure if Dad thinks he's a genius for twisting that adage around to work for him and his belief that without his protection, dragons will end up under a scientist's microscope. And now, with the reminder of what it was like growing up here, I could just kick myself for handing over all that hard-won independence. Even if it's temporary.

Why did I ever come home? I'll always be a failure here. And how can I help Max if I'm not strong enough to help myself? My eyes water with self-loathing, but I clear my throat and shove those feelings where they belong so I can move to the next paper. There's a neat stack of completed grades beside my peppermint tea, but too many left to do, given the late hour.

Gah! I wish I had a cappuccino, or anything caffeinated, to get through this pile. I'd never sleep tonight if I gave in, so I stick to the peppermint tea, something that won't keep me up, but makes the room smell like Christmas. With temperatures cooling, I can daydream about the coming winter wonderland.

A sharp clatter below my feet spooks me, the racket jarring my now cooled tea. It splashes my hand, dousing my pajamas and the future gamer's essay sitting in my lap. *Lovely! Another mark for this crap-tastic day.*

Leaving the grading, I head for the kitchen and snatch a towel to clean my mess. The load of pent-up frustrations this week causes my movements to jerk more than normal. "I should get to bed," I grumble, scrubbing at the tea on my shirt a little too hard. One heavy-handed yank on the water nozzle tops off tonight's karma by dousing my chest with a stream of cold water. "*Great!* Who left the sprayer on?"

The back of my teeth grind back my curses to the universe. I wonder if I pissed off some grand Karmic god or if I'm paying for Dad's karma. Sighing, I rip a long strip of paper towels from the holder and blot the giant wet spot. "At least I don't have to worry about a tea stain." *Only a wet t-shirt contest.* Maybe humor would help me... focus on the positive and all that.

Heck, at this point, the siren call of my bed sounds better and better. I toss the towels in the trash, and head to collect my things in the parlor. Just outside the kitchen, an echo of footsteps warns me seconds before our basement door flies open. It narrowly misses my face, but it's Kris's guilt-stricken eyes that stop me in my tracks. Anger radiates off him, at complete odds with the raucous energy below. He falters when he sees me, those moss-colored eyes turning contrite as they drop to the red discoloring his hands and forearms. As soon as I notice, his eyes flicker through a kaleidoscope of color, his dragon expressing every emotion that rolls through that hard head of his. At least it looks that way to me.

"Abi... hi." He scans the hallway until he catches me zeroed in on his hands, trying not to throw up.

"Is that blood?"

At my shriek, Kris rushes the door closed, cutting our conversation off from the rumble downstairs. "Yes."

That's it? No excuse. No explanation. The lack of emotion is frightening.

I'm left staring at his no nonsense chiseled face, trying to hide my shock. He stomps around me with a grunt of annoyance that ticks me off. I'm hot on his heels; I can't convince my feet to do anything else. But I'll be damned if Kris gets to walk away, like being covered in blood is completely normal.

I follow him to the kitchen, standing right beside when he yanks the faucet to its hottest setting and buries his hands underneath. I watch Kris scrub blood off his rippling muscles for an awkward eternity before finally stepping close enough to pour a generous stream of dish soap over his forearms without a word. His sharp eyes cut my way, questioning. I know he's waiting for my ire—my judgment—but I bite my tongue and focus on the swirl of red pooling in the bottom of the basin.

There's no time for a mental freak out until I get some answers.

Unfortunately, the gross factor means I'm not much help with cleaning, but while Kris is busy washing, my eyes rake over every inch exposed. I scour for any visible mark or wound that would create this much blood. Nothing. The only scratches on his body are his very bruised, very busted knuckles.

I have to ask... "Are you okay, Kris?"

To my surprise, Kris's face burns crimson, from his shaved hairline to the thick scruff of five o'clock shadow lining his jaw. One I've wanted to lick for months now. Especially when that sexy muscle ticks in his cheek, usually when he's angry... like now.

"What did you do?" The question is out before I think twice and Kris reels back.

He eyes me with a flash of regret and... shame. "I was challenged, and I won. That's all you need to know."

"Screw that!" I cross my arms over my chest to fight my temper. "You will not come into my kitchen, covered in blood and... and dismiss me." *Not again.* I wait the big thug out, knowing he'd never hurt me. Who cares if I look like a pouty toddler? I'm tired of being in the dark.

Somebody better explain... and soon.

This house is a cesspool since Mom died. And Dad gets worse every year. He thinks I'm too innocent to know how deep he is, that I'm too precious to hear the nastiness they talk about. *Sure...* like I'm a blind idiot. I've got no idea Dad traded his soul for power and money. *Right!*

I know there never used to be this much violence. Or maybe I have been blind. I know Kris's life should scare me. It just doesn't. I'm just tired of all the lies. I wish I had a normal father, one with a boring office job and a briefcase. A father whose worst problem was an addiction to emails during dinner. His business associates would be the balding, stick-in-the-mud types instead of these imposing figures with scars and scowls. Some of the unwashed men that walk in here look right through me with their cold, dead eyes. Like the weakling I am.

I side-eye Kris's stubborn profile, amazed that I never lumped him in with the others. My sixth sense says he doesn't have the same blood thirst they do. Not that the man is innocent. *Hello, exhibit A...*

the mess of blood coloring his hands after God knows what went on downstairs.

Kris sighs, frustration that I won't leave him alone deflating his shoulders. Silence stretches thick between us, but even though I'm annoyed, I can't just leave him like this. *Can I?*

"Abigail, I'm fine. You should go," he says, his voice laced with sadness, tugging at my heart. My need to care for Kris washes out the anger.

I hold my breath against the stench of blood and take over for Kris's rough cleaning. I hate that smell, but he's scrubbed for a bit with no progress. If anything, the angry red scratches crisscrossing his skin look worse. I wipe Kris down with a lot more care than he showed, and when there's not a drop of blood left, he snaps off the faucet. I hand him a dry towel, ignoring that put out look.

Get over it, I'm hovering. I toss the—now disgusting—dishrag in the trash and wash my hands, all the while listening to the vacuum of our breath in the silence. With no other distractions, I prop a hip against the counter and lift an eyebrow... waiting. "Explanation anytime now." My snark is in full force tonight, feigning a power in this situation I don't normally feel. *"Ugh! Kris!"*

He ignores my outburst and braces over the sink with hunched shoulders. His head falls, studying the death-grip his fists have on our countertop. I'd feel guilty, adding more to his burden, except my thoughts are stuck on the corded muscles twisting and flexing in very sinful ways. His frustration does wicked things to increase his sexiness and spike my hormones to volcanic proportions. I gasp for a much different reason, beginning with the heat settling in the lower half of my body. My lungs suddenly feel too small.

I've had fantasies of these arms for as long as I can remember... since I secretly doodled hearts in my notebook with K+A. Since those vivid dreams of my first kiss cemented Kris's face as my fantasy man, even though he was older and way out of my league. The problem is that Mr. Arm-Porn laid out in front of me is a lot more dangerous than skinny pre-teen Kris. This one is a mountain of eye candy now, a sweet sundae hot enough to melt on the coldest day in the arctic.

With the sleeves of his gray Henley rolled up and his arms clean, my eyes fixate on the black ink exposed, dark and brooding. Shadowy flames lick the tanned skin, highlighting every twitch, every ripple in those thick forearms before they taper to nothing at his wrists. I'd swear even his wrists flex with the power in his grip. I didn't know wrist muscles could flex. *Kris's do.*

Every instinct screams to ease Kris's stress. I want to be the one who comforts his beast, the wildness inside him, but Kris has always been untouchable. That's my only excuse for why I reach out now, for why my hand caresses the sinew of muscle popping under that tight cotton. However, Kris's sharp intake of air at my touch freezes it. My heart sinks. I'm scared to move, too afraid I'll upset the tightrope we walk.

When Kris's head drops forward in defeat, I wait for the inevitable, for Kris to open his mouth and let me down easy. *Go ahead, Kris... I'll just melt into a puddle of mortification at your feet.*

"Kris." My voice cracks, barely a whisper to my ears. No response. Those mercurial green eyes avoid mine, probably hoping I won't ask questions I have no business asking. "Kris!" I say, this time stronger, battling the darkness that's dragging this perplexing man under.

"Don't." *What?* There's no doubt his voice is a warning.

I've never pushed my luck like this. It's why I'm kept in the dark, why everyone in this house treats me like a breakable child. *Everyone except Kris.* He's always been different, never raised his voice or looked down on me. He doesn't belong under my dad's thumb.

"Talk to me." I keep my hand where it is, not willing to back down when I'm this close.

If Kris knew how often I caught him feeding the stray cat in the backwoods, or the times I saw him help a bullied kid after school, it'd embarrass the mess out of him. But those secret glimpses showed me Kris's heart and built my childhood crush to an obsessive level I can't shake. I always felt special seeing that softness behind his teenage angst. It's the same now. Evidence of Kris's roughness is clear as day, but *I* see the toll it takes on him, the pain creasing the corners of his eyes.

"Why?" The word grinds past his clenched teeth, his hands tightening on our metal sink until it creaks. The sound might as well be a grenade from the way Kris jerks.

His gaze locks on the finger sized divots in the sink. His lips turn down, the guilt and embarrassment a huge contradiction for such a big, tough personality. It's hard not to laugh.

"Kris... the sink's fine." I smile, the yearning to soothe Kris's anxiety too strong to ignore.

His impressive shoulders turn my way, his eyes burning. A small sliver of hope grows. Call it a delusion from standing in the swirl of testosterone coming off Kris. Especially after years of admiring the man from afar, wishing he'd look at me the way he is now. I thought our five-year age gap was too huge for Kris to see me as a woman. I guess things have changed.

Being the center of Kris's focus is exhilarating. Then again, that man is a brooding master. Like now, he's quiet, but the heat in his gaze is something I've never seen aimed my way... it's a hunger lighting the jade center of his eyes with a ring of gold. Kris stalks forward, his guarded expression doing an about-face, softening as his confident stride closes the distance. My mouth drops open. I search for anything intelligent to fill the silence, getting more frazzled as the air thickens between us.

My throat is the Sahara.

I swallow. Time slows as reality sinks in. My heart might finally get what it wants. I glance up, Kris's height eclipsing me. My breath catches at the full gold transforming his irises. Those bruised knuckles lift to stroke my jaw, memorizing the curve.

Kris has gotten away with no explanation and I let him, too entranced with his sweet touch. I'd expect a guy like Kris to move fast, focus on the finish line, not emotion. I was wrong. The warmth in

Kris's eyes when he lifts under my chin, pausing for permission, floors me. *How does he not know?* He's had permission for years.

"Abi..." He whispers my name, one arm wrapping my waist, pulling until our bodies press close.

Don't stop now.

I wet my lips, anticipating those thick fingers sliding behind my neck, twining in my hair. My eyes roll to the ceiling. It's the gentle way Kris cups my head, guiding it back so that, with our height difference, he fills my vision, from the breadth of his chest with that intoxicating scent, to the straining muscles in his neck that lead to the sexiest stubbled jaw with his high cheekbones and little cleft in his chin. All of it starred a featured role for every wet dream, every fantasy-fueled, self-induced orgasm I've ever had. Now, it's right in front of me.

God, please don't let this be a dream.

The passion electrifying every nerve ending tells me it's not. Even my dreams don't produce this raw heat radiating. I'd never do justice to those green eyes in my fantasy. Kris, in real life, turns everything primal. To ease the rush of wetness coating my thighs, I clench them together, fighting the urge to wiggle in my embarrassingly short pajama shorts.

A slow grin spreads across his face before his gaze drops to my lips. Time stops completely, my mouth falling open in shock, but a half second later, his mouth crashes into mine.

It's not the sweet kiss I imagined from his touch, not a slow tease. No, this kiss is raw... pent-up tension and years of longing flowing between us.

My craving has me vibrating in his hands, clenching his shirt in my fist, hanging on for dear life while Kris devours my mouth, his tongue plunging, fighting with mine before pulling back to nibble at my lower lip... my top lip. I can't keep up, can't stop the whine from pouring out. I need more... need to be closer.

Climb him.

A burst of light hits the back of my eyelids and I fling them open, jerking as if electrocuted. *What the hell was that?*

Kris's hands gentle, sliding to cup my face, holding me as if I'm precious while his thumb strokes my cheek, searching. He looks shell-shocked, same as me. My thoughts are a jumbled mess. All I can think about is how his breath warms my skin like melting honey, how those sinful lips are red and swollen, calling for a soothing, gentler kiss.

"Kris, I…" I'm not sure what to say, but the rasp of a throat clearing startles us apart like two naughty kids caught necking.

"Well, well." Red stands at the kitchen door, his mouth cocked in a nasty smirk as he takes in the scene in front of him.

Kris recovers faster than I do, his eyes hardening as he straightens to full height. He tucks me safely behind him as he turns to Dad's head henchman, primed for battle.

Red only chuckles, the cruel sound sending chills down my spine. "Tsk, tsk, Baldy. Didn't know I'd be interrupting something up here." Those cunning eyes laser-lock on Kris, watching our body-language with piqued interest.

When my hands twist in the fabric at his lower back, subconsciously leaning in for support against the vile person in front of us, Red sneers.

His dead eyes pop to Kris, sucking every ounce of air from the room when he shifts into work mode. "Dixon said to get moving. Let's go."

Kris glances at me over his shoulder, all the warmth from earlier gone. My heart stops. *Does he regret kissing the boss's daughter?* Kris has his *'working'* mask back in place, hiding any feelings I thought were there. He strides toward Red and slaps a massive hand on his back, harder than needed. He pauses for a fraction of a second, a challenge warring between them before Kris rumbles a warning under his breath and walks out the door.

Not a single look back. I'm wrung out after that interaction while Kris walks out without a care.

This time Red's laughter is genuine when he catches my put out look as I track Kris's muscled behind out the door. "Don't worry, little one. It's open season now. I'll be 'round later if you need company."

I gasp, fighting the instant gag reflex as Red struts out the door. His filthy wink leaves me gaping in disgust, my stomach turning at Red's comment. Worse, Kris's detached escape ruins my erotic buzz from that kiss.

Abigail, you know better than to hope with these men.

I'm past hope at this point, but the sadness that settles in after zaps all my energy. I leave the kitchen messy, not giving a care to clean up anyone else's mess. I'm going to bed. *Screw them all!*

Chapter Four

Kris

FIVE DAYS AND I'M still kicking myself over that kiss. It shouldn't have happened.

The hell it shouldn't. She's ours.

Okay, it shouldn't have happened in her father's house, with the man and most of my brothers warring downstairs. No excuses... I lost control. And because I was weak, I plastered a target right on her back.

To walk away from Abi in that kitchen and leave her with Red was risky. Actually, it was one of the hardest things I've ever done. But if that obnoxious oaf got the slightest whiff of how much Abigail affects me... it would wave a red flag in front of the bull. My interest in Abi would serve as a challenge—a game—when she's the exact opposite.

I only trust a few of those guys. At least in any tangible way. A few would defend Abigail if push came to shove—because of Dixon. Red is not one of them. Red needs to think I don't care about Abigail.

So, as difficult as it was, I walked out of that kitchen... for the illusion. I knew he wouldn't go after Abi with Dixon downstairs. *Even he's not that stupid.*

Dixon's number one rule since Abigail hit puberty... no hands, hormones, or anything else go anywhere near his daughter. He made that clear. Hell, he threatened to tie us down and chainsaw our wings off. *She's protected property.* He'd growl if he ever caught our eyes straying her way. As much as I despised him considering her property, the callous warning was enough for most men.

It was for me too... until recently. Until that first summer she visited from college. That's when controlling myself became an issue.

As a teenager, Abigail Dixon was just a little thing, too young... too shy. The frail one who never came into her dragon powers. Our job as Dixon's men was to protect her on the streets. And the guys did, even the ones who talked behind her back. I never made fun of her weakness. In fact, a few of our lower guys received an introduction to my fists when their mocking got rambunctious enough for Abigail to hear. I'd hate if she judged her differences by someone else's insults.

Then, a few years ago, Abi's tiny frame filled out. New curves called my attention to places I never dared look before, like the girl changed overnight. No more knobby knees... her new lean lines and sinewy muscle created a big problem below my waistline.

Whatever spinning class or yoga bullshit Abi got into at that Ivy League place did her body more good than a glass of milk. I've tried to ignore my craving for Abigail, to convince my cock to want someone else, but I fail miserably at every turn. Alcohol didn't help. My dragon straight refuses to be with another woman.

And now that she's home full-time, Abigail has gone past what I can tolerate. I can't function around her—nor her father—when my soul says to mark every flawless inch of ivory skin as mine. Worse, that shit grows stronger every time we breathe the same air. Why is it so hard to deny an attraction to someone I've known half my life?

It has to be her.

Shit! I stop pacing, my eyes darting to the bottle of cheap whiskey I stocked for the longer stake out. *Looks like I'm cracking that bottle quicker than I thought.*

I prepared this time. This Podunk town doesn't have much, but even a crappy motel room is better than sleeping on the hard ground. I raided the tiniest country store I've ever seen for supplies and now a load of junk food covers my dresser... nuts, chips, and protein bars. And the important stuff, like the largest bottle of Jack I could find. It burns like hell on the way down, but it'll save my mind from replaying *the* kiss like a broken record when I should be sleeping. I'll never function this week with Abigail's lips rolling on a highlight reel, driving me crazy.

Of course, my dragon has no issue lusting after the curves of little Abi Dixon. We're stuck in a battle of wills: my overwhelming need to protect Abigail, with my dragon's temptation to see how hard of a pounding she could take.

Is she a hellcat in bed? Did some stuffed-shirt up north figure that out? The idea of some little prick touching my Abigail scorches my blood, the fury making me see stars.

My Abigail? Seething, I fight against my dragon's urge to cleanse her too brilliant mind—and heart—of anyone who isn't me.

No! Abigail is too smart for me. We will not bring her down to our level. His fiery huff lets me know his displeasure with that argument. Every time I think about not being good enough, it hurts.

Ironically, Abi would never put herself above anyone else. She's a brain, but a sweetheart first.

I fill a disposable cup with the cheap whiskey and frown. There's one niggling suspicion rolling around in my head, the only reason for my dragon to crave Abi and no one else. Why he visibly recoils from the rest of the floozies hanging around our crew. All of them are pretty enough, even hiding behind several layers of face paint. But he only wants one.

Abi wouldn't be caught dead in a miniskirt, though. She doesn't throw herself at boys for a crumb of attention. She has class and my dragon freaking loves it. Hell, I've never seen the girl go to a party, let alone break curfew. She's not easy... doesn't even slut herself up for Halloween like the other girls. Most women use the holiday as an excuse to wear as little as possible. They just play it off by naming themselves naughty *'insert boring profession here'* and get away with it.

Now, the thought of Abigail embracing her naughty side—just for me—is something my cock wants to witness. All my blood flows south, not caring if we're in a dingy motel room that smells like mold and old bodily fluids. *Dude! There's nothing I can do with this tonight! My poor cock!*

She's fated. The words drop an atom bomb in my head, confirming my worst suspicion. The adrenaline spike negates the two shots of whiskey I've had so far. I never thought of mating, not in my world. I've scratched itches, sure, daydreamed of a certain blonde beauty. But mates are fantasy I believed in as a child before my world burned around me. Not now.

Now, I'd never bring someone I care about down to my level. Not the way my life is.

The iron wall around my heart cracks. I flop on the checkered bedspread, ignoring the creepy crawly sensation from my head touching the musty fabric. If Abigail is my mate, I'll need every resource I have to win her, all my strength and brain power. Dixon has that girl so far under lock and key that even Abi doesn't know how deep his reach stretches.

Speak of the devil. Her father's ring tone chimes from the bedside table.

"Yea, Boss?" I sit up, needing all my wits for a conversation with Dixon. I swipe along the scruff on the back of my head, using the comforting texture to relieve a crumb of the anxiety his voice causes.

"Any news, Kristopher?" *So much for niceties.*

"Not yet, sir. The girl is on some reservation with her family. So far, her life is boring as hell."

Dixon grunts, not finding my commentary as funny as I do. "Any cops?"

"Not that I've seen. None of her people seem concerned. She's not holed away in her house either. She seems like the *one* magical unicorn who can actually keep her mouth shut." I laugh, but it sounds stilted even to my own ears. Dixon grumbles in the background, too low for me to hear through the phone, but I stand and pace anyway, using the four-square-feet of open space in the tiny motel room to work out my anxiety.

Fuck! Dixon needs to call off this mission and give me the go-ahead to come home. I don't know how much boredom my brain can handle before it starts entertaining itself with thoughts of a sprite little beauty with blonde hair down to her ass.

"Look, Boss. I see nothing going on with the girl… only normal family shit. Has Doc been able to make any progress with getting her back to Tennessee?" Whatever Dixon's plan is with this girl, it'll be easier to go unnoticed at home where she isn't surrounded by her entire family.

Dixon's laugh booms through the phone, prickling the hairs on the back of my neck. "That dumb ass can't do anything right, but we're… motivating him."

"Okay…" I drag out the sound, waiting for the order to return home. "Well, I can't get close to this chick here in town. She goes nowhere alone. I think we should stand down here or people will notice."

"Leave the planning up to me, Kristopher. Give it another few days, then get your ass home. I need your skills if Jon-boy can't handle the vet." The line goes dead without waiting for my agreement, or my sign-off.

I'm completely sober after talking to Dixon. I pour another glass of whiskey and let the burn of the amber liquid numb my restlessness at being told to heel. My weight flops back on the lumpy mattress, stretching my legs nearly to the end. *God! I dread sleep.* From the eighties headboard arching behind me to the scratchy bedspread, not a single part of my body is comfortable in this tacky monstrosity. Even the cheapest person on the planet would question how this shit hole survived without redecorating in the last thirty years. There's zero chance I'm climbing under the covers tonight. *Why test the bedbug gods? Seriously.*

I question why we're surveilling someone who was just in the wrong place at the wrong time, spying on family time. It's a kick in the balls to watch people my age laugh and go about their lives free of the darkness in mine. Top it off with having no control over what I do with my time, or who gets punished, and it hackles. Especially when another, more pressing mission calls to every cell in my body.

Groaning, my head thumps the dense wood behind it. *When will this feeling go away?* Smothering my hunger for a certain forbidden beauty is damned impossible, especially now that I've had a taste. My desire for the woman shreds my insides, tearing me apart piece by piece until I listen and give in. *Should I?*

Unable to stop myself, I sit the forgotten alcohol beside the bed and reach for my phone, opening the few sneaky photos I've collected of Abigail over the years. Her angelic face fills the screen and I smile, unable to fight the pull of those crystalline eyes and perfect porcelain skin. My favorite photo—one I visit often—caught her wild blonde hair, lighter than the sun's rays, flying in the wind behind her on the way to school. I never mind stakeout duty when it's guarding the only person alive I'd protect with my dying breath. And she had no idea I was there.

Inevitably, temptation clouds my better judgement and my hand strays south, pressing against the pain in my throbbing cock. It jumps, greedy for more. My eyes close, lowering my shorts to free my swollen cock for a few strokes. If it were Abigail's hand wrapped around my length, I'd be in heaven.

As it is, I stroke to the memory of her lips. Every tug, I envision her hand. Every squeeze, she's watching, a private performance just for my Abi. I bite back a moan as the fantasies take over. My eyes fixate on my phone, imagining Abi is here, riding me with that silky hair creating a curtain around our heads. My chest heaves as I stroke faster, letting the angel face I want to devour carry me over the edge with a silent release. I lay in bliss for a minute before dragging myself to the bathroom and cleaning up.

After, I change into a fresh pair of clothes and climb into bed, resigned to spend the next week here. I might as well rest while I can, because once I get home, I'll be in for the most important mission of my life. A small kernel of hope takes hold that lulls me into dreamland. In my dreams, Abi isn't just a wild fantasy... She's my future.

Chapter Five

Kris

DAYS LATER, I WAKE swamped in sweat.

I'm hot-blooded like all dragons, but I thought sleeping on top of the covers would save the overheated dreams since I can't sleep in the nude on the job. It didn't. I tossed and turned all night, my t-shirt strangling my torso like a goddamn straight jacket. My stomach growls, feeling the effects of my liquid dinner last night.

What's the chance I'll find a halfway decent breakfast taco in town? Only some serious grease will soak up the effects of the cheap whisky.

I squint. The goddamn sun's searing my eyeballs. I don't know what's worse in this hellhole, the cracked blinds or the scratchy comforter. "*Ugh!* I need a shower." I groan, ignoring the assortment of mystery stains under my bare feet when they hit the floor. *Okay, stains win the crappiest hotel award.*

I cringe on the way to the bathroom. The tiny glass stall they call a shower is only suitable for cleaning smaller humans, not my six and a half feet of dragon. But the faster I wash off last night's stench, the faster I can knock out Dixon's orders and get home. I'm in for the fight of my life... not only to win over an angel I don't deserve, but somehow, I have to convince her father not to kill me as well. It's going to take a miracle.

Holy shit! I need coffee for this!

To wake up my overly tired corneas, I set the shower to scalding before hopping into the cloudy haze of steam filling the small cubby. I grab one of the tiny bottles of soap and give myself a five-minute scrub down before toweling off. It's better than nothing and my mouth is already watering for that first cup of coffee from Talon's bakery. *That place is the shit!* And the one vice I gave into on my last recon, a tool to blend with early morning window shoppers. They'll overlook a tourist—even a tatted up one—if I blend with the other overworked assholes.

You are overworked. An irritated growl fills my head.

Not going there.

Usually, my target hangs with her doppelgänger, I assume her sister considering their matching dark braids and big doe eyes. The only other person I saw Miss Nosy out with is a spiked-hair skinny dude. He nipped at her heels all day like some love-sick puppy. It's a little pathetic if you ask me, but what the hell do I know? Maybe that schtick works for him.

I'd follow on Abi's heels all day, my dragon offers unhelpfully.

Shoving his voice down, I grab my wallet and jacket for the short walk to main street. Dragons don't need jackets, but it's another tool to offer cover. The world expects someone walking the streets in the nip of fall to guard against the cold. So, I will. Just underneath, I'll secretly melt like a snowman on a tropical beach.

Another day of boredom in this *too-homey-for-its-own-good* small town. I don't expect any intel I don't already know. My target is as vanilla as they come. Hell, she'd make a scoop of ice cream look like a caramel-glazed sundae made with endangered buffalo milk. *Are buffalo still endangered?*

Gah! Who gives a shit? My dragon laughs at me inside my own head.

Clearly, mass boredom has stolen my fucking mind. "For Christ's sake, my species is all but extinct. Who cares about the rest of them?" My voice is the only noise on the empty street, except the annoying chirp of excited birds. Those birds would get the shock of their lives if I could fly over the main drag instead of hiking there.

Ten minutes and a sheen of sweat later, I'm walking out of an overly peppy bakery with a coffee and breakfast sandwich in hand. Sadly, there are no tacos, but I take to the shadows with my loot and stroll, stealth mode, behind the scenes. Going out of sight in the square is difficult given my size and sleeves of tattoos. I stick out almost everywhere: the park, the library, all those tourist trap places locals and tourists love.

"It's a *goddamn* Hallmark movie," I grumble, tucking myself at the edge of an alley to watch traffic pickup on the cobblestone *downtown* street.

This place is bubblegum on steroids, from the ice cream shop with that old-fashioned awning, to the wood benches waiting for people to mingle and chat. Even the greasy spoon diner on the edge of the square looks ripped out of a history book with its tacky vinyl booths and car themed decorations.

I take a sip of my coffee and lean against the brick wall I'm using for cover. The chick-boutique isn't open yet, so there's no threat of nosy customers asking questions. Judging by the plate-glass window displaying purses and mannequins with flowy, bohemian-type dresses and lace-covered table overstuffed with yard sale rescues, whoever does shop here would not take kindly to my type of loitering.

I wonder how long I have to putz around the square before I cross paths with the snoopy vet. *The girl's gotta eat, right?*

Three hours later, after walking down Main Street four times, I'm less confident. Business owners are noticing and there's still no sign of the girl. Don't all girls shop on a Saturday... run errands... something?

I want to avoid her reservation at all costs. I don't need some hunter firing in the air and taking me out. "This fuckin' dead-end is not worth catching a bullet," I grumble, heading toward the hotel. I'm not staying here another day. If I get nothing out of this whole day, I'm going home. Dixon will have to deal.

After grabbing my leather go-bag and checking out, I pop off a text to Deacon. *This mission is toast.* He responds immediately: *Get your ass back home then, bro. Mikey's got the house loaded for a party tonight. Girls! Girls! Girls!* I can practically hear his life-of-the-party announcer voice and shake my head.

No girls! my dragon growls, clawing at my chest.

Dammit! Irritation creeps under my skin. I'm tempted to ignore common sense and take to air just to shut my dragon up. My feet are getting me nowhere. *It's four in the freakin' afternoon!* I check over my shoulder. There's a green, rusted-out dumpster that would be decent enough for cover. In a split-second decision, my feet take me down the dingy, foul-scented alleyway, away from the random people walking the street. I stash my coat and t-shirt inside my bag and tuck it behind the garbage mess, ignoring the rotted leftovers and rat feces at my feet.

All I need is an hour and my wings to knock this shit out fast. Transitioning as an ancient lineage is goddamn time consuming. The dragons who fight their inner beast struggle the most. Not me. I *hate* feeling vulnerable, so I embrace that shit. Even though shifting feels like lava burning under my skin. My life depends on forced shifts and mastering my body—in both forms. If I don't, some other asshat's gonna take me down. Still, my wings hurt less and are faster to get me in the air.

Concentrating, I imagine the length of my rust-colored wings, the cool air tickling as I fly. Within seconds, my shoulder blades erupt with the powerful scalloped muscle, only a small hitch of breath giving me away in the eerie darkness. My jaw locks against the pain, grinding the back of my teeth to stay silent. Gradually, the burn subsides and I stretch my leathery hide behind me, preparing for flight. With a smile, I snap their length toward the ground and rocket above the tiny downtown.

Flying is the greatest high I've ever had.

My lungs tighten, mist slapping me in the face as I breach the low-lying stratus clouds. The air is thick up here, but between people shielding their eyes from the rain and the assortment of umbrellas blocking their view, I can circle above without a damn person noticing.

It should be a good plan.

But hours later, I've circled the entire town and outskirts and... nothing. I can't imagine this girl sleeping the day away, unless she realized we're following her.

Fuck! Stalking this chick is a goddamn waste of time.

Let's go home. My dragon is bored. Only one thing is going to make him happy.

I've done what I can do in this map-dot town, short of crossing the line into hurting a girl who doesn't deserve punishment. And that idea turns my stomach.

As corrupt as Dixon is, he's squeamish about taking people out unless absolutely necessary. It's a promise he made to his late wife after she tried to coerce him out of the business. He couldn't give it up while she was alive, but vowed to a sort of hustler honor code... no women or children. And because she was always terrified of someone finding him out, he agreed to minimize any useless attention on the dragon species.

That concession is my conscience's saving grace.

Over the last few years, Dixon's partner—who acts like his shit doesn't stink—has pushed our crew for sketchier and sketchier money-making schemes. Things I'm not ok with. Dixon held off, sticking to casinos, money laundering, and the like. But that leaves Earl's human trafficking bullshit across the eastern states to the Georgia boys. That I even know that much makes me gag. It's why I hate this current mission. I just can't turn it down.

"Goddamn exposure threat," I growl into the air. That's the whole reason I'm here, protecting Dixon's Mafia at all cost. I can't ignore her risk. If our crew slips up, Dixon's partner would have our heads... zero fucks given to our conscience or our code.

By my third circle of the mountain, I'm bored out of my mind. My body is strained. "I'm calling this shit." And goddammit if I don't catch sight of the vet-girl's red SUV after turning back. She's at the same little store on the outskirts I shopped at earlier this week.

I groan. "This better be the last time I snoop on a woman shopping for groceries." There's not a single cop in the area, which is what Dixon worried about. Nothing even hints at this girl being a threat. *I'm done.*

I just need proof of how vanilla this chick is for Dixon, so I don't end up back in this shit-hole.

Eying the cinderblock building, I tuck my wings and swoop to land, staying in the shadows for cover. I can't go in the store, because my shirt is back at that nasty ass dumpster. Plus, the girl would recognize me, guaranteed. She made me that night at the clinic. I know it. All week, I stayed at a distance. I can't have Miss Nosy connect the dots. To say it's made gathering intel difficult is an understatement.

From the side of the building, I ready my phone for a few easy photos. Except, just as I focus on the sliding glass door, a thud vibrates the gravel behind me and instinct drops my center of gravity in a flash. My leg sweeps behind me as I turn, crouched and bracing for an attack on whatever predator snuck up behind me.

Unfortunately, in my haste, my phone skids across the pitted asphalt with a screech amplified by shifter ears.

Chapter Six

Kris

"Off yer game, kid?" That snide voice catches me off guard.

How the hell did this foul asshole creep up behind me? That blustering landing could have woken the whole town. Especially with Red's cackling laughter.

"No chance, Red!" I'm doing a piss-poor job of hiding my annoyance, but damn if that insufferable man doesn't test my patience. He's way too likely to draw attention... attention with regretful consequences for bystanders if they saw him fall from the sky. Red's laughter cracks louder, irritating my dragon, who huffs inside my head.

"Aww, Baldy, I think you are." He slaps me on the back, that mocking tone as irritating as the faux-brotherly bullshit.

I shove by him and grab my phone from the dirt, inspecting each side for cracks. It's an old piece, but I ignore Red's satisfied smirk when he takes out his latest model. That bastard spends no money on his family, but he's perfectly happy to steal or blow money on anything he wants.

My instincts sing on high alert. And they never betray me.

That Red could track me in flight at all... not to mention sneak up on my ass, pisses me off. The anger has rubbed my nerves as raw as a dock rope after a hurricane. Not ideal in one of the south's largest criminal societies. And Red knows it. The victory shining from his eyes leaves no doubt in my mind; this sick fuck is gonna run straight to the boss.

"Screw off." My lip curls, wishing I could bite this fucker's head off. My dragon growls, his low rumble agreeing with that idea. Yet somehow, I refrain from knocking those tarter-stained teeth loose.

"What's the matter, kid? Something blonde and bendy twisting up yer mind?" His beady eyes crinkle with perverse laughter, the sound fracturing the silence of the night. He's downright giddy at making me squirm, thinking he got the best of me.

Let him mention our mate in that tone one more time. I will gut him. I stop my dragon's words. Abigail is my quickest trigger... obviously my dragon's too.

My Spidey sense says to watch my back with this one. There's no honor among thieves. Red would rat me out in a hot minute. I can't have him doing that before I have a plan in place.

"What's your beef, Red? Dixon's daughter is off limits. You know that."

"*I* know that," he says, his raspy voice setting my defenses on edge. "Do *you* know that?" After years of smoking, Red's laugh now sounds like a phlegmy cough. "I never said I wanted *the lemon.*"

I growl, my temper spiking at hearing Abi's old nickname. The crew labeled Abi '*the lemon*' behind the boss's back. When she hit puberty and hadn't shifted, the guys took to disgracing her as a half-blood, too weak and too human to live up to Dixon's legacy. The boss never knew. But I never used that name.

I narrow my eyes at Red. His twisted glee over ridiculing Abi verifies who I always suspected gave her that nickname. *God! That man's a weasel to the core!*

"What are you doing here, anyway?" I ask, forcing my voice to steady. If Red sees what riles me up, he'll use that to go after Abigail. I'd unleash hell in his world if he hurt her as part of some sick game. It's a dangerous balance.

"What do you think? I sniffed you out." His nose sniffs dramatically. The dumb ass trying to rile me up like a goddamn comedian. *Red's up to something.* His ruddy face lights up when he catches my glare.

As if the man could smell anything over his own stench. He has to be nose-blind already, because that nastiness is damn sure invading my space.

A hum of mechanics interrupts our bitch fest. Red follows my eyes to the messy head of ebony hair walking through the sliding doors, arms loaded with groceries. Those jogging pants sag on her waist and the t-shirt clings too tight like she outgrew it years ago. The whole girlish picture makes me extremely uncomfortable.

Still, I have a job to do.

My hands level the camera at our target, snap a few shots of a normal girl going about her normal business. Then a wide-shot of the parking lot to show no cops before firing off a text to the boss. My wings itch to lift off, to leave Red and his putrid smell on this side of the mountain.

"I'm out." I bite my tongue and tuck my phone in my back pocket. Somehow, I hold what I'd prefer to say... *screw off.* The smarter option is not to ruffle Red's feathers—if dragons had feathers. The glow in those hollow eyes perk up like a kid waiting for Santa on Christmas morning. He wants me to engage. He won't get it.

Red's face falls and I brace in case he gets any overly ambitious ideas about taking me out. He's not paying attention to me, though. His pointy nose aims at the parking lot, dragging in air by the lungful like he found the cure for cancer. My curiosity wins. What the hell changed his mood all of a sudden?

"Bear," Red snarls into the darkness, his volume ricocheting off the back wall of the grocery.

"Shut the fuck up!" I hiss, tucking my wings tight to my back in case his noise draws unwanted attention.

Red doesn't acknowledge my warning. He's too busy taking his own photos of the girl and her huge new guest.

This guy's my height and—I can't believe it—but a little wider than me, a rare find in the human world. I never want to say Red is right, but my nose smells bear. They always smell faintly of the woods. No matter how they try to disguise their scent, trees and earth cling to them just like their bulky muscles. And neither disappear in their human form. Those boys are huge. What worries me is our girl's familiar greeting. She's a bigger danger than I expected if she's friendly with a shifter. This guy's a mammoth-sized complication to my exit-strategy.

Alert Dixon. There's no way around it. I can smell her interest downwind from twenty feet away. It saturates the air. "Mates..."

"Bullshit, they haven't mated." Red's argument dies on his lips, those beady yellow eyes flashing annoyance. "Stop thinking with yer dick, man. You got your wrong head in the game."

"I know they haven't mated, dumbass." I can't stop the irritation from seeping in my voice, but both eyes stay trained on the bear's interaction with our target. The big guy just turned this *game* on its head. "Red, come on. Even you can smell that. She's his mate."

Red's double fists knock my chest—his pitiful attempt to shove me back. News Flash... it doesn't work.

"Bull. Fuckin'. Shit." Red's contempt grits between huffs of air, like he can deny fate just by exhaling it. "I think you're going soft, Baldy. Mates are fairytales... make believe."

How can Red deny something that's a cornerstone of shifter culture?

I stare for one frozen moment. It's not macho to want true love. I dare anyone to question my manhood over believing in fated mates. There's an unfortunate trail of battered bodies in my wake that proves plenty.

"I'm not ashamed of believing in mates, Red." *My parents were mates.* I may not deserve a mate after everything, but I'll be damned if anyone makes me question if they exist. Especially not a redneck like the one in front of me.

I glower. "Make believe, huh? You mean, like dragons, were-wolves... or that fuckin' bear standing over there?" I nod my head at our target and her partner, not even trying to hide my laughter. Red's face colors. He doesn't like my mocking. Or maybe because he knows I'm right.

"Fuck you!" Red spits a wad of brown tobacco to the ground, aiming for my feet and missing. His face sets in a scowl. "You know what? Fuck the bear, too." Red gives me his back, scrolling his phone for I don't know what. When he finds what he's looking for, his fingers fly across the keys, typing faster than a high school kid spreading gossip.

"What the hell are you doing?"

"You worry about you, Kristopher. I'm getting shit done." His sick laughter wipes away my humor faster than a Black Racer slithers.

My face sobers as I stride closer, looming my six and a half feet over Red until his head lifts. Those sinister eyes fall level at my collarbone, and he hisses through clenched teeth. "Son-of-a—" His curse cuts off, cracking that cocky façade in the face of a larger aggressor.

My dragon celebrates the victory of shutting Red's mouth. *Cower, you bastard.*

"What did you do, Red?" I shake my head, malice coating my voice. "I'm so tired of his shit," I groan. Red is ten years my senior. Why does he act like an overgrown adolescent?

His spine straightens, tension deepening the valleys at the corners of his eyes. It's impossible to hide emotions from a shifter. And Red's heart rate just kicked into high gear, telling me I need to watch him.

Red knocks past me, giving himself space in the darkness. "Nothin' for you to worry about, Baldy. Remember yer place. I did what I had to." His meaning is clear. Red is a nasty son-of-a-bitch, but he knows my skill. I'll kick his ass. But that chip on his shoulder has been there since Dixon brought me into the upper circle years ago.

Fine. If he wants to take off the leash, then so will I.

Unfortunately, a bitchy retort won't get me anywhere with Red, and the comeback dies on my tongue anyway when the stench of fear and adrenaline wafts across the parking lot. I glance over, where the agitated bear stands, his spine rod straight, head searching in every direction for the source of his mate's stress. He smells it on her as much as we do.

What the fuck did Red do?

"He's looking for danger, goddammit."

Red only chuckles at my warning, his enjoyment over tormenting the girl obvious. "I only sent a little warning. Nothing to get yer knickers in a twist." He waves his phone in my face, wiggling the screen side to side like a misbehaving child taunting his prey. Red's senile laugh shows how detached he is, that he doesn't see the danger of an angry bear protecting his mate.

My eyes follow the words on Red's blurring screen. *Shit!* My stomach ties in a knot large enough to stabilize Quint's boat in Jaws.

Red: Don't think your new boyfriend will protect you, vet girl.

"What the fuck, Red?" I hiss. "When did you get her number?"

Cursing, I pace behind the cover of the grocery wall. The girl's shifter boyfriend is on red alert now, scouring the parking lot for trouble. That will end in an inconvenient, mismatched battle if Red and I aren't in full shift. And since I don't have his scent anymore, I assume the wind has changed. "Shit."

"Stop being a pussy," Red grumbles, his freckles standing in stark contrast against the anger darkening his face. "I got the number from the vet. We paid him a visit and got a hold of his files."

"Who gave orders to engage? Dixon doesn't want the girl touched unless we confirm a risk."

I'm not surprised Red would compromise a peaceful mission just to stir shit up. He's obviously been more active behind the scenes than I realized. Pissed, I grip that scrawny arm and jerk. His gaunt body moves with more force than I expect, throwing us deeper in the shadows.

An angry growl hits me in the face, but since I'm hauling his body like a naughty toddler, I just laugh. Red swings his arm ineffectively, those druggy-muscles having no power in his battle for freedom. "Tsk, tsk. Red, you samplin' way too much product, man. You're weak." He scoffs, swinging harder like it's going to have any effect on his freedom. His widely known drug use is why he's a figurehead for Dixon—faux management—but a weakling isn't useful in our world.

Dixon says, as long as he's not harmful, he stays. And since the alternative is joining with Earl, we all put up with it.

But Red's crossing a line now, blatantly getting in Dixon's way. I cringe, having seen Dixon's explosive temper when one of his crew goes rogue. The boss doesn't care if it's an accident or on purpose; let anyone hurt a woman or child and there's hell to pay. He lives in fear of betraying his promise to his wife. He vowed never to execute anything like the abuse she endured as a child.

"What's the big deal, Baldy? I raided her place, texted her. So the fuck what?"

Red swings, attempting to free his arm. It connects with my shoulder—no pain—but the little twit pisses me off. I hold tight, my temper elevating from working with a man with so little control.

Shoving his ass in front of me, I only release Red when we're out of view—and sniffing range—of the shifter. He flips on me the moment I let go, spitting a nasty wad of tobacco at my feet. "Fuck you, Baldy! Dixon takes too long. You two pussy-footin' like you got pigtails and pink tutus." Red scoffs, wiping his hands down the front of his shirt, like somehow, I wrinkled the flannel uniform he wears.

"Dixon's orders were recon, that's it," I grind out.

"Dixon never should have promoted you. You're a disgrace to your wings," Red spits out, hatred dripping from every syllable. He turns, done with our conversation and obviously ready for his plan. He stops at the end of the building, gritting his teeth against the pain from the impending shift.

His bony body stretches, the beginning of our tough leathery skin coating his freckles in a reddish hue just before he stretches his wings. Red's stark eyes attempt to scold but grow annoyed at my lack of intimidation. "You know what, Baldy... fuck Dixon. I searched. I raided. I might have enjoyed a little ransack, but the bitch is mine to do with as I please." The desire to knock Red cold takes over like some sixth sense and I step forward, laughing when Red retreats further. His derision for us all is clear from this conversation. His voice drops, rumbling in the darkness. "I'm gonna finish this bullshit... soon. Count on it, Kris. If Dixon can't do it, I'll coordinate with Earl and take care of business."

That threat is the final ice in my veins.

Behind our standoff, gravel crunches, pulling my attention to the tires spinning for a speedy exit. I'm frozen in time. My eyes falling to where the bear stands in human form, eyeing the surrounding trees with suspicion. I feel his apprehension in my chest, noticing a slight lift the moment Red takes flight.

With his poisoning presence gone, I need to contact Dixon, warn him of Red's AWOL status. But I can't, for the life of me, turn from this distressed man, like he's a kindred soul. From his paranoia to the yearning gaze at his girl. He locks on the horizon for a while, watching the spot his mate disappeared with desire and desperation tainting the air.

I feel ya, brother.

Chapter Seven

Red

WHERE DOES THAT OVER-MUSCLED piece of shit get off?

That coward thinks that just because Dixon treats him like the second coming, like the goddamn son he never had, even though I'm the one who's been by his side since he and Earl joined their gangs together. Back when not a one of 'em had a dime to their name.

Now, this meathead thinks he can boss me around, that I give two cents about his recon orders. *Fuck recon.* I should be the goddamn boss, not that spineless Dixon. Then we'd be acting like the badass dragons we are and not pussyfootin' around.

I'm itching to move. Can't stop thinking about it, even after meeting with Earl in Georgia. There's a plan at least, but all this waiting around is for people who don't know how to get shit done. *Give me the job! Take my goddamn leash off!*

Still pissed, my dragon steams the air through clenched teeth as we land in my backyard. It's one a.m., dark enough that I'm not gonna go change in the forest like those whiny bitches in Dixon's gang. Any nosy humans in my neighborhood can bite my ass.

Groaning, my eyes blacken at the edges, narrowing into a tiny tunnel of vision through the pain of my wings retreating. My serpent-like dragon muscle condenses into human-form, the weaker, bonier version of myself I hate. If I had my way, I'd live as a dragon and not suffer this torture transitioning back and forth. It's bullshit to have to show the world weakness, to get run over by genetic freaks like Kristopher, who grew to a behemoth size.

Damn. I wish I could go back to the day his parents bit the dust and stop Dixon from taking that shrieking boy into his house! *What the hell was that?* Earl issued the hit, and I waited until the color drained from their faces to sneak out, not even touching that dumb kid twiddling some video game on the couch. *My reward?* That dumbass was my underling for the next ten years.

And now the bastard thinks he's above it all.

Screw him! I growl, stumbling through my backdoor with a curse to my unsteady feet. My body throbs for hours after a transition back to human and, like everything else tonight, it pisses me off.

I smack the light switch inside the door, searing my sensitive eyeballs with the kitchen fluorescents. Immediately, I notice the absence of my dinner. Going over to the microwave, I pop the door open in case she prepared leftovers. Nothing. Oven... nothing.

"Where's my goddamn sandwich?"

That bitch didn't leave me anything. I'd bet my left nut she and the kid ate and went to bed without even thinking of the one who worked and put that food in their bellies. I don't give a shit if she had a headache this morning when she called. She has one damn job... take care of our house. That includes my dinner.

If she doesn't see me for three days, there better be food waiting for me just in case I come home. My dragon uses all my damn energy. *Now, I want my fuckin' dinner!*

With my mind set, I take the stairs two at a time. Time for a wake-up call and a little lesson in what's expected in this household.

Chapter Eight

Abigail

I'M ONLY GIVING MYSELF thirty more seconds to debate if this is a smart idea.

The street is quiet enough. But that doesn't stop the sense of dread making me question stepping out of the car. Yes, most of the homes have seen better days, but that's not why. I'm not that much of a princess.

Still, their overgrown yards and peeling paint show a complete lack of care in the neighborhood. A few have rusted swing sets and broken toys in the grass, tugging my heart that any child lives here. A few homes down the street stand out against the other rundown shacks, like people are moving in and remodeling the neighborhood. Their maintenance shows: fences mended, mums sprinkled through flower beds and porches for the fall.

Unfortunately, I'm parked in front of the former, one with dead bushes instead of a freshly raked yard. With weeds covering every inch of flowerbed and every bush overgrown and scraggly. There's not a bud of color brightening the place. Wood-rot shows through the chipped paint on the porch and all across the side of the house. Some boards pull away, their nails failing with lack of care, creating an easy entry point for plenty of bugs and vermin from the outside.

At least the only busted window I see is in a dormer that exposes only the attic to the fall chill that's set in.

The whole place is so dilapidated, I wonder if I wrote the kid's address wrong. *Maybe it's vacant.*

There's only one way to find out.

Before I talk myself out of it, I leave the safety of my little sedan and walk to the faded blue door that I bet was cute once upon a time. If I sit debating the potential safety issues, I'll never do this. It's not just the porch boards popping under rusted out nails, and the crooked handrail hanging at an odd angle. Worse is the pack of teenagers at the corner. Whatever they're smoking isn't enough to hold their attention. Ten eyes turn, five leering smiles aimed my way with a symphony of belly laughs and back slaps, that way boys do when pretending to be men.

"Woo. Hoo, baby."

"Hey, mama. Over here."

"Day-um, boys... I could toss that one over my shoulder and run."

I ignore their cat calls... a near impossible thing considering butterflies ravage my stomach when I give the boys my back. In my pocket, I finger the metal attachment on my keyring in case one of those idiots tries to carry out that last thought.

The cold steel is easy to carry, but provides more power and, let's face it, more damage with the prongs sticking from my fist than my tiny hand could do by itself. Especially against much larger guys. It provides nice security when I'm alone. Because of that, I carry it everywhere. Not just because it was a gift from Kris—although I'm sure my infatuation with the hunk has something to do with my attachment to the thing.

I'm sure I read more into Kris looking out for my safety, too.

Still, I relived that day in my fantasies a lot. The night I found Kris wandering the hallway outside my room while I packed for freshman orientation. I heard the footsteps echoing closer, away... closer, away. Until finally, I walked out to figure who the hell was making so much noise on my deserted wing of the house. Even at that age, Kris's angled jaw left my knees weak, but the shock of seeing his hulking frame pacing doubled his normal effect.

Kris looks about the same as I feel, catching him outside my door. His usually hard face softens into the first blush I'd seen on the man since adolescence. Smoothly, he strides where I stand slack-jawed in my doorway.

"Here." Kris's masculine grunt is barely audible over my frantic heart rate.

Oh. My. Gosh. What is he doing in my hall?

Glancing down at my flimsy pajama shorts with the blue ruffled lace around the hem makes me wish I was one of those girls who dressed sexy for bed. Not like I'm still ten. A masculine cough pulls my attention back to those hypnotizing emerald eyes. And now, the burning skin on my face is noticeable.

Never doubt my paleness and its horrible timing to betray my feelings.

Kris scans the hallway before he passes me a small rectangular box. No wrapping... only a wide yellow bow tying the top. Does he remember yellow is my favorite color, or is that luck?

My hands tremble as I take the box, more nervous than I should be.

"Um, it's just something small," he says, chagrinned. For a second, I think Kris is going to take the box back, but he doesn't. It stays frozen in my hands while I figure out which I want to gawk at more, my mystery box or the hulking muscle standing like the best wet dream at my bedroom door.

"What is it?" I smile, giving the box a gentle shake. It's stupid, but I'm thrown off by seeing the man who hasn't looked at me since I entered high school unless assigned to my protection duty. Now, the hunk is two feet away with a dry-fit t-shirt molding to his pecs, while my girly pajamas scream, 'I have no idea what to do with your sexy body.' That doesn't stop me from wanting it.

"Open it," he says in a rush, the bossy plea breaking me out of my stupor.

My fingers shake as I untie the ribbon and tuck it into my pocket, as excited as a kid at Christmas. I lift the lid and stop, confused as I pick up the tiny tool. I turn it over in my hand, trying not to crumble under Kris's focused attention. I don't want to hurt his feelings by not understanding his gift.

What the heck is this thing? Should I know that already?

"I, ah... since you're tiny, I thought it might help you. You know... extra protection at college. While I, uh we, can't watch over you."

I've never heard Kris stammer, but that adorable way he's scuffing the back of his head takes the sting out of his reminder, both of my small size and my total lack of dragon skills. One look at the sincerity in Kris's eyes and I know he's not ridiculing. He's sincere in trying to help.

Either way, it's nice getting more than grunts and three-word sentences out of him. I miss the conversations we had before things got weird, before Kris joined my father's guys. Back when he was just the teenage boy I crushed on.

His wide, callused fingers maneuver mine to fit the little metal thing perfectly inside my squeezed fist. And I get it. The hard extension will let me defend myself without hurting my hand, not to mention giving me a hair's chance of being effective.

I shake my head and remember the satisfaction on Kris's face when I beamed up at him. It was the last time I saw him grin.

After that, when I'd visit from college, he kept his distance, and each time it broke my heart a little more until I stopped coming home. Still, I kept Kris's tool with me, believing it showed he cared on some level.

Like right now.

This tool helps me not chicken out. I've made it this far. This is the time. The worst danger in the Brewer house isn't home—daddy dearest. I overheard the guys talking on the back deck this morning and decided to pay his son a visit. Little Max hasn't been at school for three days. No call. No explanation.

Red's not here. Red's not here.

The quiet chant as I climb the steps helps block the obnoxious bro party behind me, but it does nothing to ease my sixth sense from prickling when I knock a rapid beat at the door. Nerves that I'm overstepping normal school boundaries keep every part of my body twitching, fidgeting, or jiggling like my pants are on fire. I can't stop my eyes from tracking all over the house, looking for a distraction.

Cobwebs string above my head, crisscrossing the porch ceiling to the naked light bulb in the center. If I were here after sunset, I'm not sure I'd be able to enter the crawly habitat out of fear one of those eight-legged things would decide to build a nest in my hair. *Eck! Spiders give me the heebie-jeebies thanks to an ill-advised attempt to watch Arachnophobia as a kid.*

From the state of the house, the wires hanging loose where the doorbell used to be no surprise at all. How can a kid like Max come out of this place? He's one of the neatest, most responsible… hell, one of the politest kids I know. It makes sense in a way. If the kid hates the way he lives, he wouldn't continue that outside of the house. That's the part niggling my brain. Max doesn't skip school. Yet, he's missed three days with no call from his parents, no doctor's note. It's not like him at all!

At my second knock, the door cracks open… just enough to see a few haggard inches of Max's mom, her pale skin hiding under an oversized sweatshirt. Her unwashed tawny hair hangs limp over half her face. A face that looks to have lost all its given blood in the last thirty seconds. And by the purposeful angle of her head, I know my suspicions of abuse during our conference two weeks ago are true. I'd bet my left breast that given the opportunity, she would have a pair of sunglasses to hide behind, the age-old stereotype of an abused spouse.

Even through the small opening, Mrs. Brewer smells human. Not that I'm perfect at detecting species considering I've never shifted myself, but it would make sense for a bully like Red to pick a human mate he can use, abuse, and run over.

"Miss Dixon... what are you doing here?" Her hesitant voice would make me question my visit if I didn't catch that slight tug on her long sleeves. The faded purple markings are hard to miss, even under a sweater.

"Miss Dixon! Miss Dixon!" Max grins ear to ear, his feet pounding toward the front door when he hears my name. His socked feet slide to a stop behind the frail woman standing guard of their home. Like a shattered gargoyle, no longer able to ward off evil demons from the sanctity of her home.

"Hey, little man." I risk meeting Mrs. Brewer's eyes... weary, just like the tight lines of her body blocking access to her son. His little head pokes around her waist, though her hand holds the little boy mostly behind her. "How are you, Max? Haven't seen you in a few days." I keep my tone light, hoping Max will open the door easier than his mom. My gut says she won't be as forthcoming.

"Oh, he's fine, Miss Dixon," she says, her voice strained. "Just under the weather this week. You know how it is."

Somehow, I'm not reassured.

"Yeah, stuff's always going around school." I nod, but my gears are turning, wondering if there's anything I can say to earn Mrs. Brewer's trust. She's been standoffish from the first night I met her at orientation.

My sneaking suspicion is that she knows who my father is. For all she knows, I'm one of them and going to rat her out if she mentions anything sketchy. If that's the case, it makes sense why she's tucking Max away from me. A mama bear protecting her cub.

Gently, I try again. "What is it you have, big man? Fever? Tummy ache?"

No go. Mrs. Brewer cuts me off. "It's really sweet of you to stop by, Miss Dixon, but I wouldn't want you getting sick. Max can return to school tomorrow. He'll see you then." The door tries to close in my face even as she says goodbye.

Max's smile drops as he looks up at the woman who gave him most of his features. Like someone wise beyond his years, Max squeezes her hand in support, but bravely makes his own decision to move from behind her protection. An entire conversation passes between them, twin emerald eyes communicating silently, a partnership, an understanding. Immediately, I see… these two people have each other's back, no matter what. It smooths some of my worry for Max. Until the little boy comes into full view, his thin arms wrapping around my waist in a heart-felt hug that hits deep inside.

Tears spring to my eyes.

"Thank you for caring, Miss Dixon." That sweet voice nearly brings me to my knees. Especially when Max pulls back, hanging onto both my hands. He knows what he's doing by coming in the open. There's wisdom behind those sad eyes that's hard to look at because I see it… the dots along his bicep, the fading purple circling his wrists.

Fingerprints.

His tiny face blurs in front of me. This kid has more maturity and grace than either adult standing beside him. And he's suffering for it, caught in a world he didn't choose. My eyes jerk to his mom's. I want to hide my judgment, but I'm just so angry. I can't curb the desire to hit something.

"I'm sorry," she mouths silently, shame wallowing in her red-rimmed eyes.

I open my mouth, not sure what to say, but stop when her head falls, tears finally cracking that tough exterior and spilling over her sunken cheeks. One hand pulls away from guarding the door, moving to cover her sobs in front of Max. The action causes her long sleeve to slide back, revealing a blue and black wrist underneath. It looks painfully fresh, angrier than Max's. But it's the faded yellow ones spreading out underneath that hint this isn't the first injury this month. Mrs. Brewer has a rough life. I can't, in good conscience, pile more pain on her, no matter how pissed I am that Max is in this situation with her.

"Mrs. Brewer," I start, swallowing down the emotion clogging my throat. "Can I call someone for you? A family member, a local church… anyone. It will be quiet. I promise." My arms circle Max's shoulders, holding him tight against my stomach while I plead with his mother, beg her with my eyes to let me help.

I can't take them back to my house for obvious reasons. I'd be tossing the woman into the dragon's den... literally. Her damn husband spends more time at my house than he does here. They need a place to run where Red won't track her, somewhere far away.

Max lifts his head enough to look back at his mother with a hope that breaks my heart. But she just shakes her head.

"There's no one, Miss Dixon. My family didn't accept my marriage to Clint. We haven't spoken since Max was born." Regret for her life choices is clear, but no one deserves punishment like this. Still, Mrs. Brewer straightens her shoulders, wiping the wet tracks from her face before extending a hand to Max. "Come on, little man. Let's let Miss Dixon get on with her evening."

He nods, blessing me with one last smile as he lets go of my waist. "It's okay, Miss Dixon. I'll be at school tomorrow."

I'm torn. I want to grab this kid and run away from this sadness. Life has obviously beaten down his mom if this ghostly pale woman accepts her life with a morbid self-punishment. What happens to Max if he stays? Will Red beat the sweet innocence out of him, too?

I glance down at Max's confident, sad smile. "Don't worry, Miss Dixon, I'll take care of mom." His conspiratorial little voice is the last crack in my heart. I watch him turn and wrap his mom in a hug, making me both proud and worried at the same time. No matter how well intentioned, Max can't protect her from a full-grown man, let alone one with dragon strength. And he shouldn't have to.

With a little wave, Mom and son leave me frozen on the porch, long after the door shuts in my face. Until the cool fall air sinks into my skin and I notice the street's fallen quiet. The teenagers have gone, and the void of outdoor activity is noticeable without them. There are no kids playing. No people walking their dogs or coming home from work. Even the crickets took a hiatus from life in this neighborhood.

The emptiness sends chills down my spine as I climb into the car. There's a rain of depression across the whole night, blanketing my mood like the fresh drizzle spritzing my windshield.

Why is life this unfair?

My inadequacies as a dragon plague me the entire way home. Nothing I think of is within my power to help Max and his mom. By the time I turn down the half-mile driveway to my dad's house, my confidence is at an all-time low. I haven't felt this down from seeing that giant, secluded mansion since Mom died. I knew then this house would never be the same. I just didn't expect it to turn into a prison... one I loathe to call home.

Outside, the home is a beauty. The ornamental landscaping and tall, southern style columns would make a historian salivate, wondering what secrets these walls hide. *If they only knew!* Because inside those brick walls, I'm trapped... stifled. Wondering what trouble I'll walk in on consumes me, fills me with dread every day until I'm emotionally exhausted.

If anything, tonight is a wake-up call. I can't stay in this house; stuck in a life I didn't choose. Is that why I worry about Max? Because I see where this life leads.

But how can I expect him to make changes? I'm not brave enough to do it myself.

'If you always do what you've always done; you'll always get what you've always got.' My mother's words carry me into the house. Even if she was quoting Henry Ford, she still motivates me from the grave.

Chapter Nine

Kris

"So, you got nothin', kid?" Boss booms in the confines of his sizable office, jarring my nerves. Waiting for his wrath is like waiting for the chair to fall with a noose around your neck. Hell, the room feels like waiting in the goddamn principal's office.

"Not nothing, sir. I followed the girl for a week, watched what she did, who she hung out with. She's boring as hell, boss. Just another girl home visiting family." Dixon glares as he walks to the rollaway bar in the corner, pouring himself a glass of scotch from the glass decanter there. My temper rises, having to repeat for the third time that there's nothing to get from this Cherokee girl.

Red's crazed laughter rings from the couch in the back where he's spread, covering double the space than his stunted frame needs. *Overcompensating much?* My fists clench, desperate to knock that satisfied smirk right off his ugly mug. It's obnoxious how a grown man lights up at catching his brother-in-arms off guard.

That Dixon has Red in his office at all, instead of razzing me in private, is a low blow.

My dragon rages fury in my head, scratching and stomping until I want to beg my beast for mercy.

Lucky for Red and lucky for my brewing headache, the boss interrupts our stare down, his impatience plain as day. Dixon moves to perch on the edge of his mahogany desk, the lines in his mouth drawn tight. "Sit," he says, pointing to the couch. It's a command—not a request—and the boss expects no argument.

I don't give him one.

I fall in line and lower myself on the opposite end of Red, waiting for the ass chewing I expect. No way I'm relaxing back like the idiot beside me, not when Dixon himself stands a leap away from us. My ass perches on the edge of the cushion, elbows braced on my knees, bouncing. Whatever tolerance I held these last twenty-ish years has left. It's broken. Even my dragon agrees, roaring straight chaos in my head.

I'm sick of this life! Sick of our punishments being bodily harm or death instead of a pink slip like normal people. Sick of doling out punishments. I glance down to my right hand, stretching and retracting my tight fingers. The bruises have healed, but the scars spidering across my knuckles write their own story of how brutal it is to be the enforcer for Dixon's mafia.

On the outside, Dixon's the picture of relaxation, his crystal glass held to his lips for a slow sip of dark liquor, the calm measured heartbeat that doesn't skip while he tortures me with deep, careful consideration from a few feet away. Only I'm not fooled by that calm façade.

My dragon huffs, heating the air I drag in my lungs, making it hard to breathe. He's paranoid watching the boss's twisted mind work through the ways we failed him and what he'll do about it. It's unnerving.

To ease suspicion, I grind the back of my teeth to control my beast and slow my knee's vibrations. Dixon's gaze shifts, his burning sea-colored irises releasing me from their scrutiny and locking on his number one.

"*Red!* You said this girl has a bodyguard." The sniveling weasel grins. Dixon's insinuation is clear... our stories don't mesh up, but I can't tell which of us he's questioning. Considering Red got back early to deliver his dirty report ahead of mine, I'm not surprised. He painted me as weak, no doubt. In this organization, weakness is a quick way to die.

Dixon's head flips between us both before sticking on me. "Seems a bodyguard is a giant fuckin' billboard, Baldy. The chick obviously heard something she shouldn't. Don't ya think?" His voice is terse, only expecting one answer from me.

The tone torches my skin, like a thousand fire ants having a field day with my dragon. The dragon who's desperate to take vengeance on the backstabber beside me. I shake my head, keeping my movements controlled so Dixon doesn't see the steam waiting to blow out my eardrums. "It wasn't a bodyguard, Boss. The dude was her mate."

Shock jerks Dixon off his rear.

"Mate! What the hell, Red? Didn't think I needed to know that?" The challenge hangs in the air, aimed at Red, thank fuck. Still, my body stays coiled, wondering why the hell Red's silent when he should pray for mercy. *Idiot!*

Their stalemate only breaks when the sound of crunching gravel in the driveway pulls Dixon's to the window. His lead footsteps thrum a steady beat, completely at odds with my rapid heart rate. When a sigh deflates the rigid lines of his shoulders, my agitation eases, too. Only one person makes the boss go soft... Abi.

Red, however, doesn't know when to shut it. Or when a ticking time bomb has already defused. No, his smoked laughter rings across the room... seconds before that pint-sized combat boot shoves right inside the moron's mouth.

He stands for the door, ignoring my presence like I'm a fly just buzzing his ear. "Like I told Baldy, mates are bullshit. That shit ain't worth mentioning."

A roar sounds from across the room as Dixon's body catapults past me and into the back of Red. The second in command hits the floor, flattened under Dixon's knee that's steadily applying pressure between Red's shoulder blades. The smaller man groans from the boss's weight.

"Watch your mouth." Dixon's face burns crimson, straight hatred melting his earlier iced façade. Slowly, he bends menacingly close to Red's ear, keeping one hand fisted in the back of his hair with just enough force to keep his cheek wedged against the floor. "Just because you didn't wait for your mate, doesn't mean I didn't find mine." That growling whisper awakes goosebumps along my arms, and though I'm double our boss's height, I still have a level of respect—or fear—for the man. One that Red's learning the hard way from his prone position.

I've seen Dixon's temper in the past, so I play it safe and eye their showdown still as a statue from the couch. Not a sound from my lips when the boss yanks his prey's wrist up to a twisted position in the middle of his back. Not a twitch of movement when the older man lifts to his feet, jerking the mullet on Red's head until he stands with him. The man normally controls a room with the power of his reputation alone. It's not rare to see his dragon strength exert without a shimmer of his skin. Dixon doesn't need his dragon close to the surface to be dangerous.

With that thought, I try my damndest to hide my smirk when Red goes into full blitz mode, his body swinging left and right to get out of Dixon's grip. It does nothing. *How fuckin' weak is that man?*

When my nemesis finally stops fighting, his red eyes blaze with a mix of betrayal under his embarrassment. Only Red doesn't have the balls to respond with aggression to Dixon. If I didn't think the man so disgusting, I'd pity him. It's a hard fall from grace, being manhandled by our leader as if you're a nobody.

Like you haven't spent thirty years under his wing, doing his bidding.

Once Dixon physically carts Red to the door, he lets go of Red's hair and jerks it wide. His voice drops low against Red's ear, warning. "You know, Red... I should have known a piece of scum like you could never understand the power of a mate. Watching how you treat your family all these years has been disgusting and I let it slide too many times." Judging by the hiss of air coming from Red, I assume Dixon put a pointed twist to Red's wrist to emphasize his words. "The next time you decide to punish your wife, Red. The absolute. Next. Time. Think about this conversation. It won't only be her mistakes that get punished."

With that, Dixon shoves his man through the door, satisfaction tilting the corners of his lips when Red thuds hard against the opposite wall. He straightens quickly, tugging the hem of his already wrinkled flannel like it'll do any good. That disheveled appearance wasn't strictly Dixon's fault. It's his complete lack of personal hygiene.

The pure murder that darkens his eyes, however, that's Dixon's fault. Red knows that he's out-manned, but he wisely controls that normally explosive temper.

"You both deserve each other." Red scoffs, attempting to steady his panting breaths. "I'll get this done myself." With anger wafting off him, Red storms down the hall, leaving the two of us somber in his wake.

When Dixon walks behind his desk. "Follow him. Make sure he doesn't do something stupid." Resignation makes his voice hollow.

"What about the girl?"

"I'll get the vet on her. The doc has upped his numbers like we want, but he needs help at the clinic. If we confirm she's clear, we could use her help... underground." Dixon grabs a sheet of paper, shaking his head as he hands it over. It's a log, organized by addresses with labels and codes, none of which I understand. What I *do* understand are dollar signs. That's a lot of cash. Dixon taps the paper, huffing a frustrated breath. "Earl's pressuring to elevate our shipments. And Red's all for it, but there's no fuckin' way I'm going along with this game."

Dixon studies me, but I've got nothing. This is the first time I've seen the inner workings... What do I say? "What does this mean?" I trust Dixon won't think me stupid for not following his train of thought.

"I gotta prove the distribution we have is fine, Kris." *Shit! He used my real name.* "I agree with you on the girl. I see the threat and her mating a shifter means we watch our backs. Earl's freakin' the fuck out, but this is my territory. I want to see if we can work with her, keep an extra doctor on hand, you know. Especially if the vet lost his marbles. But I need her under control first."

I nod, completely over my head, trying to plan this as a lone wolf... or lone dragon. "What if she won't come back? The vet's sloppier than we thought. From the conversations I've overheard, she doesn't exactly like working there." Dixon shakes his head, like the idea of keeping her under our thumb stresses him more than if we could just off her.

"Yeah, well... we'll cross that bridge when it burns in front of us. The doc patches a good bullet hole, but it's looking like he can't keep his hands out of the cookie jar, either." He nods at the sheet in my hand. "That's not gonna fly."

Chapter Ten

Kris

AFTER GETTING MY ORDERS, I should be out the front door, but my gut pulls me toward the parlor instead. It's Abigail's favorite spot and for the life of me, I can't stop my feet from heading that way.

She's hurting.

My dragon senses his mate's despair from the other side of the house, which worries me that our connection is so powerful. Especially when I can't control his urge to follow our mate, to make sure she's okay.

We can't have her.

That's my daily mantra since Abigail returned home—count them—four months ago. Every time I want to give in, I fight it. But every day the argument gets weaker.

Old Kris would walk out of this damn torture chamber. I'm under orders to track Red. Disobeying a high command in Dixon's Mafia comes with heavy repercussions. Some I've dished out myself. I know how hard our men punish when directed from the top. That's one problem messing with my head, the guilt over those memories. The times I hurt guys I once cracked a beer with, or like the vet... someone who helped me in the past. Whether he saved me out of obligation or fear, I don't care. It still eats at me. If I were a religious man, I'd say Hail Mary's until my balls turned gray.

Hell, I doubt even that would make a dent at this point.

Only when I walk into the parlor does it hit me. Abi's pure perfection sitting in that over-fluffed chair like she does every day after work, that messy blonde hair piled in a twisted bun on top of her head. I just want to dig my hands into it, let it loose. Set those curls free around her shoulders the way I love. But there aren't enough Hail Mary's in the world that would earn me rights to the beautiful girl in front of me.

Stop thinking that!

It's bad enough I can't take my eyes off the woman. I'll be damned if my hands go anywhere near her. I tell myself that every day. And most days it works. Except the times she sighs like that. I hate seeing her shoulders drop in defeat, like the weight of the world sits there. It's all I can do to remember my promise when my fingers tingle to touch her just watching the woman work.

Then she goes and bites those damn fingernails, and the tilt of her arm drops the ribboned strap holding her pajama top up. Softly, it slides off that delicate slope of porcelain skin, making my mouth water. The urge to follow the wayward strap with my lips, to pull it back up with my teeth is overwhelming. Any excuse to sample Abigail's skin. Forget the wrath from Dixon.

Oh sorry, Abi. I broke every finger on our last job, but don't worry. The punishment was worth it. Hah!

My dragon groans internally, thinking about the half an hour he wants to spend worshipping that line of exposed neck. Thankfully, Abi's so entranced in her laptop, she doesn't know my slow death in her doorway.

Take us closer.

Okay, I'm only not arguing because I need to know if those fuzzy shorts are as soft as they look. I see those damn things daily. And the way that baby blue material stops just below the curve of Abigail's ass, the amount of leg on display riles my dragon up something fierce. He screams to claim, to mark her so every other male in this house knows she's taken.

How would those toned lengths feel wrapped around my hips when I sink into heaven?

Abigail's face twists comically, her brows furrowed as she clicks through page after page on her laptop. The adorableness temporarily distracts me from my NC-17 thoughts and into a more PG-13 that at least allows for polite conversation since my feet won't listen and walk out the door.

"What are you so focused on?" I try—and fail—to hide my laughter at Abi's startled squeak. It cuts the silence in the quiet room, lightening the awkwardness of my surprise visit.

"*Jesus Christ, Kris!* You scared the crap out of me." Abi glances up, the blue in her matching pajama top morphing her compassionate eyes to the color of the sky.

I laugh. "Now, there's a picture." The sarcasm slips out before I can bite my tongue and I cringe. *Shit! I sound like a twelve-year-old.*

Abigail's slight smile rewards my off-humor, relaxing me as I watch a pink blush work its way across her ivory skin. My cock stirs. Immediately, my mind wonders how far that shade of pink continues. Does it spread across her perfectly pale body at other times, like when she comes?

Before my eyes, Abigail's shoulders tighten and I see the moment she remembers who I am, her tease of a smile fading. My paranoia grows watching her eyes flit back to her computer. I just can't tell if she doesn't want to look at me, or if she doesn't want me looking at her screen.

Dislike or distrust... which is worse?

Stop bitching! I tell my dragon. *Abi doesn't know us well enough to make a judgment call.*

We can change that.

Damn that teasing bastard.

My internal debate lasts only a second longer, until Abi tilts her delicate face my way, eyes asking the question neither of us dare. Her face shows the same shameful pull mine does. That possibility calls me forward, Abigail tracking my actions as I walk closer. Her fingers curl protectively around her monitor the closer I move, like she needs to guard it from me.

What the hell!

Anger surges, but I shove it down, cutting Abi some slack, considering who we are to each other. When I sit in the matching chair, instead of invading whatever secret she's hiding, Abi's breath exhales, nailing me right in the chest.

How is she scared of me?

I thought we had an understanding; that she knew I'd never hurt her. Hell, I protected her from school bullies... and the ones in this house, too.

At times, in my early teens, Abigail was the only person I could confide in after losing my parents. She listened to my pain. And for the first year I stayed here, she was my friend. Granted, she was five years younger, but Abi's gentleness always drew me in. That I've slid so low in her mind, it... it fucking hurts.

I don't care if I have no plans to claim her, fated or not. My would-be mate thinking so little of me is a rejection even my bitter heart wasn't expecting. It's a kick in the gut. A deep sorrow tightens my chest knowing I don't deserve Abi.

Shit! Coming in here was a mistake.

Abi straightens herself, sitting a little taller, watching my fidgeting hands struggle to appear calm. Her scrutiny feels like ants crawling down my neck. When my brain registers those delicate lips curling at the corner, I relax slightly. I watch as she licks the wetness from their plumpness, sipping her tea as casual as can be. I wish, more than anything, I could do the same.

"Can I help you with something, Kris?" that smart mouth interrupts my train of thought.

Nope. Not touching that.

Distraction.

"Whatcha working on with that sourpuss on your face?" I circle a hand over my scrunched up, overly exaggerated frown, trying to joke my way out of this awkwardness.

Abi's surprised squeak isn't exactly what I wanted, but I'll take her indignation over the defensiveness any day. Abi's posture relaxes slightly, but I hate that flash of annoyance when she sees me. It was quick before her eyes flitted back to the screen, almost looking paranoid at my intrusion.

This is absurd! I laugh at our ridiculousness, the first full-bodied laugh I've had in years.

Abi's head jerks my way, her eyebrow arching in disbelief while I try to get a hold of my temporary insanity. That surprised gawk reminds me of who I've been all these years—her dad's minion. Clearing my throat, I calm myself, despite my cheeks heat with shame. There's a reason she's paranoid. I'm not the buddy anymore. I shouldn't be sitting in a chair half my size, with a girl too pristine to touch. My humor fades fast.

I'm about to get up when Abi's smile cracks through her tough scowl, easing a bit of the discomfort over making a fool of myself. After a long pause, where a million turbulent emotions pass through those baby blues, she puts me out of my misery.

"I'm doing research." Her features school with a determined stubbornness I've never seen on Abigail's angelic face.

When her eyes flit back to her screen, my head blares warning bells. More so when she finally breaks down and tells me about her day. My jaw locks, not wanting to blurt anything upsetting. But I'm damned certain from that story that something dangerous is about to come down on Abi's head.

Over my dead body! My dragon wakes at the calling to protect our mate, his shimmer hovering under the surface. I push back his interference, but knowing my dragon is alert makes it hard to focus.

"You're gonna think I'm stupid." Abi hardens her voice, prepared for an argument. I can tell from how her eyes narrow in on me, waiting.

"Kris, I have to do something. I dropped by a student's home today. He's been out, with no call... It worried me."

Sea-green eyes plead, slightly off color from their normal hue. I search, curious about what's different. Abigail stares, studying me the same way I study her. Lucky for me, years of training blank my expression carefully while I wait for her honesty.

"And what happened?"

The rock in my stomach knows already.

"Well... a lot of things. But the biggest is how bad this kid and his mom are being hurt." She waits, eyes boring into mine with righteous indignation. "By his father." *Shit!* "I came home and started researching shelters, churches, any place that can help them here in town."

Double shit!

Abi sees the recognition in my face, the warning. Her mouth falls open, her disbelief and betrayal hitting me square in the chest.

"Abigail..."

"Kris, did you know about this?" The hissed question is much softer than the snap of metal when her laptop slams closed. The glare hardening Abi's normally sweet eyes is too much. I knew she didn't have me on a pedestal or some shit, but confirming her disgust, her judgement, is more than I can take.

Turning away, I scan the hallway. No one can overhear this conversation, for her safety and mine. "Abigail, you need to stay out of this," I say, standing. My conscience is desperate to space from the accusation in those gorgeous eyes.

"You knew!" Abi's outrage nearly topples her laptop with how fast she jumps from the chair. She settles it safely before those tiny feet stalk me across the room.

Even behind my back, I track her approach. My shifter ears pick up her increased heart rate, the rapid gasps of air that let me know how blindsided she is by all the horrible things happening right under her nose.

I hate it, but Dixon insists on his daughter staying protected from it all. She's not supposed to know any of his unsavory activities.

Though, I wonder what sort of grip the boss has on reality. He thinks he's fooled his ivy league daughter, which is ridiculous considering the thugs walking in and out of here at all hours. *The girl has ears, dammit.*

"How long have you known?" I turn at the soft question, finding Abi's petite little body standing rigid in front of me. Her hands fist at the hips I'd wanna grab if she weren't currently glaring daggers at me like I've grown two heads—one of them being the Devil himself. "Answer me!" Her voice vibrates with anger.

Immediately, my reflexes snap. One arm wraps low on Abigail's waist, pulling her flush against my body in self-preservation. My hand muffles a string of PG-13 curses and screeches, blocking the outburst from drawing unwanted attention to this parlor. Murder colors Abigail's livid eyes, tinting them with a faint purple hue that leaves me confused... again.

Abi can't shift.

I guess the desire to cut off my balls has a caffeinating effect on a latent dragon.

"Quiet!" I hiss, clenching my jaw against the desire warming my blood from Abigail wiggling in my hold. Watching my mate grow, having her scent closer than ever before, is pure torture. Even with disappointment clouding her eyes, I still want her.

"Goddamnit! You've got to stay quiet, Abigail." My frustrations boil over, the harshness in my voice surprising us both. Her eyes widen before glassing over. *Fuck!* I fight through the guilt. I've only ever spoken softly to Abi... when we've spoken at all.

At least she stopped fighting.

Resigned, I remove my hand—and my hold—confident Abi won't scream now. She must understand how difficult this is. She lives with these people. Lowering my voice, I admit what I wish I didn't know. "Everyone knows, Abi. The guys, Red's men... even your father."

Her gasp burns my lungs like her pain is my own. And when she grips her chest, protecting her heart from breaking, I feel that too. I hate bearing bad news, especially to someone as sweet as Abigail. But she's not a child anymore. No matter what Dixon thinks. My body's incessant craving for her womanly curves is a clear fuckin' sign.

With her lips pressed tight, Abigail backs out of my space, shaking her head. Again, she turns, squeezing her temples like just looking at me hurts her head.

Shut up. You're going to make her hate us! my dragon warns, his temper flaring.

But I can't back down. If putting my foot down keeps Abigail out of her dad's mess—or Red's—it's worth it.

Unfortunately, I can't stay strong when Abi's head dips. She whips around, scrambling to collect her laptop and teacup—scrambling to get away from me as fast as she can. Those delicate shoulders tremble with silent tears, signing my death warrant, because I know without a doubt, I'll give up everything to protect this woman.

I'll give my very last breath.

Abigail's heartache slays me. It's the only excuse I have for stepping forward, for wrapping my arms around my tiny siren. I can't help myself.

Even as she struggles, shoulders twisting, jerking in the steel trap I have her wrapped in. "Abigail... shh... easy, baby." My whispered words against the top of her head offer comfort, turning this precious gem in the circle of my arms. I'm not sure who I'm comforting, really. There's not a doubt that my dragon—and my racing heart—calm just holding my sweet mate close.

Hell, I doubt the girl can hear my words over the sobs wracking her body. A driving call to comfort my mate takes over, but with Abigail fighting me, I offer the only comfort I can... I let those small fists slam my chest. Let her abuse me to release the poisonous anger, the betrayal.

Self-hatred washes over me. Even accidentally causing my mate's distress feels like a boot to the balls. I deserve Abigail's strikes, though they barely ripple the water or cause any pain. Nothing hurts worse than her scent of despair in the air. Still, her battering slows as her fists tire of battle. They come to rest against my stomach, semi-guarded in her stance. But with my arms still locked around her softness, Abigail's sobs get lost against my chest, her sad sniffles muffling in the front of my shirt.

"How can you guys just… let it happen?" she asks, sagging in defeat. Even buried in my hug, I hear the accusation and my arms go slack. It hurts.

"It's not that easy."

I lift Abi off my chest, needing space from the confusion tearing me up inside. My dragon protests the moment I step away, forcing me to turn away so Abi doesn't see his irritation and mistake it for my own. Those bottomless eyes already hold too much disappointment. The hole in my heart can't take anymore. And it sure as fuck can't take Abigail's tear-stained face. I deserve it, but that doesn't make it easy.

These last fifteen years, I've run on autopilot. In my head, the life-debt I owe Dixon puts a pretty little mask on the questionable actions and business I conduct on his behalf. Except, none of it is a life I can offer a mate, so as hard as it is to pull away, my dragon needs to accept it.

"I didn't say it was easy, Kris. I asked how. How can you let it happen?"

"Abi," I start, before snapping my mouth shut. How do I explain the crazy hole I've dug for myself? Does my rule of 'no women or children' matter if I turn a blind eye to their pain?

Would Abigail understand that stepping in on a brother is suicide? Or am I just as guilty for turning a blind eye, no matter what I tell myself? My stuck brain can't organize the right words. And pretty soon it doesn't matter, anyway. Abi pushes off my stomach, backing away to a safer distance for us both.

Shit! We're lucky Dixon hasn't walked in on us already.

I sigh, knowing I can't give Abigail what she needs tonight. My only need is her safety. That's the only way I'll stay sane. So, I level her with my best, no bullshit scowl. The 'listen to what I say' look I hope makes her see reason. "Abigail, I know you don't understand, but it's important you trust me on this. I'll work on our little situation, if... and I do mean *'if'* you promise to stay out of it."

Her sarcastic laugh sounds as hollow as the defeat in her eyes. "Don't do me any favors, Kris. You might hurt yourself." Venom rolls from those soft pink lips crossly. I watch them thin into a hard line as she dismisses me, stands with laptop in hand, and walks away.

It's minutes before I can turn away from the empty doorway, snapping back to reality. Losing Abi's softness is a slap in the face. But I have orders. I need to follow Red, whether I'm doing it for Abigail, her father... or myself.

The hardest part is knowing I'll find something despicable when I get there.

Chapter Eleven

Kris

OKAY. WHERE THE HELL are you?

I've spent the last two hours hovering over the trees, circling Red's haunts by the process of elimination: his home, that run-down bar on the outskirts... nothing. *Shit!*

Tracking Red would be less of a Where's Waldo if I had done my damn job earlier. Instead, I followed my hormones and now the only other idea in my head is far-fetched. But if Red were smart, he would have left Dixon's tongue lashing and gone straight to his nightly duties. Not that he has a lot of actual responsibility anymore. Red's the laziest goddamn boss around, delegating any job possible to his team. However, he is required to check in on that team.

My dragon's rumbling laughter shows that even he thinks I'm giving the weasel too much credit. Still, I pass over a few collection points and my jaw nearly hits the ground. Red is actually making rounds—at the vet clinic—at midnight. Only, the clinic isn't on Red's route, it's mine.

What are you up to, you snake?

I bite back a roar over Red stepping on my turf and tuck my wings, hurriedly swooshing to land behind the building, under the cover of dark. Nobody's out at this time of night. It's the sleepy part of town, which is why I plan my visits this way.

Normally it hides my wings, so I don't have to shift in the damn forest and walk the two miles here. Tonight's rush is more volatile than my sheer laziness. I need to get inside Red's bat-shit crazy head... ASAP. Before he does something that gets the rest of us noticed by the authorities.

So far, Dixon's dragons have operated under the radar, almost functioning separately from our counterpart in Atlanta. The two sides fractured when Dixon's wife died, and he started questioning their way of business. Earl's entire lot is too flashy—too sadistic—for Dixon's taste. Red fits a lot better with the gang down south than he does here in Tennessee. Except for his horrible style in clothes, those are way too white trash for those fancy boys.

Bullshit like this is exactly why I don't trust Red. No more than a stranger off the street.

Standing here whining won't do any good.

On that thought, I pry open the broken lock Dr. Michaels hasn't fixed yet, pausing with every squeak of metal in the quiet night. Part of me loves that the doc never takes care of shit; the other part wants to buy the man a can of WD-40 and teach him some shit. Sneaking is against my M.O., but once I'm in, I carefully muffle the click of the emergency handle closing behind me.

In the back room, that croaking laugh I know so well rings over Dr. Michaels' panicked jabbering. "Wh-what if Dixon finds out?" The tremble in Doc's voice shows exactly what I suspected. He's more nervous than conniving. *This is all Red.*

"You let me deal with him, old man," Red says, his cocky voice filling the hallways. "You just keep funneling me our little gravy on the side and I'll worry about knocking down the obstacles."

A slap of skin, three times, lets me know Red's location. He's hovering over the doctor's desk... his signature move. Threaten and intimidate with a brotherly—not brotherly—slap on the back. The move lords his power over whomever he wishes, pushing them, coercing his prey by cornering anyone weaker. Basic rules: accept his terms or risk a beating.

What the fuck? How long has that traitor worked behind our backs?

"What do you want me to do?"

"Get that bitch back here, for one. I gotta deal with her away from that bear she partnered with."

"Bear—" the Doc squeaks, but Red cuts him off before he can ask anything else.

"Nuh, uh, uh, Doc. I'll worry about that. This is my game now." The venom dripping from Red's voice shuts the doc up quick, all the while pissing me off.

That little shit would have been protected. He should have told me.

"Yeah, sure. You bet," Doc says, scrambling. Confusion pitches his voice, but he agrees readily, clearly accustomed to following Red's plans. That poor choice is gonna be the death of him one way or another.

Dixon's gonna love this!

Before I let my temper loose, I need proof. Tapping the voice memo on my phone, I record the tail end of Red's spiel, grinning when the jackass digs his grave deeper. Dr. Michaels has proved himself nothing but a weakling, but Red... Red is the backstabber.

We need a plan.

Quickly pocketing my phone, I head out back, not stifling my noise as well as I did on entry. Instead, I snap my wings wide, taking to the air on a mission. This war is inevitable, but it may just be the last piece to an exit strategy... if I work my advantage with Dixon.

Red has to go down, that's for sure. And if I secure Dixon's legacy, it'll be easier to break the news that I'm out... for good.

And, if she'll have me, I'll be taking his daughter with me.

Chapter Twelve

Kris

I KNOW OUR BUSINESS occurs under the cover of dark. But after leaving Red's clandestine meeting, it sucks having to wait until morning to meet with Dixon.

He used to be king of the game. Now the old man sleeps while the rest of us do his bidding. And it's fine if he doesn't stay awake until two or three in the morning. It just sucks royally when I need to talk to him and have to wait for breakfast.

By six a.m., I've waited as long as I can. I'm at his door, my brain and bloodshot eyes running on three hours' sleep. But the burning in my corneas is working its way to my temples. And I'm expected to be ready for the day? Hell, I've run on less.

What I'm not ready for... Abi answering the door in a fluffy yellow robe that barely covers her thighs and curlers twisting all that platinum hair in all kinds of odd angles off her head.

Fuck! She's amazing.

I'm blaming her pile of fresh morning sexy for my grin, for cracking my sleepy façade like a lightning bolt, waking my ass up. Abigail's sexy sweetness lightens the load of stress on my shoulders. And if it didn't, the embarrassed squeak she let go before shoving the door, trying to slam it in my face... that would do it.

Quickly, my foot jerks to block the doorway before Abi can lock me out. Her huff of annoyance nearly breaks my barely held laughter. She's too perfect, hiding behind the thick oak door, so I don't see her in all her morning glory.

"Nice try, Princess. I got a full view of all that beauty."

"Kris..." she scolds, slapping the back of the door in frustration, her head poking around under a mass of curlers. When our eyes meet, Abigail's skin burns scarlet. Only shifter senses could hear the frantic rhythm of her heart.

My hold is slipping. The warning daggers flying from this little thing are damn adorable. That look, like she'd burn me alive given the chance, pushes me over the top and my laughter bursts right there on her daddy's front porch. It sounds slightly psychotic and a little short on common sense given the tiny ball of rage growing right in front of my eyes.

Abigail violently swings the door open, crossing her arms in a way that pushes her pert chest up a little higher, wreaking havoc on the other side of my self-control. The part—ahem, my dragon—that wants to drag this ball of fire against me and kiss that scowl off her face. Every ounce of blood leaves my brain and flows south, imagining those soft lips, remembering what it was like to take them.

Taking a step back, I drag a lungful of air in with my eyes locked on Abigail's. I'm banking that a hard enough stare will keep that angry gaze from sliding down and seeing my bulge threatening to break free for a good morning handshake. Clearing my throat, I re-focus on why I came and ignore that tempting peak from the gap in Abi's robe when she shifts.

"Is your dad up?" I ask, offering what I hope is a calm, cool—*not* cock-centered—smile.

"Dining room," she says, warily pointing one pink-tipped thumb to her left. The other hand nudges the door wider, giving me room to enter their two-story foyer in search of Dixon. Every step inside the door strengthens the delicious smell of milk and honey that draws me closer involuntarily.

Unfortunately, the moment I mention Dixon, a tense anxiety chills the air. While I stalk toward the source of my favorite smell—Abigail's freshly showered, goddamn delectable body—she turns her back, shoulders tense and robe cinched closed at the neck as she rushes up the stairs. I stand there watching her go, the steady plop of feet growing distant on the wood and tormenting my dragon.

Follow our mate. Claim her now!

What the hell? That wouldn't go off well.

If I go after Abigail, she deserves courting. Then she'll have to admit the inevitable. We belong together.

Except claiming my mate is not something I see happening. There's constant danger around me, and Abigail's sweet heart is way too pure for a man like me, one with so much blood on his hands.

Speaking of...

Pushing thoughts of Abi to the back seat, I go in search of her father. My senses say trouble is about to pop like the Hindenburg, so it's almost anti-climactic to find Peter Dixon eating his plain morning bagel at the table, exactly where Abigail said I would. Before I open my mouth, he drops the newspaper he's reading to the table with a snap, letting the silence in the room become deafening under the blood rushing through my ears.

Dixon calls me out before his eyes ever lift to greet me over the lip of his coffee cup, as if he'd been waiting impatiently for this conversation, like my loitering wastes his precious time. I'd ask how he knew I was here, but that's a stupid question for a shifter. Either it's my scent in his house or Dixon's natural foresight talents, but the part that worries me most is wondering if Dixon knows how long I stayed out there chatting with his daughter... and if he senses what I desperately want from her.

My mate.

Giving me a slight nod, he leans back in his chair, getting comfortable with the slightest paunch on display as he spreads wide, sipping at the black coffee that's dragging me in the room by a nostril. "Gotta stay informed to start the day, Kris," Dixon says, patting a meaty hand to his newspaper, as if we're bros breaking bread and talking politics.

"Grab a cup, son." His voice is firm, calm. A quality I don't expect by the end of our conversation. Still, when Dixon gestures to the buffet in the corner, I follow like the blind, led by the heavenly aroma of dark roast. The smell alone does wonders for my overly tired mind this morning.

Except, the boss hasn't invited me into his personal space since I was a kid. And my shoulders are knotting under the extra stress, waiting for whatever shoe Dixon's going to drop. My visits to this house are usually in some form of training, education, or work. At least since I came of age around fifteen; old enough to handle minor tasks in Dixon's gang of merry assholes.

When I have news, I deliver it, receive orders, and go on my way. Dixon has been a hermit in this house since his wife died. But altering our relationship now, inviting me for coffee and calling me son, raises my hackles.

Does he know I want his daughter?

With slow steps, I carry my cup to sit beside my suspiciously quiet boss, aware that every step fills me with dread the closer I get to that giant mahogany table. "Thank you, sir."

At least its mammoth size puts ample space between us. That damn thing takes up most of Dixon's dining space, yet somehow looks perfectly natural under the cathedral ceilings and ornate moldings in here. It's like Queen Victoria and Texas married, had a baby, and it puked its larger-than-life designs all over Dixon's house.

His astute eyes take in my nervousness. Assessing. But my anxiety doesn't seem to bother Dixon. His demeanor remains the complete opposite, the picture of calm as he waits for me to relax. I see how Dixon's patience worked to his benefit all these years. I've had men piss their pants when I show at their doorstep. Store clerks hover their fingers over panic buttons when they see my tattoos and buzzed head. Sometimes it pisses me off; sometimes I use their judgment to my advantage.

However, all that badass intimidation does me no good when two minutes of silence in front of my mate's father have me willing to spill the beans. Of what... I don't know. But it's the worst—and the best—interrogation standoff I've ever experienced.

"Fill me in." Dixon's stern voice breaks the silence.

A statement, not a question. *Okay.*

Swallowing, I push down my anxiety and steady my voice. "Well, the gist is that I tracked last night and found a few things concerning." Dixon's expressionless, waiting. "So, uh, I checked his route and a few bars and couldn't find him." Eyebrow lift. "Basically, Red was at the vet clinic chatting up the doc, and I overheard the dumbasses conspiring to syphon money off the collections." I wait, watching surprise flash briefly in Dixon's expression.

"Nonsense." His hand waves back and forth, swatting the idea away. *Like it's that easy.* "Why would Red go behind my back?" I see Dixon's temper building, getting incensed the more he rolls the thought through his head. "He's second in command, goddammit. I taught him everything he knows."

"I think that's the problem, sir."

Dixon's fist slams the table, his red eyes flashing murder in my direction that quiets what I was about to say. That man's anger is dangerous, not something I want aimed my way. Do I step in before this all blows up?

I never thought Dixon would lose his touch, but he's letting his men run roughshod. The lack of control helped Red collect a group of like-minded assholes and they've gone rogue, undercutting jobs, bringing attention to the dragon species we just don't need.

"*Fuck!* What's going on out there, Kris?"

Dragging a hand across my face, I fill him in on the details—at least what I heard—of Red's plan. I have no idea what they said before I arrived, but I don't want Dixon to realize I didn't leave immediately, like he instructed.

Dixon jerks to his feet, nearly toppling his chair. "How the fuck did that happen? Seriously! The vet is *your* responsibility, Kris. Yours!"

That booming voice, which normally snaps at other people, is pissing me off and white knuckling my fragile coffee cup isn't helping much. "Talk, boy. How the hell did Red get the better of you?"

I cringe. *Where does he get off?*

"Sir, with all due respect, I've been off chasing my tail, tracking Doc's employee. I haven't had time to keep tabs on Red."

"That employee *you* let eavesdrop on our business, you mean? The night that put our entire operation at risk if I don't handle her, you mean? Handle the way I promised Beth I never would." The man glaring accusations at me now is not the one who sank into a pit of depression after his wife died. No, this is the ruthless boss he was before meeting Beth. The one I heard stories about, who worked hand in hand with our more ruthless counterpart in Atlanta. This is the boss who understands our business is kill or be killed. Nothing else.

My skin prickles with awareness as my dragon senses the increased danger in the room and prepares himself for a painful shift in case we need to defend ourselves.

It takes a beat to peel my hands from my coffee cup, my stomach churning nuclear acid over this conversation. *I'm tired of this life!*

Now, I'm not only watching my back from our enemies, I'm watching for our own men.

"Boss, I get it. My game slipped that night. But, sir, if Jon-boy hadn't been stroking his own ego, the girl wouldn't have heard anything, Doc wouldn't be betraying us, and we wouldn't be playing catch up. He's the dumbass that escalated a normal visit into a beat-down." Each word is louder than the last. If I'm signing my death warrant, so be it. "Boss, I'm a goddamn babysitter out there. There's other stuff I could—" A quick palm in the air stops my defense mid-sentence. Dixon's heated glare warning that I'm about to overstep.

"Boy, you've always been my favorite, but don't go trying to break rank."

Me. Favorite?

I raise an eyebrow, but Dixon stops me, his palm acting as a shield, as if that alone will keep my mouth shut. "Look, I've got pressure coming up from Georgia. They want us to expand our... goods, which leaves me in a tough spot. I ain't working the stuff Earl wants. No way in this fuckin' world." Just the thought tightens Dixon's features, his eyes crinkling at the corners, his lips thinning. The large crease in his forehead aging the man in a matter of minutes. The previous cocky version of our boss would never admit defeat, not this easily. But recent years have beat Dixon down. Now his piss and vinegar personality is just... stale.

Dixon's shoulders bunch as he walks to refill his coffee. "Kristopher, if I didn't think you could handle this situation, I wouldn't put you in this role. You're young, tough... my most reliable man." He stops to grin over his shoulder. "Plus, that level head keeps you a step above Red. Every goddamn time."

He must read my confusion, because Dixon's chuckle grows, making this meeting sound like a fun little breakfast, not the dreaded third degree I expected. One thing still bothers me...

"Why is Red your number one, then?"

Dixon's shaking laughter fills the room as he circles behind me. "Boy... come on! Keep your enemies close. Rule number one!" I stiffen at his pat to my shoulder, not loving my vulnerable position at the table. *Is that what he's doing now? Keeping his enemy close.* Except, this seems like a father placating a small child. I don't like it.

With one last pat, Dixon is back in his chair, his voice dropping to a conspiratorial whisper. "Your job is going to get us a step ahead of Red. If that moron thinks he can pull the rug over my eyes..." he scoffs, a mischievous glint hits me over his coffee cup. "He's got another thing coming."

"What does that mean?"

"We're gonna get the girl," he tuts, like it's the most brilliant idea to pop in his head. "We'll use her to get to the Doc... or at least get some info from her we can use." I cringe at Dixon's giddy smile.

"Sir, the girl's protected by a bear. They haven't mated, but I smelled it. If they do, it'll be harder to get to her."

A cold smirk turns my way before the newspaper lifts, covering his face like our conversation's over. "Then you'd better get out there, boy."

With that blatant dismissal, his housekeeper, Lydia, comes out of nowhere, swiping my cup on its way to my mouth. They must have some secret code, because Dixon's long-time caregiver swoops in to clear the table with such finesse, such a placating smile on her face that you can't be mad at her. Within minutes, it looks like I never sat there.

Unsure of what more to say, I stand, hurrying through the ornate archway that leads to the hall, racking my brain for who I can trust in our organization. Dixon's new mission will require walking a tightrope of control, balancing intimidation with self-discipline, discretion with extraction. Only two guys in our gang get shit done when asked—without going hothead. I trust them like brothers. That's Deacon and Mikey.

The rest of the crew are Red's discount minions.

Unfortunately, my lack of concentration slams me right into Abigail, who's frozen just outside the dining room. Only my quick reflexes keep her from hitting the floor, but not before she flies backwards from the impact with my much larger body.

Shit! How much did she hear?

Chapter Thirteen

Kris

"Abigail!" I drop my voice to not alert her father to another eavesdropper. But Abigail's shaking her head, those soft blonde curls swishing around her shoulders. Frantically, she jerks at my hold on her arms, even though I only grabbed her to save that pretty little ass from the marble floor.

If only tears weren't swimming in those endless blue eyes. They make it hard to deny the lovesick fool my dragon has turned into. She makes it too damn hard.

Thank fuck! Abi's dressed now. The small blessing lets my brain function clearer without that tiny robe short circuiting every thought. In that pencil skirt and silk blouse, she looks like the Abigail I've watched for months. She's not a sexpot... she's classier. Crimson lipstick and a dark mascara are the only signs of makeup on her face. So why can't I put her back in that little untouchable box she's lived in all these years?

Abigail's presence lets loose a whole other set of problems. She's the sweetest embodiment of a naughty-teacher temptation. And I may know better, but my brain is working overtime against my hormones. It's getting harder and harder to do what I know I should and not what my dragon is pushing.

My best scenario will be piggy backing off this situation with Red. If I work out the boss's stress and stop whatever coup that little group has planned, I'll have leverage. That has to win me some points. But is it enough to accomplish the impossible?

I don't care how you do it. She's ours. My dragon is no longer quiet about his needs, and it'll be easier to take control as a man before his spirit does it for me.

My fogged brain slowly clears to recognize the abject horror on Abigail's face. She shakes her head, tears flowing freely as she begs. "Don't do it, Kris. Please!" The desperation in her voice confirms the worst. She heard. I wish I could say I was above following her dad's orders, but I can't. At my hesitation, her demeanor changes, anger taking over to fuel her fight for freedom. Those sky-colored eyes glow with the faintest rim of red around the irises and I stare in disbelief.

We fuel her. The smugness in my dragon's voice almost makes me smile, but somehow, I hold on, knowing that would toss my seething beauty right over the top.

Maneuvering Abi with one hand, I guide her away from her dad as gently as my dragon-powered impatience can.

"What the ever-lovin' he—"

Ugh!

At the end of my rope, I cover Abigail's mouth, effectively muffling whatever argument was about to fly from those tempting lips. Too bad my highhandedness doesn't stop the stream of curses from wetting my palm. If eyes had the power to kill, I just pissed Abi off enough to turn her normally peaceful blue orbs into laser death rays, fit for an epic sci-fi movie.

"Abigail, hush." With the slightest squeeze of my hand, I urge my girl to quiet down, shaking my head that she's still ranting.

Although no actual words get past my hand, Abi continues to squeal behind it, her breath becoming irregular and getting worse the harder she struggles. I've never seen Abigail—a normally sweet soul—turn so violent. But if she doesn't stop, Dixon's gonna walk out and find me manhandling his daughter... which likely leads to him breaking my neck on the spot.

Desperation spikes my blood pressure and before I think twice, shifter speed is moving us through the hall, aiming for the kitchen, half a house away from the boss's prying ears. The quick motion throws Abigail's body against mine, aligning her soft curves with my hard ones. It's perfection, sweet torture. The force of nature that's taken over my thoughts, my decisions, is something I've never felt in my twenty-nine years.

From Abigail's fingertips digging in my shoulder as she holds on, to her sharp intake of air when her feet lift from the ground, it all puts naughty thoughts in my head.

What else would pull that wicked sound from this beauty?

Hell, I'd love to hear that sound for real. For me. To lay her body bare, granted the freedom to nibble, to bite... free to mark as mine for all to see. In my dreams.

In real life, I'm starved for just one. The one whose perfection is too good to be cursed as my mate. The thrill of her soft skin brushing my front—even accidentally—is enough to send every ounce of spare blood straight to my cock, without a piece of clothing removed.

Shit! I'm in deep.

In the kitchen, Abi still grips my shoulders, her panting breaths wetting my palm until guilt forces me to lower her feet to the floor. I'm not trying to piss her off. I'm not trying to hurt or control her, no matter what she thinks I'm capable of. This one person is all I have left in the world, even if she's clueless to her value.

I'd break my fucking arm before I'd hurt her.

Cautiously, I remove the hand covering Abigail's mouth, praying she doesn't scream after my rough handling. Relief washes over me when no screams come. Breath seething... yes. Eyes flaring... yes. But no screams... win!

Still, I won't exhale until she understands. With that wild look in her eye, I can't let her body away from mine... not yet.

With obvious frustration, Abigail pushes against my chest, fighting for separation. "What the hell do you think you're doing?" she asks, seething through gritted teeth. Thank God she's not screaming for my head.

"Abi, you can't blurt things out like that with your dad in the next room." Hell, I'm nervous with *several* thick walls separating us, so I keep my voice low, hoping Abi gets the picture and does the same.

"Why not?" Abigail's tiny hands shove my chest and I let go, not wanting to upset my mate any further. Immediately, losing her heat is noticeable and my fists clench, wishing I could hold the pissed off angel pacing in front of me. I get her frustrations, but my sole concern is keeping Abigail safe. If it requires towing the line a little longer to get out of this game, I will. *Fuck! I'm tired too!*

My eyes track Abigail's movements. The dainty fingers tugging her hair. Those pink-stained cheeks that darken with every step, mumbling under her breath as she struggles to reign in her freshly ignited temper. Because deep down, she knows I'm right. Even if her stubbornness doesn't want to admit it. Finally, Abi slows, turning those incensed eyes on me with more bravery than I've ever seen from this woman.

She knows we won't hurt her.

That thought would make me smile if it weren't for Abigail's crossed arms and defiant glint in her eye. The dread in my gut when she issues her quiet threat leaves no room to challenge. This is the gauntlet throwing down. It's step up or step out time. There's not one doubt in my mind which one I'll choose. Sanity's overrated, right?

Plus, I think I've lost the ability to deny my mate by the sheer will of my dragon alone.

"Kris, I will tell my dad the same thing I told you. Neither of you had better touch that girl. Whoever it is!" Abigail swallows thickly. "My mom would roll over in her grave."

"I get it, Abi. I really do." My chest tightens. How can Dixon be so blind to think his daughter is ignorant of his business? Especially when it happens right under her roof. This tightrope walk right here is what is dividing our ranks. And now I have to keep some vet tech chick quiet and battle my own demons. Dixon wants the impossible. To be a good man for his daughter and late wife, when the exact nature of his position makes that impossible.

"Abigail, your father wants you protected from his business. It's why we keep his secrets and pretend it's all on the up and up." I shake my head, frustrated at walking on eggshells for too long. Unfortunately, my words don't make a dent in Abi's death glare. She's itching for a fight and part of me doesn't blame her. "Come on, Abi. It'd break his heart if he knew you knew."

"Bullshit, Kris! I'm not a little girl anymore." Fresh anger electrifies the air as she steps closer. Hands on her hips. A wild challenge in her eyes. That angry huff lifting her chest with every breath. It creates a dangerous concoction that wakes my dragon, who barely holds onto control whenever Abigail's in the same room.

I step closer. "Oh, trust me, Abigail. I am very aware you're not a little girl anymore." My hand itches to reach for her and I don't stop myself this time.

Moving slowly to not frighten her, both hands come to rest on Abi's hips, softly at first, then pulling with force to bring her close. Close enough to feel the part of me that aches for every second in her presence. The sexiest gasp warms my neck, her lips parting when she rubs against my need, standing hard and desperate between us.

Recently our glancing touches haven't been enough. It seems staying away is no longer an option. My dragon has taken over and doesn't care if Abi's too good for us. He's turned on and ready to claim.

"Kris—"

Sensing Abigail's worry hanging thick in the air, I decide to stop whatever baseless excuse she's about to offer. Before she can utter another word, I drop my head to lock on those luscious lips, needing a taste more than I need air at this moment. I don't rush.

This kiss isn't the hurried passion of our first. It's not wild... it's yearning. A consuming need to mark Abi as mine, to show her my heart in a way she's never seen.

I desperately need to wash away those horrible thoughts in Abi's head about me.

For that reason, I keep our kiss soft. Just a soft drag of my lips... a sensual caress that pulls the sweetest sigh from my sweet angel. That wisp of breath tickles my lips, freezing me centimeters away. I watch Abigail's lashes shutter closed, my eyes drowning in her parted lips, those flushed cheeks.

Holy shit! The mate fate picked for me is beautiful!

This delicious torture is too much. She's too heady this close. I'm afraid if I dive in, it'll ruin the moment. Until Abi's pink tongue flicks out to wet her lips and I'm done for. She's a magnet, pulling me. My lips caress first, lingering to test before I nudge her head back for better access. That she allows it shoots a thrill through my body that stiffens my cock. I forget all the reasons we shouldn't be.

Could we have been together all this time?

She wants us... you feel it. My dragon seems to think so. Then again, patience isn't our species' strong suit.

I take in Abigail's panting breath, open and willing in front of me, and I know it's too late. My efforts at gentleness are shot to hell. With one hand twined in Abi's hair, I hold on tight, causing Abi's eyes to flutter open. Her lust grows with mine, glowing from inside, a beautiful shimmer that causes my dragon to purr.

My mate.

Yes.

No longer denying it, the fingers gripping Abi's hip twitch, firming their hold. At her soft gasp, I give a quick tug, bringing those slim hips flush with mine... sweet temptation. The slightest smile teases Abi's lips. This mischievous little thing has me fighting my knowing grin.

Carefully, I let one thumb snake under the hem of her shirt, rubbing soft circles along the exposed skin there. Abigail's responding shivers are my heavenly reward, the vibration thrilling my inner dragon, who wants to explore a lot more of Abi's flesh than I'm allowing.

When she leans forward, hands sliding across my stomach in her own exploration, I nearly explode. To wait for Abigail's exploration is pure torture. When one of those hands scratches up the ridges in my stomach, I break. It's on.

I barely control the growl of pent-up lust, my raging hormones taking over. Sexual tension drives the urge to darken my angel. And Abi's glazed eyes aren't helping. Of course, my sweet Abigail strokes the vibration in my chest, her soothing nature seeking to calm.

Except, the moment those slender arms wrap around my neck, excitement heats my blood. Before I can stop myself, I lift Abi's weight to the countertop, pushing that tight pencil skirt up so I have room to step between the welcoming spread of her legs.

I dive in for a sip of her morning coffee. Sweet, dark... heaven with the deepening of our kiss. Abigail's bottom wiggles to the edge. The lace at her heated core presses against my middle in a wanton little dance.

I let the friction burn, ramping my need for this woman higher, lighting the fire in my blood that's spurred on with every desperate whimper. Her response encourages my explorations. But when my hands slide to Abi's backside, squeezing the tight globes in a rough caress, she startles. I'd laugh at that adorable squeak if my pent-up craving for this woman wasn't about to explode.

"Abi, do you want this?" I ask, nibbling the line of her jaw.

"Hmm," she purrs, obviously caught in the same trance I am. It's reassuring, but not what I need. I've lost the precious control that kept me away. One look from Abigail, that slight tilt of her head nuzzling my hand, and I'm gone. *Is she with me?*

Because this is a life-or-death risk.

Gently, I gather the hair falling over my hand in a twist, using the long, silky length to draw her head back and give my lips more room to explore. Purposefully, I let my breath tease over her ear, making sure I have her full attention. "Abigail."

"Hmm."

"You know this will be trouble." A light nibble to her earlobe marks my words, making Abigail's fingers twist in the front of my shirt.

She's gripping like she doesn't want me to leave. And her panting breath doesn't offer any arguments to my exploration either, so I slide down to enjoy the fresh scent below her ear. The one driving my dragon wild.

The air is thick with our ragged breaths, but I barely hear it over the thrumming in my ears. Time freezes as my other hand lifts to cradle Abi's head, taking in every detail like a starving man denied for years. The curl of lashes resting on her cheeks. The tiny freckles dotting her nose.

I memorize every curve, every mark on her beautiful face. Even the sliver of a scar running under her hairline at the temple. That one I remember from the first year I met Abigail. Some punk pushed her off the top of the slide after school and since our school ran Kinder through twelfth, I was there to see it. I was also there to give the kid a shiner for picking on someone smaller than him and walk a bleeding Abigail home.

Bending, I place a soft kiss on her temple. The memory ignites every ounce of anger I felt that day seeing Abi hurt.

"Kris." My name is soft on those berry-colored lips, and I trace their crease, now stained from my kisses and not her lipstick.

Instinctively, my thumb strokes the thumping pulse of blood at her neck, admiring Abi's increased heart rate under the soft skin, waiting for the words that tell me to stop. All I see is the pulse of her excitement. The sensation is heady to my dragon. He wants to claim that spot with our mating bite. Especially when the sweet scent of Abigail's arousal reaches my nose, branding me as deeply as I want to brand her.

Dragging in a breath, I try to control my desperate need for this woman. "What do you need, my love?" I want to hear it... need to hear it.

A pink stain crawls up her neck, making me smile. In typical Abigail shyness, she bites her lip, not answering my question. But her legs tightening around my hips lock me close. It's all the answer I need.

With fire burning in my veins, I scrape the morning scruff I didn't take time to shave along that soft curve of shoulder exposed at her collar. I don't trust my teeth anywhere near Abi's neck for fear of damning us both.

Inside my head, my dragon is bucking to get out. Until a little whine hits my ears and I panic that I've gone too far. Especially when Abigail's hands fly to my head and tug it back. My hold on her hair loosens immediately and I open my mouth to apologize, but Abigail cuts me off. Her frenzied eyes bounce back and forth between mine, stretching my anxiety to excruciating lengths until, in one swift move, her lips lock on mine. Surprise snaps the tight leash I have on my control, breaking my last shreds of willpower.

Emboldened, I take over the kiss, reclaiming Abi's mouth harder this time. One hand dives back into Abigail's tangled hair, now wild from my fingers, as I brace her head against the power of our kiss. Chaotic hormones course through my body, every instinct urging me to pull Abigail closer.

I blame that pull for my other hand sliding to her lower back. I blame it for pressing until her hips join mine in a slow, steady rhythm. I blame it for why I pump my length against her sex over and over for some much-needed friction. And when her moan muffles under the dance of our tongues, I blame *that* for ignoring the danger of being doors away from her father and lowering Abigail's enticing body flat to the countertop, anyway.

What the hell am I thinking?

I know what I'm thinking. I'm thinking about my mate spread in front of me like a buffet. I'm thinking about that shocked gasp when her back hit the chilled surface. And what other fun would pull those sounds from her. I'm thinking about those blunt nails digging into my forearms while I hold her in place. How the tentative pump of her hips grows bolder with each stroke of my cock.

The magic of watching Abi use me for her own pleasure becomes more than I can take, releasing my primal growl to echo through the kitchen. It's torture. Her innocence... my desire. The combustion of heaven and hell wrapped up in our inevitable passion.

Overcome, I yank Abigail back close, drowning in her lips one more time. I need a second longer to bask in the mate I can't have. Dixon will hang me out to dry for tainting his princess. The fact that our arousal hangs thick in the air means any of the dragons that roll through this house daily could easily sniff us out. She'll be pissed, but I need to be stronger than my dragon's will.

Fuck! I should win an award for pulling away with pre-cum dripping from my cock. That's how goddamn close I am to busting a nut like a teenage boy.

It takes excruciating effort. But a smug satisfaction puffs my chest when it takes longer for Abigail to drag her eyes open. I smile, stroking her flushed cheek, waiting for awareness of our location to sink in.

"Abi, your dad is down the hall." I keep my voice low, but I see the moment her walls shutter down, alarm flashing across her face.

Is she remembering what brought us to this room?

It shouldn't hurt so bad when she shoves my chest, giving herself room to jump off the counter. But it does. Especially when those hazy eyes clear and Abi levels me with an ominous glare, crossing her arms as if trying to protect herself from letting me in again.

"You're going to do it, aren't you?" The venom in that sweet voice is foreign to my ears. And when she wipes her swollen lips, erasing our kiss, it's a dagger to my heart.

"Abigail... come on." My eyes plead, hoping she'll understand. *I don't have a choice.* But the silent communication falls flat. I reach for her hand, but she jerks it out of reach, turning her back on me so I don't have the slightest chance of reading her expression.

"Don't." Anger hisses through clenched teeth, but when Abigail opens her mouth again, the emotionless void in her voice is worrisome. "Kris, you can't help him. I knew my dad was... into stuff..." Her head falls, shaking like she doesn't believe her own thoughts. "But I-I never imagined this."

If only, baby.

My shoulders sink with regret. "Abigail," I call, my voice firm. I wait until she turns and fight to not to let those sad eyes crack my heart. "There's a war coming, baby." I step closer, ignoring her shaking head for one more chance to stroke the soft skin under her chin. "I have to go."

Before I finish the sentence, she's blinking back tears. The weight of the world sits on my shoulders when I turn, leaving my inconvenient mate standing alone in the kitchen.

Chapter Fourteen

Abigail

Two days later, I'm still fuming. At my father. At Kristopher.

The hormones vibrating through my body mean nothing. They haven't caught up to my anger yet. I refuse to think about Kris's lips. He's my father's thug. That's it!

Gah! Running a hand through my hair, I grip the back of my head, fighting against the mortifying memory of rubbing myself all over that infuriating man. Of letting his hands pull my hair, opening for him. I didn't fight it at all. I let his lips—his skill—outweigh my clumsiness with men. He was too much to resist.

I know I shouldn't hate myself for giving into the massive crush I've harbored for years. It makes sense to be powerless against his pure sexiness. Those smoking green eyes, those thick, muscular thighs and tattooed arms. What woman could resist when they burst out of those snug t-shirts?

The difference is, he *can* resist me. He knows I hate what he does, still he walked away to do whatever despicable thing my dad had planned.

Well, you know what? Two can play this game. I am my father's daughter, right?

I haven't talked to him since the morning I eavesdropped. I can't look my dad in the eye knowing he would kidnap a girl. It doesn't matter who she is or what she did. And since those bozos won't see reason, I'm on a mission tonight. Assuming Kris followed through on Dad's orders, I need to know where to find this girl.

My conscience can't handle someone getting hurt. Not if I can stop it.

Lucky for me, my dad's office matches the rest of our neurotically organized house. I just don't know what I'm looking for. His empty desktop gives me nothing. No telephone because we don't have a landline. Dad's laptop never leaves his side. The desk is void of pens because that would mean clutter. There's not even a calendar. *How does a busy man not have a calendar?*

The only exception on his desk is the silver filigree frame propped in the corner. A black and white wedding photo from thirty years ago.

I pick up the one feminine touch in this room, a photo of Mom and Dad in their wedding attire, embracing like lovebirds under the large oak tree behind our house. I run a finger over my mom's long veil billowing behind her in the breeze. My dad gazes at her like she's everything he ever wanted. Like she takes his breath away, while her hazel eyes shine pure happiness for the camera.

Maybe if Dad still had that, I wouldn't be snooping in his office praying he hasn't done something horrible. My mom had a confidence, a knack for keeping him in line that I don't have.

Love makes us a better version of ourselves, Little One.

Setting the picture down, I block out my mom's voice. Saving this girl is too important for an emotional distraction.

I start with the top drawer, but all I see are all pens, pads, and paperclips. "*Gah!* Why is my first thought some dorky alliteration?" I mumble, not expecting an answer, of course. Still the need to whisper strong, even in an empty house.

Must be some sneaky intuition tattooed in the criminal DNA. Like a proverb somewhere says, '*ye who sneaks, must make no creaks.*'

I don't quiet my laughter but move on to the next drawer. There's a few files and notebooks with Dad's chicken scratch that would take forever to decipher. Not exactly an easy clue for where they'd hide a person.

I grow tense moving to the next drawer. This one holds a small, biometric gun safe like every other home in rural Tennessee. But the vacuum of silence in this office is unraveling my nerve to search. Every squeak in the drawer rollers pierces the air. Every *tink* from the metal handles jerks my eyes to the door. Tugging, I get stuck with the last drawer. Of course, it won't open. *Why is this drawer the only freaking locked one?*

Groaning, I flop into Dad's leather office chair, resting my head against the cushion. *Where else can I look?* The rest of Dad's office is a bore. I know Dad wouldn't risk bringing the girl here. That would sink too low.

Melancholy washes over me and I turn my gaze to the dark window. Even the moon's glow mocks me tonight. The one bright spot in the night sky, breaking through the wispy clouds that hide the stars from below. I've never gotten to fly, to see above them like the others.

Usually, I don't think of it. But sometimes on these eerie nights, I know I'm missing something. That morose thought needs to go. I get down to work, this time searching for a tool that might help. *Bingo! Paperclip.*

Stretching out the metal, I bend the end until it looks like something that will pry open the locked drawer. "Fingers crossed those *Law and Order* reruns taught me something good." My mumbling as I try to remember how criminals do this on T.V. helps my brain not completely freak out. It takes a lot more twists of the clip than Hollywood shows, but finally something in there gives.

The drawer pops open a few inches.

"Whoop!" My voice rises with my little happy dance, celebrating my lock-picking success. Instead, feeling on the verge of *something* and motivated, I tug the thing open and get down to business.

My thumbs fly over the hanging files jammed in there, pulling out any that look official and not just jammed with disorganized receipts. One file I sit in my lap with paper certificates and handwritten invoices. I skip the files with people's names handwritten on the tab and go for the brown expandable folder hiding in the back. *Looks interesting.*

Picking that one out, I unravel the elastic band holding it together and flip through thick sections stuffed with legal documents, loan documents, and deeds to property I've never heard of... Knoxville office buildings, warehouses in Tennessee, North Carolina, Georgia.

Pulling out an official-looking page with unbelievable numbers written on the top, I scan across a bunch of legal jargon until I get to the signatures at the bottom. One is definitely my dad's, his barely legible script scrawled in a crooked loop, clipped to the back. I don't recognize the address, it's just some rural road, but the note transfers a roughly described hunting cabin to my father, in lieu of money owed. It sounds like a shabby, one-room shack from the note, but it looks like it's Dad's now.

Sitting the folder in my lap, I flip through the rest in the drawer, but find nothing that looks as important as what I have. Until my finger catches on a dark leather notebook mounted in the back. Gently, I loosen the Velcro strips holding it in place and bring it to my lap with the other folder. The cover is soft under my fingertips; however, the pages inside raise the tiny hair on the back of my neck.

There must be twenty pages of names, handwritten credits and debits filling the lines beside them. Yellow highlighter marks the larger numbers, but it's the red ink marking through certain names that draws me up. I recognize these townspeople from my childhood. Not a single name is alive today. *Is that why the red mark?*

Bile surges up, threatening to make a mess of my dad's office. I grab the file of deeds and cash accounts and rush for the door. My heart's pounding a La Bamba beat in my chest. *Go. Go. Go.* I urge my feet to hurry, feeling like any second hell's going to rain down now that I've seen Dad's secret files.

Sadly, I'm three steps from safety when Dad's massive oak door flies open, startling a cry of surprise from me that rings my own ears.

"Whatcha doin', darlin'?"

Red.

That nasty drawl from Dad's second in command is the last thing I want to hear. Hell, finding Red in that doorway is worse than seeing my father.

The second he steps into my dad's office, I know. Those beady eyes slide across my body, make me feel stripped bare... dirty. Until he recognizes which notebook I have clinched to my chest and his eyes narrow, the flat brown morphing to a dull yellow as suspicion grows.

With a flick of Red's arm, that heavy door slams shut, dropping a sledgehammer on my hope for a peaceful exit. I step back, my brain scrambling... any excuse for my presence. *Think!*

I just can't find a reason I'd be holding the most incriminating evidence in my hand.

"Little girl, I said... what are you doin' here?" An evil grin spreads across Red's face when he repeats the question. It's predatory, forcing me to drop back farther to get away from that disturbing glint in his eye, the pure joy of our situation. He obviously sees my retreat as some sick hunting game, not my gross disgust at his presence.

With my sensitive nose, it's difficult to hide that disgust. The stench of cigarettes and animal wafting off Red doesn't need my nose to be a full-blooded shifter. A normal human could smell that stink from a mile away.

Facing the animal in front of me, I really wish I had a more *useful* dragon ability. Flight, strength... any of it. Hell, I'd go for fairytale fire breath if it'd get me out of this room faster.

Maybe playing tough is the best route.

Channeling Dad, I cross my arms and snap before the scant flash of bravery deserts me. "Mr. Brewer, this is my house. I was looking for Dad." I know from the cock of his head he doesn't believe me. Especially when his smirk sours at my tone. I stop my next argument on the tip of my tongue, eyeing the door.

What's the chance I could escape? Five percent? If Red succumbs to a well-timed leg cramp. *Dammit!*

The man's size isn't the problem; he's barely taller than I am. It's his eyes. That nastiness is the danger. That, and his lack of conscience.

Red has no limit to who he's willing to hurt. His brutal ruthlessness earned him top rank with my dad's thugs. Although, I've learned a lot these last few days about the nastiness of my dad's business. All along, I assumed my worst conflict was feeling like a hypocrite as a schoolteacher. It's hard to look them in the eye and tell them to *'Just Say No'* when my father is the pusher I warn kids about.

Everything's different now.

Taking a testing approach with Red, I soften my voice, swallowing past the lump of nerves so I can talk my way out of this. "I-I heard you guys were working tonight."

He sneers, stalking to where I've backed behind my dad's desk. "Those guys can handle the vet on their own. I'm not worried. I came to find Dixon," he says menacingly. "But it seems like you and me got other things to discuss." Red pauses, brushing a bit of loose hair behind my shoulder, exposing the skin there.

Immediately, I regret changing into my pajamas before I came exploring. With his beady eyes raking over my skin, I feel naked. They're soulless. Yellowed. Locking on me as his voice drops to a growly whisper. "Did you think you'd get away with it?"

My back stiffens. "Wh-what do you mean?"

"Your little personal visit to my home last week. I'm thinking you're gettin' a little big for your britches down at that school." Leaning back, Red takes his time scanning my exposed legs—my lack of britches—before a smirk twists his vile face that makes my body tremble. "Maybe it's good your daddy ain't here. We need some alone time to... clear the air about expectations in my house."

My mouth goes dry. A sickening dread churns my stomach as his words sink in.

"Well, s'only fair. You stick your nose in my business, puttin' these crazy ideas in my wife's head. You make trouble for my kid at school. Only right, I do the same." Red's slurred speech scares me. The way his words bleed together, dropping more g's as his southern drawl thickens with anger. It doesn't bode well.

"That-that's not what I did!" I try to slide my body out of reach as his anger grows, but I'm not fast enough.

Red's right in front of me, one palm landing on the wall by my head... hard. His arm bars my exit, trapping me in a circle of sweat stains and tobacco breath that blares warning bells in my head.

I need to talk fast. "I'm sorry, Mr. Brewer. I was trying to help. Make sure Max was okay, you know. H-he had missed a few days of school. That's all." I hate the shakiness in my voice, frustrated when Red hears it, too.

He grins, dragging one callused finger down my cheek. My head jerks involuntarily, disgusted, but I know the man's reputation. I do not want to piss him off. Red's nickname isn't from that repulsive mullet hanging off his head. It's for the crimson color his face turns right before his legendary temper explodes, before that nastiness unleashes on anyone weaker than him. I saw it once as a kid and I've feared him ever since.

Recognizing my discomfort, a cruel laugh shakes his body. "You know no one's here to save you. Don't you, princess?"

The air in my lungs freezes when he leans down, my body trembling, praying this vile man doesn't kiss me. At first, he only rubs that pointy nose up the line of my neck. That unkempt beard scratches across my skin triggers my gag reflex, my body shaking uncontrollably. The rising bile getting worse as the dinner I ate earlier threatens to return itself without my permission.

"Red, you need to let me go." My voice quivers, coming out more like a plea than an order.

He chuckles again. "Oh, do I?"

Groaning, I shove two hands into his chest as hard as I can, but the man doesn't budge. Again, I curse my failure as a dragon, for not inheriting the strength the men in this house wield to their advantage. Mom's words repeat in my head as tears of humiliation burn the back of my eyes.

You inherited my heart, Abigail. When your strength comes one day, you'll use it to protect, not to rule.

Easy for her to say. She's not here now. I'd prefer a little dragon strength to get this big oaf out of my space. Especially when Red just tuts at my pitiful attempt to move his body, shaking his head with mock disappointment.

"I don't think so, sweetheart. You've been off limits for years, but I saw you with Baldy. You two looked awful chummy in that kitchen." Red drops his head to my neck and growls for extra effect.

My entire body vibrates with fear from having this sicko so close.

He inhales just below my ear, laughing with pure joy at his power over me. "You know... now that the cat's out of the bag, don't think I ain't gonna get my own licks, *princess.*" That slithering tongue follows his words, leaving a slimy trail down my neck that builds a rush of panic inside.

Oh, God! Oh my God! I need to get out of here!

With shaky hands, I try harder to contort, gathering as much leverage as I can to push against Red's chest, praying it's enough to escape the hell of his grip. "Red!" I screech. "Mr. Brewer! Get. Off. Of me."

At every word, I shove, jerking my head away from the forceful kisses he's trying to catch. He plays like it's a game, moving whichever way my lips go. His shifter strength steps in, holding me inside his trap until I'm panting from the exertion. I don't dare ease off the pressure, though. I shove at his chest with everything I have.

When my head accidentally knocks Red's jaw, he growls. "That's the way ya want it, huh?" Humor drains from his eyes. I watch a truly evil sociopath appear before me.

I don't get time to scream before Red's free hand fists my hair, ripping its length as he tilts my head, giving him easier access to what he wants. My scalp stings from his roughness, but I squeeze my eyes shut to hold the tears.

It pisses me off having Red see me cry, seeing my weakness. The tears remain fully silent, only a sporadic puff of air showing how close I am to breaking down. Until Red growls, pouncing forward to bite the tendon on my neck... cruelly. When I cry out, his cackle mocks my pain, sneering sick words close to my ear while I sob.

"You like that, *defect*? You're not even strong enough to beat me one handed."

"Stop!" I cry out, frantically grabbing at Red's hand to pry it out of my hair. "Please, Clint... Mr. Brewer! Please... just... let me go." Sobs break free, the pain in my scalp becoming too much.

Red's shoulders shake with silent laughter at my plea, his grin back and growing as his free hand wanders to my hip, pressing in. "What's my name, princess?"

Sick terror twists my gut, but I still fight his grip as hard as I can, my own hands shaking from the surge of adrenaline. "Red. Red, dammit. Your name is Red," I scream, but I get nowhere slapping at that disgusting face.

He's gone full 'red' mode, wrenching both my hands into a trap so I can't connect a single hit. The quick movement shoves my arms against the wall so hard my head bounces off the surface, ringing my ears from the impact.

My mind registers ripping fabric... Red's hands tearing at my pajamas.

Useless tears stream down my face, my head throbbing. I know I won't be able to stop him now. I'm seconds from giving up. My muscles are on fire from the struggle. When Red's body flies from mine, his weight disappears so fast I crash to the ground.

The sudden drop is dizzying, blurring the motion around me until a crash registers through the haze. My brain fuzzes. The throb hurts to open my eyes. Whatever the sound is, I don't have the strength left to investigate, to stop whatever is about to happen to me. *Too tired.*

A wave of nausea bends me in half. I grip my stomach, squeezing my eyes shut to fight the barrage of panic restricting me to the floor.

If Red comes back to finish his attack, I hope to at least puke all over those nasty acid-wash jeans.

Chapter Fifteen

Kris

RAGE IGNITES FROM THE moment I step through Peter Dixon's front door.

Adrenaline courses through my blood, sensing Abigail's trouble. She may not be my mate yet, but after what happened a few days ago, it's only a matter of time. Her emotions are as clear as day. Even with a weak connection, it's there.

The last mile of my drive was pure torture. Her terror blasted me in the heart, forcing my foot to press the gas like a teenager on a joyride. If I'd been farther away, I would have ditched Betty—my '69 GTO Judge—and flown, but I was so close. I figured the time lost during a shift wasted more than driving.

Thank fuck I bailed early. Everything was off.

I get why Boss got twisted out of shape. His elaborate kidnapping scheme failed to set the bait for Red. Him being a no-show didn't give Dixon the chance to catch the prick in his lies. But something else bothers me. I just can't put my finger on it. My dragon feels it, too. He's on high alert and growing more restless as the night wore on.

In the end, I trusted my gut and followed my instinct. It brought my ass to this house tonight. Now, with Abigail's frantic sobs bouncing off the walls, my dragon takes over. Using shifter speed, I race the halls toward our mate and crash my weight through the heavy door where her cries are the loudest.

Unfortunately, the sight in front of me will live in the dark corners of my photographic memory for the rest of my days. To see Abigail's clothes shredded, her hair locked in Red's grip like his slimy claws have any right to touch such a beauty, strikes a fire in my blood to kill. For the soon-to-be-dead asshole in front of me, it blows the tight reins I held over my dragon.

Heat turns my blood to molten lava, my eyes burning red. *I will tear this degenerate limb by limb.* The fury makes fighting off a full shift excruciating, but I can't give Red the advantage of catching me weak mid-transition. Plus, I won't risk scaring Abigail more than she is already.

Adrenaline surges, and I grab the back of Red's hair. His mullet works in my favor to throw that vile body across the room. The satisfying thud when he bangs off the wall brings a smile. Until I watch in horror as Abi slides to the floor, losing consciousness. I'm torn. The darkness in my heart hungers to finish Red, so he can never touch my mate again. But my soul pushes me to check on Abigail, to cover the strips of skin exposed by her tattered clothing.

Get my mate to safety. You were nearly too late! My dragon fumes reprimanding my association with this lot.

A switchblade clicking open snaps me back to attention to find Red on his feet. Stupidly, his eyes only show a fraction of fear they should. The coward must feel awfully safe hiding behind a puny blade. *Like that ridiculous thing makes up for our size difference.*

"It's my turn with her," he hisses, like Abi's a piece of cake we could share. At my glare, he changes tactics. "I-I caught her snooping, man. She owes me payment for keeping my mouth shut with her Pa."

That sniveling bastard! *What if I didn't get here in time?*

My fists clench. "Does she?" He thinks that's an acceptable excuse to force his way with a woman.

I stalk forward with a shake of my head, watching Red back himself to the wall, trying to gage my next move. "Red, what *I* know is... if you *ever...* lay another *fuckin'* hand on Abigail... you better plan on leaving this *goddamn* house without it." A bitter snarl laces my words, my back teeth grinding down to sand in the struggle not to tear that black heart right from his body.

Rip his head off!

Protocol says, take Red to the boss. Dixon doesn't tolerate dissension in the ranks with anyone. With Red... when he hears about this little scenario with his daughter... it's war. He'll wish he never crossed us. And after the boss finishes with this traitor, I'll take my turn and break his life apart to avenge my mate.

Hopefully, when this is all over, Dixon's in a forgiving mood. I've tiptoed around Red for a month now, worried he'd spill the beans. I'm done. After the close call tonight, I'm not waiting another day to claim my mate. The world is going to know she's under my protection.

She's ours. My dragon's impatience prickles like ants crawling across my skin while I stand between this asshole and my mate.

Red's face gives him away, his eyes flashing indignantly that I'd dare threaten him. "How dare you?" he seethes, his anger getting the better of him. With clenched teeth, Red's knife swipes out in a wobbly lunge, sealing his date with destiny.

The overconfident arc misses my navel by an inch, the momentum knocking that idiot off balance, stumbling in a fit of desperation. I spring, taking advantage of Red's off-kilter state to twist his knife-wielding wrist behind his back. Easy. I have the upper hand, but I can't stop. I cock Red's arm until it's bent between his shoulder blades, his scream reaching pitch equal to the ones he ignored from Abigail when I walked in.

A taste of his own medicine.

"I will have her," he seethes, saliva frothing from his mouth like a rabid dog.

The threat shoots venom through my veins, tainting my blood until all I hear are our heavy breaths and Abigail's sobs. Red struggles, but my grip tightens at his words. Abi's whimper tells me she heard it too, and that's the last straw that snaps the fragile hold I have on my sanity. *There's only one way out of this.*

I jack his arm up until Red's feet barely scrape the ground, his toes scrambling as I march forward and slam his ugly mug into the wall. He howls in pain, but I don't know if it's from his face thudding against sheetrock or the pop of his shoulder when it dislocates from its socket. My beast fumes.

His head jerks back, aiming to smash my nose, but I'm too fast. My armbar smashes his cheek against the hard surface, ending any escape attempts. Still, the dumbass tries to talk past the press of my elbow. I grind deeper, silencing any quips out of that smart mouth that'll upset my mate. When he finally shuts up, realizing there's no universe where he'll gain the advantage in his current position. I pause, letting that thought sink in until he knows he's truly fucked. Only then do I lean into his ear, making sure he can hear my promise, making sure he hears my growl.

"Over my dead body, jackass." With that, I land a punch to the back of his head that knocks the weasel out cold. I release his shirt, watching his body crumple to the ground before sprinting to my Abigail. Now that I've taken care of her threat, I need to take care of my mate. The sight of Abi curled in on herself makes me want to finish Red instead of handing him over to Dixon, but her tears keep me at her side.

Red isn't as important as soothing my mate. Her shivering scares me. Hell, I don't know how badly Red hurt her before I walked in. *Shit!*

Squatting down, I reach for her shoulder, wanting to comfort anyway I can, but I stop myself. What if I scare her, too?

As gentle as my shaking hands allow, I tuck the hair out of Abi's face, pulling it away from the silent tears streaming down her splotchy cheeks. Her body shudders, breaking my heart. I can't tell if it's fear or adrenaline shaking her body, but the lingering tang of fear in the air worries me. I can't handle Abigail believing I'd hurt her the way Red did.

"Shh, baby. Shh..." I swipe at the trail of wetness, fighting the urge to wrap her in my arms and drag her out of here. Frantically, I scan her body for visible damage. "Abigail." My voice softens, willing my girl to recognize me, to feel our connection and open her eyes. When my gaze travels back to her face, red-rimmed eyes hit me in the gut, pleading, searching. "We need to go, baby."

At my urgent whisper, her eyes dart over my shoulder, finding Red's knocked out form drooling on the floor. Quickly, she scrambles to her feet, knees trembling so hard from the panic, they nearly buckle. I catch her weight, steadying my mate in my arms, but the joy only lasts a second before she's gone.

Abi yanks away, her face scarlet as she fights to secure her torn clothing in a way that'll cover her body from view.

"Baby, we don't have time to play coy here," I say, unwinding my belt.

Abigail lifts one prettily arched eyebrow instead of shying away. *Okay.* My mouth drops open when her eyes stray to my hips. Thank God this situation is the one and only that doesn't cause an erection around this woman. I can't imagine hiding it successfully with her scent lingering on my skin.

Flustered, I cough to cover my giddiness over Abi checking me out. *What the hell am I thinking?*

I shake myself out of that idiocy and stalk back to Red. My belt works as makeshift handcuffs, not fool-proof, but it should hold Red's hands behind his back until I can call Dixon. Which I will do the *second* I get Abi out of this house. Her safety comes first.

With Red secured, my urgency kicks into high gear. I walk toward my anxious beauty and cup her elbow. "Let's go." I start for the door, hoping Abi will give in for once without a big argument. No such luck. Her arm jerks from my grasp.

"I don't know, Kris." Her lip trembles as those watery blue eyes flicker back and forth between me and Red.

She doesn't want to be close to either of us.

"Come on, Abigail." I fight to soften my approach. My voice pleads despite the pent-up rage coursing through my body. "We need to go before he wakes up. Your dad needs answers before anyone kills him." I pause, swallowing past the gravel in my throat. "But Abigail, if he lays another hand on you, I won't be able to control myself."

She gasps, the sound hoarse from her earlier screams. The apprehension on her face solidifies the rock in my gut over the things I've done. All in the name of duty. All for her old man. Now Abi has a clear picture of how unsavory our world can be. *Does it matter if I try to live by a better code... when I can?*

My heart constricts.

Waiting for my mate to decide if she trusts me cracks my soul wide open. Red might as well have knifed me for the pain it causes. I resolve—putting my foot down now—that I'm getting out of this business... however possible. "We don't have time, Abi." Taking a deep breath, I step back a few inches, giving her space to decide.

I watch her arms wrap her middle protectively. I wish it was for comfort and not fear. Or that it was my arms she'd seek for shelter.

I already know I'm not worthy of her love today, but I need her trust. "Abigail, you have to know I'll protect you with my life. No matter what."

"Kris?" Abi's tone is gentle, hesitant. But it's when her eyes flicker to mine and immediately back down, I realize the problem. Heat still seers them red. *God! I'm such a fool!* Abi needs to know the man, not the beast, is in control.

However, after what I walked in on, cooling my temper is harder than I want to admit. But if I don't, she'll never leave with me. Which is why I focus instead on her plump red lips and the delicate curve of her nose, using Abigail's softness to school my red eyes back into their normal shade of green.

When I finally feel cool, I extend a hand, giving Abi the option to grab or not.

"You're safe with me," I say, praying she hears my sincerity. I need to get her to safety. I don't want to piss her off doing it, but I will.

Thankfully, Abigail leaps into my arms, shocking the hell out of me. Her face buries in my neck. "I know," she whispers. "I know, Kris."

Hallelujah! I lift my mate's legs to wrap my waist, cocooning her sweet body in my protective arms. *I'm never letting go now.*

I give myself a minute to savor Abigail clinging to me like a baby kitten, dragging in a lungful of her honied scent. But only for a minute. I can't lose myself in that sweet smell or in the arms clinging to my neck like a lifeline. Not yet. I need my wits about me to hatch a good enough plan to get us out of this mess.

My eyes fall to her dad's ledger lying open on the floor. It's going to be an uphill battle to win Abigail over, but I'm ready to fight. That determination pushes me from the room before I can second guess myself.

First step is getting the hell out of this house. After that, I'll deal with Red... then her father. I don't know which is going to be harder.

Chapter Sixteen

Kris

THE FIRST STEP ACROSS Abigail's threshold, she leaps from my hold. Startled, I cover the goods, protecting them from flying arms and legs as she hops down with a renewed fire lit under her ass.

"Whoa, Abi." My voice croaks, battling a barely controlled hard-on from holding my mate in my arms. After her earlier trauma, my lack of control triggers a bastardly amount of guilt. Discreetly, I shift my denim, praying Abigail doesn't notice my dilemma or mention it. "What are you doing?" I almost laugh at the incredulous look in those aqua eyes.

"What's it look like I'm doing?" An angry, agitated snort follows, making me grin despite the flush of embarrassment working up her neck.

When Abi pulls various drawers open, tossing t-shirts and under-things on the bed, that's when I have to look away. How does the sight of a few lacy garments fry my brain? I have no idea, but I'm boring holes in the ceiling, nonetheless. Listing out batting averages like my life depends on it. Who knows... it might. If I don't get my misbehaving cock under control, I could scare Abigail into never trusting me again.

"It looks like spring cleaning. Pack a bag, woman. Let's get out of here." Her scowl throws some duct tape on my fractured concentration.

"I *am* getting out of here," she huffs. "And I'm bringing enough that I don't have to come back here... ever."

My shoulders tighten. This is going to fast-track any plans I had for Abigail, but I'm not surprised. Not after tonight.

I nudge my head toward the closet and grumble a lazy agreement. Who knows if she'll be back here or not? I haven't thought that far ahead.

With her back straight, Abi disappears inside her closet, undeterred by my attitude. After only a few minutes, she's back out with a new tank top replacing the torn one and a bulging gym bag. *She's still sporting those goddamn pajama shorts*. She tosses the bulging bag on her neatly made bed, not saying a word to me. The thing looks like it has a month's worth of clothes shoved inside.

I shake my head and lean into the doorjamb, my arms crossed as I watch Abigail retreat into her attached bath. Drawers bang inside, cabinets slam... it's like she gives zero fucks anymore about being quiet or hiding.

Our mate is fiery!

Pride swells at seeing the shift in Abi. While I will protect a tearful Abigail with my dying breath, this ball-busting version who puts me in my place is my favorite. Partly because I know she only lets her confidence shine for me.

Abigail's actions become rushed. She zips around the room, flitting to different hiding places to grab an armload of trinkets for her bag. The top drawer of her nightstand opens, only to snap closed again when she realizes my eyes track every movement.

Laughter rumbles in my chest, my dragon wondering what Abi's hiding in that drawer. Her eyes dart to mine, challenging, and every part of me craves to answer that challenge. If I could just sample those sweet lips again. They're wet from her gnawing at them while she packs, showing as much nervousness as those damned, pink-stained cheeks. Both have my fist clenching to take control. My skin is feeling itchy.

Get her underneath us.

What the hell! Battling my dragon's urges against the pressing need to get Abi out of this house takes every ounce of my self-control. *Goddammit! Do you not remember the trauma she endured tonight?*

We'll make her forget.

My God! If my dragon had his way, we'd grab Abigail and take her on the same ruffled comforter she's had from childhood. But he needs to chill until we figure out the rest of this shit. My brain is already flying in circles as it is just standing in this bedroom.

"Where do you plan to go?" I ask, wondering if she has a place in mind. It would really help this whole spur-of-the-moment escape we're attempting here. The question stops her mid-dig at the girly white jewelry box on her dresser.

Abigail's confused stare turns to me, the excitement dulling momentarily in those pretty blue eyes. A tiny gold locket her mom gave her for her tenth birthday dangles from her fingertips. She wore that thing every day until the chain broke. Pursing her lips together, she snaps back into action, moving to tuck the fragile necklace in the safety of her bag's outer zipper.

With fallen shoulders, Abi turns to me, exhaling a long breath that appears to zap all the energy from her lovely body. "Kris... honestly, I have no idea where I'm going." Her voice wobbles briefly before that stubborn chin pops in the air with a touch of her earlier defiance. "Do you plan to stop me?"

Hah! That question is preposterous. She really thinks I'm that entrenched with her father that I'd turn her in.

How would she know? My dragon snorts, reminding me of my failures to secure our mate's trust.

She will soon. I'll fix it.

"No, gorgeous. I'm not stopping you." I stalk closer... right into her space and grab the packed duffle from her hand. My smile feels like a victory. "I'm coming with."

To check its weight, I lift the bag up and down before I sling it crossbody over my shoulder. Abi gapes in shock. I love her delightful mix of confusion and skepticism. How she opens and closes her mouth like she wants to argue but stops herself. That furrowed brow calls for my fingers to smooth. Instead, I tip her lips closed with my finger. *Self-preservation!* That flick of tongue peeking out is already a tease, one I can't do anything about anytime soon.

For a few seconds, Abigail and I partake in a standoff. I'm not sure what made her think I'd let her go off on her own, but at my raised eyebrow, Abi gives up and changes course for her laptop bag and purse.

"Nope." A lighthearted tsk-tsk softens my command, but Abi's irritated glare still tries to skewer me. Chuckling, I hold my hands up in mock innocence. "Don't shoot the messenger. Just don't pack more than I can carry."

With her back to me, I swear Abigail mumbles something snarky about know-it-all men, but before I can defend myself or explain, she's flipped on her heels and hitting me full force with the power of her anger. Fisting hands fly up in front of her face, squeezing empty air like she's pretending it's my neck. The muffled scream that squeals between those clenched lips would panic a lesser male, thinking his woman's gone bat-shit.

"Kristopher," she grinds out between her gritted teeth. "I know I'm little, but I can carry my own flippin' bags to the car. I'm not that damn useless... I swear!"

I sigh, knowing she's gonna hate this part.

"You can't drive, Abigail. Your car has a tracker. We're flying."

"What!" Her screech tweaks hearing again, but I stand firm, watching Abi's face redden, a touch of it turning those blue eyes into shimmering amethyst. My head cocks. *What is that?* She's shown signs of transformation a handful of times now. I can't brush it off anymore. Is her dragon really showing itself? After all these years.

Abigail strides forward, poking a finger at my chest in challenge. "We'll take your car, then." Abi's arms cross over her chest, coming just shy of stomping her foot with a pout while I shake my head, fighting the smile struggling to break free at that bossy tone.

"My car is jacked, too," I admit, knocking the wind out of her sails. Abi's lips draw together, debating another argument, but we don't have time. My patience is on thin ice, knowing we need to be out before Red wakes up. Or before her dad gets home and I lose my chance to get a leg up on this situation with Abigail.

The air electrifies between us as we stand, just inches apart, waiting for the other to crack. Clearing my throat, I admit, "Look, Abi, like it or not, he tracks us all. I don't like it any more than you do, but—"

"You have a choice in it," she mumbles, rolling her eyes.

Ignoring that lie, I push on. "Either way. I'm getting you out of here... tonight, Abigail." I pause, dropping my voice as I step into her honey-scented space. "But I need time to figure out the rest of the plan. Until I do, we can't have your father or Red tracking us down. Or them sending the rest of the gang after us, either."

"Ugh! Fine." I'm so close that even that soft huff of annoyance tickles my neck. It doesn't make that pout any less adorable.

"So..." I grin, deciding to poke the dragon a touch... tease Abigail into that nervous blush I love. Solely as a distraction, I tell myself, to get us back on a level playing field. "Do you need to pack anything else?" I ask, reaching for the bedside drawer Abi had slammed shut.

"No!" Her shout hits simultaneously with a slap to my hand.

I laugh with a full-belly chuckle at how fast that lithe little body lunges between me and the unknown. I've barely grazed the handle before Abigail locks onto my wrist and tugs as hard as she can.

Unfortunately, her desperation floods my naughty mind with all sorts of visions for what mysteries she hides. Things I don't dare think about unless I want to have a tough time walking. Especially with Abigail panting, her manicured fingers digging into the muscle of my forearm.

Don't piss her off! my dragon growls.

He may not like the glower coming off Abi, but I love the absurdity of her thinking she could stop me if I really wanted inside that drawer.

Still, it is nice to have this spunkier, fighter version of Abigail back. I didn't like seeing her crushed under her fear.

Aiming my cockiest smile at my girl, I feign innocence, knowing it'll annoy her. "What is it, little one? Something you don't want me to see in there?"

"Gah!" Abi shoves at my chest, but instead of moving back, I scoop her into my arms cradle style and get ready for flight. "What are you doing?" she asks with a shriek at the sudden change in elevation. Her tiny fist smacks my shoulder while I shush her increasing volume.

"We need to get this show on the road."

"Yes. But again... what the hell are you doing?" She's wiggling her delectable ass in my hold, creating the worst pleasurable torture I've endured in my lifetime.

I pause, squeezing tighter to halt my mate's innocent cock-tease. "Can you suddenly fly?"

"No." The word growls from her lips, grinding out like it physically hurts to admit that defeat aloud. *Okay.* She's sulky, but at least her legs aren't kicking for freedom now.

"All right, then." I don't fight my smile as I secure my precious bundle in my arms, walking through the French doors to her second-floor balcony. It overlooks the backyard. I know because I've stared up at these doors for years, wishing I could climb the trellis outside like some dark prince yearning for his forbidden princess.

"This is so surreal." I leap to the marble rail and concentrate, my teeth grinding to hide the flicker of pain from my wings breaking the skin on my back. Abigail gasps at the sound of tearing fabric. "*Dammit!* Another shirt gone." This woman scrambled my brain cells. After our little sparring match, I didn't think through my errors in clothing, during the flight or after.

Tucking Abi in tight, I stretch the muscles of my wings and leap effortlessly into the night sky. Her arms lock around my neck like her lifeline as we soar higher, her breath catching when we pass through the clouds, the cool wetness slapping us in the face.

"Wow." Abigail's awed whisper pleases my dragon as I hide us above the shielding clouds. He's getting harder to control with the opportunity to protect his mate. My skin tingles, his wildness threatening to burst through.

Now's our chance.

Down. I bark internally, focusing on the softness in Abi's eyes to calm his spirit. Her fingers lightly stroke under the tattered fabric at my back as her eyes take in the sparkling stars above. I don't think she's aware of rubbing the space where human skin meets dragon wing, but the sensation is sending shivers through the rest of my body.

See. Enjoy our mate's touch. You won't scare her!

I squeeze Abigail a little tighter, enjoying her fingers scratching at the scruff on my head. Those sky-blue eyes hold so much meaning, I can't look away as I take us on a side-winding tour of the skies. I don't want our adventure to end yet.

Chapter Seventeen

Abigail

When Kris lands sometime later, I have no idea if it's been thirty minutes or three hours. Being my first time flying, the exhilaration of soaring the night sky distracted me from everything else: my earlier worries about Dad, the crippling fear of Red... the pain.

Problem is, I'm more ticked off now that my dad never took me flying.

"I'm busy, baby girl."

"But Daaaad! Dragons are supposed to fly, and I don't have my wings," I whined, dragging out his name and stomping my little ten-year-old foot.

"No, Abigail. I don't have time to fly you around for fun." His dismissal hurts. Daddy never has time for me, and Mommy can't fly either.

This sucks!

"Let Kristopher take me, then. He's out back wrestling with the guys. He can fly me." I push down the butterflies fluttering inside my tummy at the idea of getting to hug Kris's neck in the sky.

But Dad crushes that dream with a slam of his fist on his desk. "Over my dead body, Abigail!" His bellowing voice fades as he storms into the backyard, leaving me alone in our quiet house... again.

I'm pulled out of the memory by Kris gently returning my feet to the ground outside of a small cabin. Though my eyes won't drag away from the beauty of the heavens above. I'm not ready to give it up.

"It's beautiful." I sigh, wondering how to thank Kris for this amazing gift.

"Yes, it is." Kris's breathy voice rumbles low in his chest, the sexiness drawing my eyes away from the sky. I flush when I find his green eyes glowing in the darkness, focused on me. I look away to hide my smile. *How long have I wished for Kris to look at me that way?*

"Where are we?" I hate to break our trance, but the tension between us is just too much.

He must agree, because Kris immediately straightens and moves for one of the darkened cabin windows. Unfortunately, that means my hips lose the warmth of his hands and it dawns on me. I'm still wearing the tiny pajama shorts I wore earlier—before Red—when my night only included a plan to get information and go to bed.

When Kris turns back, his emerald eyes sear into mine. His face scrolls an emotional billboard of naughty thoughts, those eyes sending a sudden rush of wetness to my core that leaves me wondering if we'll get to finish what we started in the kitchen. "Where we are is somewhere you won't be found. That's all that matters until we figure out our next steps."

He saved us earlier.

That fleeting thought makes me smile, but when Kris sees I'm not putting up an argument, he goes back to hunting through the various rocks strewn beside the porch. Thankfully, in his distracted state, Kris misses me ogling his tight ass bent over, the stress-worn fabric of his jeans stretching tight across those solid thighs, sliding up to cup his backside. *Who could resist that?* I've wanted this freedom to stare since I hit puberty.

Gah! This man is beautiful torture.

I'm still drooling when Kris stands, holding a tiny key in the air with a victorious smile. My cheeks flame after he catches my eyes glued to his rear, but his do too, so I don't feel as bad. At least Kris keeps any of his usual smart-aleck comments to himself. Which helps me pretend I don't want to dig a hole as big as China and crawl into it.

Win.

"Is this place yours?" I ask, reaching for a distraction. My eyes track Kris up the steps, purposefully keeping above his narrow waistline instead of tormenting myself with that biteable ass.

At the front door, he pauses, and I think he's going to say it's none of my business. Instead, Kris head falls, eyes squeezing shut with his hand fisting the knob. I watch with fascination as those powerful cinnamon-colored wings that brought us here shrink and disappear into his shoulder blades.

After a few uneasy moments, his eyes meet mine. "It's your dad's place." The memory of those deeds in Dad's office twists my stomach. I dropped the files during Red's attack, so all my proactive efforts got me nowhere, except in some remote cabin with the man of my dreams.

Could you really turn in your own father?

Okay, doubt... shut up!

After everything I learned this week, my conscience should be on board with getting justice. My resolve should be granite. Would I be something other than the defective daughter of a mob boss?

Kris glances at me knowingly before quietly pushing the door open, his apprehension becoming apparent in the rigid stance of his body as he scans the interior of the tiniest cabin I've ever seen. I follow, because what else is there to do? But it helps stop my spiraling funk.

The smell of dust and mildew are thick in the air, choking us both the moment we cross that threshold. I pinch my nose shut, waving a hand in front of my face to clear the staleness from my sinuses, but Kris is more proactive. He speeds over to one of the few windows in the open room, tossing it open for fresh air.

Within a few minutes, the scent of pine and forest fill the small room, clearing my mind enough to look around. It doesn't take long. In one sweep, I see a double bed in one corner, a single row of kitchen cabinets on the back side containing a sink, a range, and a countertop microwave... and one God-awful plaid couch perched in front of a tube tv that must be twenty years old.

Smirking, I glance at Kris, who's distracted from our dingy surroundings by his raid of the kitchen—if you can call it that. He immediately dropped my bag on the Formica, two-seater table in the nook to hunt for supplies in the drab cabinets.

"Is there a bathroom in this place?"

"Uh..." His head peeks from under a cabinet to nod at the only other door in the room. "There," he says, sending a disarming smile over the counter that flutters the same butterflies in my stomach he gave me as a little girl.

Holy cow! I'm in trouble.

Before I embarrass myself, I half-run to the bathroom and lock myself in. I need a moment of privacy, considering my brain feels like a bag of marbles this close to Kris. Given what we ran away from earlier tonight, I'm damn sure gonna need a clear head to deal with whatever shitstorm's bound to fall on us.

I suck in a cleansing yoga breath, gripping the small powder sink to regulate my panic. Exhale. Repeating the process, I take in my wind-blown hair in the oval mirror, which shows barely a scrap of my reflection through the hazy film that shows both its age and lack of care. The obvious dark circles under my eyes are hard to miss, though. They are accessories that show exactly how little I've slept this past week. Pretty much since I got on board with changing my life. It needs to happen. But all week has been a battle of conscience. Yes, I want to get out of my dad's protective bubble, but I haven't been as gung-ho about the quickest way to accomplish that.

Earlier tonight, I thought I was ready. I was dead set on finding evidence to turn my father in to whichever authority would help. I've been completely furious with Kris for going along with Dad, assuming he was just another thug willing to do his bidding. Hell, I thought I stood a chance at saving a perfect stranger.

You could if you'd accept me. A quiet voice whispers deep in my head. For the first time, my conscience seems to have a mind of its own.

Confused, I shake my head, feeling like a wet dog stepping out of the bath. When my eyes focus again on the mirror, there's no mistaking their shine. The center glows with a quick flash of purple. *What the—?*

Blinking several times clears the blur, and when I reopen, they're back to my normal blue hue. *Okay, I have finally lost my mind.*

Shoving off the sink, I rethink the wisdom of alone-time and decide the small living space with Kris's hulking presence is oddly my safer option at this point. The stress is obviously turning me wacky. And if I can't trust my own thoughts, watching Kris's muscles flex while he works in the kitchen seems like a viable—and enjoyable—distraction.

Growing giddier by the second, I head for the worn couch in what passes for a living room and drop myself on the threadbare cushion. In my head, I saw myself curling into a comfy—and hopefully sexy position—to wait out Kris's scavenger hunt. So, when he'd finish, he'd be so overwhelmed, our passion would put a brighter ending on a rather shitty day.

That would have happened if reality weren't a succubus bitch!

In real life, my heavy flop on the couch produced a puff of aged musk and old man farts that make it hard to breathe. It's a legit struggle, but I do my best to not cough, waving one hand to clear the air while I debate the sanitation of the cushion I'm sitting on. A surprised laugh barks from the kitchen, its sexy rumble hitting me low in the stomach until Kris's spiky blond head pokes over the counter and hits me with a raised eyebrow.

"Tummy problem, princess?"

While I'd love to slap that quirked brow right off his smug face, I settle for narrowing my eyes into the most menacing look I can manage while holding a straight face. But his twisted grimace is too much, and my grin breaks loose, loving that he nauseously suffers from the same putrid odor I do over here.

"Har, har. Hilarious, ass."

Before the curse is out of my mouth, Kris's grin spreads wider and he stands with a flourishing wave of his hand—Vanna White style—that I never imagined coming from this broody bad-boy. He's laid out our entire bunker stash across the countertop. Not that there's an impressive spread to display here.

"We have some two-year-old crackers—name brand mind you—stale cereal, a few cans of veggies, peaches, and some kind of dried jerky meat I wouldn't touch with a ten-foot pole." Each item ticks off a finger, but he holds the last one up, eyeing it like it's radioactive.

Despite not eating since breakfast, my stomach wants nothing to do with the list he rambled off. "So, uh, this place has been empty for a while, huh?"

"Looks that way." Kris shrugs, walking to our grody couch and eyeing it cautiously before sitting at my feet. He shifts them to his lap, sliding off my tennis shoes as if it's the most natural thing in the world.

To my surprise—and utter delight—Kris massages the pads of his thumb into the deep arch that aches constantly in my foot. My moan is involuntary, I swear. And the shameless way my head falls back, hitting the couch before I think better of it... that too is involuntary.

I'm almost afraid to breathe that Kris might stop. Never in our relationship have we had the freedoms together that we've had the past few weeks and part of me is afraid it's all a dream. Especially when he rubs deeper. *God, please don't let me wake up from this one.*

The magnificent way Kris lights my entire body from the inside isn't normal. He has some magical key; I think. He must, because when those strong fingers tug at my toes, the goosebumps tingling up my legs make it impossible not to wiggle.

My eyes close, feeling pampered and loving the hell out of it, judging by the purring in my head. Until Kris's massage stops, and my eyes fly open. His hands remain firm on my feet, pressing them to his lap. *Did I moan out loud?*

Then my brain registers the hard ridge growing against my heel. Flustered, my head turns to the guilty grin on the other end of the couch. *Is this turning him on?*

Kris shrugs. "Sorry, Princess. You just do it for me."

My jaw drops. What do I say to that? I don't know how to seduce a man. If I did, I would have been all over this one a long time ago. I just never expected my childhood crush to want the defect.

Don't call us that. An outraged shriek reverberates in my head.

Jerking upright, I tug my feet free, tucking them underneath me on the couch. "Kris..." I ignore his surprised grunt in favor of figuring out the craziness inside my head.

Immediately, he's contrite, looking both guilty and confused. But it's the comforting hand he rests on my shoulder that causes my eyes to blur. The tears make me feel worse. I don't want our moment to end.

"Kris, I legit think I'm going crazy." My hands shake, out of control, really, but Kris is completely calm as he leans forward, shushing me, rubbing rhythmic circles on my back.

"Abi, it's okay. I shouldn't have said that. I just... I couldn't help myself." I squeeze my eyes shut, hating that Kris feels the need to apologize.

"Don't." My voice cracks. I shake my head, burying my face in my hands, so he doesn't see how badly I'm losing the battle with my tears.

Kris would never laugh at us.

Ahh! I cover my ears, rocking frantically. The voice in my head needs to stop. *What's wrong with me?*

Anxious, I turn to Kris, tears flowing freely now. "Something's wrong with me. My head..." I sniffle, and his frown blurs.

A wave of nausea hits me, prickling my body like it's standing on a live wire. My fingers dig into my forehead, hoping I can press the crazy out when I feel Kris lift under my arms, bringing me to straddle his lap with no effort at all.

Through my tears, I feel those thick arms wrap around my back, tugging me into his hard chest, giving me a place to crash in a moment of weakness. Kris's body is a granite pillow for the sobs wracking my body. But it doesn't stop my face from burying in his neck for the second time tonight, breathing in his masculine scent. The tears slowly release the chaos in my head until I don't care about looking weak anymore. I'm taking comfort from the man with the hard exterior shell because he's who does it for me. I don't care about anything else.

The rest of the world fears him. *Not me.*

I could never fear the warmth in that heavy hand stroking the back of my head. The way he holds it protectively, offering comfort and understanding, instead of judgement and ridicule. How could I have ever thought Kris was just another of my dad's ruthless thugs? Guilt over that earlier judgement floods more tears, but Kris's raspy voice keeps shushing, rocking my body gently against his, easing the pain my guilty conscience deserves.

"Shh, shh… it's gonna be okay, little one. I promise."

I don't deserve those sweet words, but they go a long way to calm the voice in my head. I want to trust it'll be okay. I want to keep my body here in this perfect spot, my head on the curved muscle of Kris's chest, listening to the heartbeat of my ultimate protector.

"We're gonna find a way out, Abigail. Somehow. And we won't have to worry about hiding anything anymore." Kris's heartbeat races under my ear, but I don't know if he's excited or nervous at the idea of what's coming.

"I'd like to believe that." Exhaling, I rest my forehead against his shoulder, my hands pressing that rock-hard stomach to give myself a little breathing room. I can't bear to look Kris in the eye yet, considering the tears I've shed in his lap.

My. Childhood. Crush's. Lap.

But now, with the panic subsiding, I sit up, attempting to hide a very unladylike sniffle, only to notice the large, wet spot on the front of Kris's shirt. He doesn't look bothered, but it doesn't stop my cheeks from burning with embarrassment that my tears did that. And somehow, he still gazes at me like I'm a pristine artwork, not a blotchy eyed, runny nose mess.

Kris's thick thumbs come up, wiping the wetness from my cheeks. His heart beating like a bass drum, faster, louder. It joins the sound amplifying around me. Chirps from birds parroting through the open window. A monotonous drip of water from the kitchen that pops like a mouthful of Bubblicious. A quick scan of the room leaves me fascinated, but it also sacrifices that peaceful serenity found in Kris's arms.

I'm backsliding into panic, inching myself into crazy-land with every noise reverberating in my head. "Kris." My whisper protects from further noisy chaos in my head. "Something is seriously wrong with me." The confused tilt of his head is disconcerting, making me wiggle on his lap under that probing gaze. I bet he's wondering why he volunteered to protect a crazy woman.

"Abigail, nothing is wrong with you."

Kris's deep timbre blocks the explosive symphony in my head. If he'd only keep talking, it might stop this downward spiral into cuckoo-land. Of course, he doesn't. When Kris falls silent, the roaring in my mind resumes, like someone is holding two massive conch shells to my ears. The ocean sounds drown me, my hands shaking with the fear of losing my marbles.

Calmly, Kris swipes away the tears that haven't stopped overflowing, never once laughing or telling me not to feel. His touch reassures, a shocking contrast for such a hard man to have such a soft touch. That tenderness ignites my veins into a flowing physical pain. It takes over everything, crumbling my foundation like a stick of dynamite lit on my life.

Eventually, my fog lifts and I realize Kris's lips still move with not a word sinking in. His eyes immediately darken with worry when he realizes I can't hear a thing he's said for however long he's been talking.

What the hell is happening to me?

On my next breath, I'm off his lap, dragging in air that's too hot, into lungs that are too tight. My hands brush up and down my arms, but it doesn't calm the flames licking under my skin. By the time beads of sweat accumulate at my hairline, I feel like I'm melting inside, my body burning from the inside out.

Bolting for the open window, I do the last thing I ever imagined... I strip my tank top, letting the chill of the mountain air blast goose-bumps across my overheated body. Because, without the option of crawling out of my skin, I need the relief of less clothing to cool my temperature. I can't even think about being topless in front of Kristopher.

"Abi... Abigail." Kris clears his throat, picking up my discarded shirt and following me with his bulk of sexiness. This close, his powerful, woodsy scent hounds me, melting my body with every breath pulled into my lungs.

Ugh! This is not helping cool me off.

Bending at the waist, I practically shove my head out the window, gripping the dusty sill in a desperate search for cool air. Kris stands back, giving me space but stays close enough—I think—to stop me in case I'm trying to jump out the window. At least, that's what I assume from his freaked-out expression.

"Abigail," Kris calls, his gruff voice pulling me from the fog in my head... slowly.

Unfortunately, no matter how soothing his timber is, the closer Kris steps, the more my body seems to revolt on itself. The sensation of bursting out of my skin is almost unbearable now, my knees trem-bling, demanding all my focus to remain upright. Tenderly, Kris grips my chin, breaking my death grip on the windowsill and bringing me to face him. I'm transfixed on those turbulent emerald eyes flashing concern with a touch of... amazement.

"Abi, have you *ever* shifted before?"

Hah!

"No!" How dare he ask that?

Kris knows the ridicule I've suffered not being able to shift. A sudden burst of anger roars deep inside my chest, startling us both and shaking my lungs before it moves up, almost tickling my ears with the strange sound. Sadly, Kris doesn't look affected in the slightest, not by my irritation and not by the daggers my eyes fire his way. Neither hit their mark.

Worse is the small smile tilting the corners of Kris's lips as he stands there... staring.

That's enough. I jerk my chin from his hold, hiding from those all too seeing eyes.

Piling my hair on top of my head, my shaky hands hold the tangled mess off my neck for some relief. If my brain were functioning correctly, it would have my feet running out of here. But no, the only distance I can bear is turning my gaze out the window, leaving me sweating in front of the one person whose sex appeal drives me crazy and whose arrogance irritates the hell out of me.

Hell, I'm standing in front of this tattooed god topless, shaking, sweating, and... panting. And since I never wear a bra under my pajamas—I don't have enough breast to need it—Kris is devouring every inch of skin on display. My nipples harden at the desire in his eyes. Will he finally stop this back-and-forth game now that we're alone?

Nope. That boat crashes with Kris's resolute sigh.

He slides my discarded top over my head, crushing any hope we'll get off our sexual merry-go-round anytime soon. Debilitating self-doubt has me second guessing every encounter these last few months. Moments I thought would lead somewhere special, only to wither away. Every look from Kris. Every touch. Every assumption I made that he's a dark knight, misunderstood but overall a good man with a protective soul.

Yeah, the shame burning my cheeks strips away whatever hope I had for Kris. Either he's not interested and a liar or he's a freaking tease. One second, he's eyeing me like a prime porterhouse steak.

The next, he's covering my exposed body like it's radioactive. *That's not a blow to my ego at all when all I want is to strip him naked.*

Ugh! I hate sarcasm and now I'm using it nonstop! It's too much. *Too much!*

My hormones have obviously short-circuited something. The volcanic temperature that coursed through my body not five minutes ago must have skyrocketed them out of orbit. Now, only pain remains, and my mind wants a distraction. Because stupidly, my heart wants what it can't have.

Frustration takes over, triggering a deep flight response. My mind begs me to run. To strip... to fly?

Before I question that last thought too hard, I scour Kris's face. My brain might say run, but my heart pushes for something else entirely. With Kris's eyes vulnerable for once, letting me read every emotion firing in that cunning mind of his... the confusion, excitement, happiness. An elephant-size load of feelings packs into the bright gold flecks around his pupils. The opulent shifter color sparks his typical shade of green into sparkling jewels, making it impossible to look away.

So, I don't.

I pounce.

Chapter Eighteen

Abigail

Jumping off the biggest ledge of my life, I attack Kris's lips with a power I didn't know I possessed. He catches my weight mid-leap, bracing under my hips as our passions collide. It's a clumsy mashing of mouths. Me in his arms, practically climbing Kris's muscular frame like a koala latched onto a stalk of bamboo. My hands grasp his rock-hard shoulders, hanging on for dear life.

Kris's passion takes over, slamming my back into the wall behind me. His grip anchors my hips, though I wiggle, desperate to be closer. The electricity zinging across my skin is like nothing I've ever felt, burning me from the inside out with longing. If I could smother myself in Kris's scent, in his heat, that itself would soothe the crazy desire flowing through my veins.

When I scratch my nails into the short hairs at the back of Kris's head, reveling in the buzzed texture, he growls and my core floods with arousal. I cherish this freedom to touch, to explore the finely tuned muscle straining Kris's shoulders. With Kris vibrating under my hands, I feel powerful. As our kiss heats, Kris's tongue dives deeper, tasting. Stroking teasing touches before withdrawing to nip at my lower lip.

It's heaven. It's hell. It's complete torture.

My power slips after that knockout kiss. The hormones overwhelm, flooding my body until a keening moan fills the room, the sound needy and frenzied. It triggers something inside Kris, a snarl my only warning before he takes control and strides forward, pinning my arms to the wall under one of his massive hands.

I whine at losing my ability to touch, but the confinement doesn't feel like earlier. For the second time tonight, I'm trapped against a wall, except I fought Red's revolting touch. With Kris, I'm frustrated, fighting because I can't pull him closer.

"Kris..." I plead, moaning to the ceiling.

A smile softens his features as his head dips, that wicked mouth resting just below my ear and inhaling my scent with a sigh. My breath stutters, waiting. Who needs oxygen? All it takes is one erotic lick to my pulse point to light an inferno in my blood. Kris's free hand trails down my arms, leaving a trail of goosebumps that have me writhing in Kris's much larger presence, craving his closeness.

Everything about the man overwhelms my senses... His hands, his voice, that masculine scent of fresh soap and aged leather, with something else entirely unique to Kris. Around him, my world lights up, vivid and bright, threatening to seize my lungs. The effect short-circuits my nerve endings, amplifying everything. Like the stark contrast of cool sheetrock to my scalding skin. It prickles and I gasp for air.

"Easy, baby. Easy," Kris says, his voice hoarse. One callused hand strokes my jaw, his thumb bracing my chin up, understanding what I need without my asking. His expression teeters between giving in and riding the roller coaster of passion between us and protecting me by controlling it.

Guess which one is going to piss me off?

His eyes search mine, for what, I don't know. I concentrate on sucking in ragged breaths, filling my lungs with this man who lights my nerves on fire. Kris's lips thin, a harsh exhale tickling my cheek as his head falls to mine. Those green orbs hypnotize my soul, slowly burning me under that intense gaze until my legs tremble, barely able to hold vertical as a new wash of pain blisters my back.

"Shit!" he growls as my breathing labors. Reluctantly, he pushes off the wall, breaking our spell of lust. "We need to get you outside." With no effort—and no fight from me—he lifts my body in a cradle carry, using his shifter speed to rush to the front door.

Outside, darkness has settled in. My clammy skin sizzles in the night air like sweat hitting asphalt on a scorching summer day. At my gasp, Kris squeezes my legs against his chest, comforting my distress with his powerful arms. It washes a surprising calm over me, distracting my body with the better mission at hand... my craving for a taste of Kris's jawbone. The urge to bite along that sexy stubble is powerful, more than the pain lancing my back. I'll deal.

Desperately, I wiggle in Kris's arms, breathing through the pain to position myself within reach of his neck. My hands grip the back of his neck, not caring where I sink my teeth into. The manic voice inside my head just says it's imperative that I do.

Except, when I lean in, inches from my goal, Kris pulls back, and I lose his supportive pressure under my legs. A quick shot of disappointment darkens my thoughts, so I can't even enjoy sliding down the front of Kris's hard body. But his next movement, when he peels my hands from his closely buzzed head, drops me to rock bottom. The disconnect releases a sad little whimper, ratcheting my vulnerability to hysterical levels.

We need him. A voice inside my head whines. I wiggle harder to back up, not liking how my body betrays my thoughts.

Between the drama and unknowns in my future, the pain wrenching its way through my body, and Kris's repeated rejections, I can't take anymore. Everything's so out of my control. The way it's been all my life!

That thought shifts my mood quickly, sending an indignant roar into the starless September sky.

"Shh, little one... calm down."

Famous last words, buddy.

Unfortunately, I'm not strong enough to fight when Kris restrains my shoulders, keeping our bodies a few inches apart so he can bend to look me in the eye. *If he's so damn interested, why does he keep pushing me away?*

It's unnerving to have the man of my dreams peering into my soul yet looking at me as if I'm a science experiment. By the time Kris finishes his exasperating examination, I'm seething. My shoulder jerks, trying to release his hold but having no luck.

"Let me go!" I want to be strong, but my voice weakens when tears blur my eyes. I'm tired of having my desperation on display. The humiliation of it eats me alive. But Kris pulls away with no effort, not at all suffering my same torture.

Finally, he takes pity and pulls me into the circle of his arms. One of those massive hands presses my head, his chest offering a fleeting comfort. It's quick. Only a few seconds before he grips my upper arms and pulls away. *Great! I'm a flipping rag doll.*

I'd laugh at the feeling if it weren't for the somber set of Kris's lips. Their thin line traps the words like he doesn't want to say them. I stare up, waiting for some explanation for why Kris is doing this. My gut clenches, and Kris flinches at my pain, his eyes softening. "Abigail... you're shifting. Or you're gonna shift... I'm not sure."

At first, I don't hear a word. I'm too distracted by the gold flickering in those jade eyes. The heat buried there clenches my stomach with a yearning I just can't get rid of, no matter how many times this frustrating man pisses me off. *Why do I want him so much?*

Then, what he says sinks in... "What?" I laugh, but the shrillness in my voice can't hide the uneasiness crawling through my blood. "That's a cruel joke, Kris." His words pierce my heart and if my arms were free, I know there'd be an Abi sized hand blazed across his face. Struggling to breathe, I bite my lip to stop its tremble, but my body reacts anyway. It's like Kris's words have ripped off a band-aid and gutted my insides.

"It's not a joke, baby." He looks hurt at the thought. "I would never do that to you, Abi."

Bile rises in my throat, threatening mortification in front of a man I've wanted for fifteen years. My entire body feels out of control. I hate it. With a gasp, I bend at the waist and Kris lets me go, understanding something I can't quite believe yet.

"This hurts!" My stomach clenches painfully and I groan, dragging frigid air into my lungs, hoping that the cold stops my muscles from tearing apart. Because that's exactly what this feels like.

In the recesses of my mind, I feel Kris stroke my back while I pant. I reach for his words of comfort. I jerk upright as the pain slides to my shoulder, nearly knocking Kris's head. My eyes flit to the sky, praying for divine intervention for the burning sensation moving along my spine.

Somebody help me, before my body explodes.

"I know, baby... the first time is painful." Kris's whispered words bring my eyes to his. I feel the slick tears coating my skin but can't pretend to care. I'm barely able to drag my brain into focus. Steadily, Kris's eyes glow brighter, and my brain finally registers his words, *'first time painful.'*

Does he know? Wait... why would he bring that up now?

Cocking my head, I glance up, confused, only to find humor dancing in his eyes at my expression. *Jackass!* He obviously follows my train of thought, and I want to scream again. But that damnable smile is too distracting, his smirk too fucking sexy, even with my entire body lighting up from the inside. It's no surprise my body only ever responded to Kris with all that sexiness. He broke something. He's the reason my body rejects any boy who tries to sneak a kiss.

I'm about to lay into him about him taunting a person in pain when a fresh round cracks my shoulder blades, slashing skin easier than a Bowie knife. "Oh my God, Kris!" My howl sends a few straggling birds from the trees with its volume.

My breath labors, channeling a Lamaze class I've never taken to push against the pain. I drop to my knees, but Kris's hands soften the blow, easing my weight to the ground as more tears overflow. A gurgling sound bubbles from my throat, the sound of ripping flesh hitting my ears, making me cringe.

Anxiously, Kris grabs my face, jerking my head and my body towards him, his eyes locking on mine. Their intensity verges on desperation as he frantically tries to break through my panic. "Abigail... Abigail." Over and over, he repeats my name. "Baby, look at me." I blink, his face slowly coming into focus. "You're beautiful, Abi. So goddamn beautiful, baby." Kris's awed voice breathes life into me, his fingers stroking the loose hair from my face.

Every place he touches gets immediate relief from its agony. His hands soothing the burn so well, I lean in, eager for more. I would smother myself in Kris's scent, rub him like a cat in heat, to feel the comfort he brings.

More and more, my pain recedes into a dull ache. Enough that my worries of imminent death morph into relief and my head falls to Kris's chest with a gruff—and hoarse—exhale. "Oh, thank God! I can breathe."

Kris's laughter bounces my head. His relief is as palpable as mine in the way his body sags. When I feel comfortable enough to lift my head, the valley of hard muscles I just used for a pillow distracts me. One hand rests there of its own freewill until I feel the lightest tickle at my back. It startles me into turning around, something completely awkward while you're on your knees, being held by Kris's two absolutely capable hands. I still try, weirded out by the sensation.

Something bit my back? This freaking hurts!

Kris's chuckle annoys me, echoing across the open yard at this odd little cabin. He should help get whatever's on my back instead of standing there making fun of me.

"Calm down, love," he says with that know-it-all tone I hate.

"Do not laugh at me, Kristopher!" My meanest glare does nothing to stop his ribbing. It's not even worth trying with this one.

Another brush against my backside disturbs me enough to forget arguing with Kris in favor of fixing whatever the hell is fluttering across my back. The muscles and skin back there already feel odd, similar to a foot falling asleep and then tickling to high heaven when it wakes up again.

"What the...!" I shriek, twisting my head far enough to see without Kris's hold.

Immediately, I'm on my feet, screaming. A pair of bone white, scalloped wings extend from my back, large enough to block my vision of the cabin now that they're standing up tall behind me. My brain doesn't compute.

I turn a quick circle, wondering if my eyes deceive me. *Am I hallucinating?* Kris chuckles, bouncing out of the way when my wings almost slap him on one of my twirls. Thinking about how tight my back feels, I stretch the new appendages, feeling the muscles loosen wonderfully, like waking up after a long nap.

"Your wings, baby. They're beautiful." His voice almost reverent as one hand reaches out, stroking along the soft new flesh, all the way from the thicker base muscle to the sharp ivory talon curling at the tip. The smooth cartilage shivers under his fingers, my mind begging me to lean into Kris's delicate touch. It's a hard urge to fight as I watch a myriad of emotions flash across that gorgeous face.

Our mate.

A low growl emanates from Kris, and I wonder again if he can read my mind.

"How did this happen?" I ask, glancing at Kris. Shock tastes sour on my tongue. I look down where my hands grip his bicep, unable to meet his eyes for this confession. "Kris, I can't shift... I'm broken. You know that."

Somewhere inside, a scream triggers my body to crumble into Kris, soaking in our connection for a moment of relief for the pain.

"No, no, no. Never say that, baby. Not around me." Kris's raspy voice sounds pained, his arms wrapping me in safety, protecting me from the traitorous thoughts that have plagued me since I lost faith in my dragon ever making an appearance. Kris avoids the tender spots on my back, somehow knowing what I need without my saying.

I sniffle back a wave of tears, tired of these chaotic feelings swirling at once... surprise, fear, yearning... happiness. Shock. I never allowed myself to imagine my dragon or what she would look like. Over my shoulder, I watch the new wings spread behind me, amazed at their near translucent sheen. They're so different from the other dragons I know, but they're mine, and I love that.

Happy tears burst out on a laugh. I swipe them away, but they just keep flowing.

Kris's brow creases with concern, looking confused. "Does it hurt?" He's as helpless as the deranged woman in front of him and that makes me laugh harder, more joy filling my heart than I've ever experienced.

But I'm curious.

"Why did this happen now?" I squint at Kris, searching for answers like he's a magic eight ball. One eyebrow quirks halfway up his forehead in surprise, but Kris just shrugs, his grin reminiscent of the teenage boy I first fell in love with. The obvious enjoyment of my moment warms my heart, but... "Why didn't I change fully?" His face falls, and I jump to clarify. "I'm happy. Believe me!"

My swish of wings runs a joy through me like I've never felt before. I hope he feels my happiness, because Kris might be the only person who'd understand how huge this is. "Just... why didn't I change fully?"

That patented smirk returns, his cockiness on full display. "Give yourself time, Princess. Wings are the easiest." My eyes fire lasers at that ridiculous statement and Kris laughs, holding his hands up in mock innocence. "I know, I know... it doesn't feel easy the first time. I'm just saying that some young dragons only produce wings until they mature. It's brand new. You can enjoy it, princess."

I admire Kris's calm. Even if it bugs the crap out of me, I still couldn't imagine anyone else with me during this craziness. For the first time in my life, I feel brave. Before I second guess myself, I grab the side of Kris's face and crash my lips into his. He freezes, but only for a second before his hands slide up my neck, bracketing my face to hold it still.

Mine! A lumbering growl rolls through my head, frying my already frazzled nerves.

Chapter Nineteen

Kris

I TAKE OVER OUR kiss quickly, devouring Abigail's sweetness like it's my life's blood.

She started it. That blocks the guilt over fate inevitably pushing us together. Shoves it deep into the dark corners of my mind, the part that knows all the ways I'm not good enough for this woman.

Tonight, it's okay. Abi feels invincible, fueled by the miracle of a first-time shift. However, Abigail's tiny body in my hands reminds me of how vulnerable she truly is.

Once she moved past utter shock, I know she felt our mating connection pulling the two of us together. We haven't talked about those repercussions yet, nor what her new abilities mean. All these years, was being under her father's roof the root of her *defect,* if you want to call it that?

Dixon nearly crushed her with his control. I don't care how much I looked up to the man as a young whelp, seeing his protective shell dull his daughter's light soured my stomach. It's disheartening. Granted... the man is intimidating. Large brute shifters like myself are afraid to stand up to him.

How could I expect someone with Abigail's soft heart to have a chance?

Unfortunately, all those years of isolation diminished the value Abi saw in herself. I noticed the change over time. Every punk that ridiculed Abi took a chunk of her self-esteem with them. I'm not sure if Dixon never saw it, or if he ignored it. And while I helped with school bullies as a teen, I was no good against her father's crew... at least when it mattered.

Not anymore. She's mine now. Mine to protect.

My reward is that sweet little sound in her throat when I deepen our kiss. It sends my dragon into a spiral, all my blood heading south to my cock. He's ready to claim. Every ounce of self-control goes to shove him down. This is too important. Abigail is a treasure, and no matter how long I've suspected the truth, that Abigail is our mate, she's only discovering her power now.

Earlier, when she said she was broken, it about killed me. But every mile, every hour, we put between ourselves and her father increases Abigail's strength... and the call of her dragon. My dragon delights at the call from his mate. Her potent smell grows as her confidence grows, more so as her arousal grows.

That scent seeps into my system, warming my blood and, involuntarily, my erection. It presses into her belly, searching out relief from the aching pressure, from the torture of holding back when our mate is finally within reach.

Forcing myself to go slow, I work light kisses down Abigail's neck, needing to feel the heat of her pulse under my tongue. She sighs, but I can't tell if it's from the kiss or my soft stroke of her virgin wings. Their sexiness compounds her new confidence to drive my beast wild. If I don't stop now, our pheromones are going to be trouble. Out here in the open, any predator could find us, including Red, if he gets away before Dixon gets home.

Fuck! I forgot to call when we landed.

Abigail snaps something loose in my head where I can't think straight. But I don't want it coming to bite us in the ass, either. The last thing we need is Red hunting us down. Every instinct in my body screams that I should have killed that scumbag when I had my hands on him. Judging by the surge of anger roaring in my head, my pissed off dragon agrees.

Worried now, I pull back from our kiss, pleased with the swollen pink lips panting up at me. I need to get Abigail inside. Fast.

Squatting, I lift Abigail's legs around my waist, loving how her teeth nip the skin along my neck as I carry her inside, away from potential threats. Her enthusiasm tests my control, pushing my need to mate into overdrive and causing excruciating torture to my cock in the confining denim. I bound up the steps with Abi like my ass is on fire because those tiny little flicks she's doing with her tongue are about to damn kill me.

Inside the house, Abigail takes the lobe of my ear into her mouth and the warmth sends my mind to the many locations I'd enjoy those lips.

No, we can't yet. As much as it kills me, I'm the stronger dragon. I can't let fate's pheromones move us too fast.

Yes! She's ours!

Groaning, I guide Abigail's legs to the floor, her whimper of protest driving me as wild as her body does sliding down my front. Those normally blue eyes glow purple, making my grin impossible to fight.

"Why'd you stop?" Her blown pupils show every inner thought, even if my Abi never would.

"Because, little one, we can't go any further until you're ready."

She scoffs. "Don't I look ready?"

To prove it, Abi leans to tip toes, attempting to recapture a kiss, but with our height difference, she needs help to reach my lips. God, I would give anything to meet her halfway, to take what she's offering. In a perfect world, I would spend at least a few hours exploring her body. It would take a lifetime to sate my dragon, but we have to start somewhere.

But mating bonds are for life. If we lose a mate, or if, God forbid, she leaves, it will drive the inner dragon insane. Some waste away to nothing. Others go savage, forcing their hoard to put them down for safety. Either way, mating is not a decision I'll let Abigail make on a whim while her eyes glow with the baser instincts of her inner beast.

Her wings are still out, for Christ's sake. I need her human soul to choose me as well. Or I want her to, either way.

Glancing down, I exhale, squeezing Abigail's hips to keep her a few inches away and begging the universe to grant me willpower. It's easier to focus without her body pressing against my strangled cock. The goddamn thing needs some breathing room.

I sigh. "Baby, you went through a traumatic experience tonight. Not to mention, a huge life change. *Shit!* We're hiding in this god forsaken cabin, on the run, and oh yeah... about to go against your father *and* go up against Red." My fingers lift Abi's chin when she goes to look away. She must understand this choice before she makes it. I can't have anything else.

Instead, she jerks her chin from my grip, eyes glazed with anger and... hurt.

"Kris, believe me, I have *waited* for this a really long time!" Abi snaps her wings, obstinance radiating from every pore. Those lean arms cross defensively, plumping her handful of breasts until they torture my discipline. I want to bite that soft flesh, the slight curve peeking over her tank top enticing my dragon to ignore whatever repercussions a quick mating would bring us.

Abigail's anger is obvious. It's filled the air with a dark musk that I sense easily. She's pissed.

Why are you arguing? Take our mate! My dragon begs me to shut up, to bury myself in the willing female flesh in front of me.

She's not ready, dammit!

She's pouting. She wants us.

Just the opposite. Abigail wiggles for freedom against my arms, so I let go, never wanting to remind her of anything close to Red's trapping earlier. I need Abigail's trust.

Unable to do anything else, I follow Abi to the shoebox-sized bathroom, watching her angle her newly gifted body from side to side. Her awed face is nearly as beautiful as the unexpected wings shimmering on her back. Even if she's intentionally ignoring me. My woman is doing her best to hide her giddiness, almost crawling out of her skin, but no one can hide their inner feelings from a mate. Better liars have tried, and my Abigail is not a liar.

Shit! We have so much to talk about.

"Abigail, we have to play this smart." Our relationship got a turbo boost in the last twenty-four hours. It's impossible to hide who she is to me now, especially to the others. "I think my intentions are obvious. But, baby, too many people could burn us if they find out."

Her face twists with an adorable snarl. "What do you think I want to do, Kris? Rent a flippin' billboard?"

I don't respond, too fixated on Abigail's last twirl. She does her best to intimidate, but her sassy side eye does the opposite. The woman's inherent magnetism draws me inside the tiny, outdated bathroom, even though there's barely room for one of us, let alone space to fit with her wings out.

On reflex, she tucks her wings in, creating a wall of protection between us that makes me laugh. Thankfully, the extra room allows me to step behind her. I bring my lower half flush to her bottom as much as allowed with her wings out. One hand moves to stroke the soft skin on her shoulder, enjoying my mate's soothing warmth even if I can't have her yet.

Abigail whips around. "Uh, uh. Don't even try it, Baldy." I groan at her use of my street name, growing annoyed when she pushes against my chest to back me out of her personal space. "If you don't want me, I want privacy."

Agh! A growl of pain ricochets through my head, but I let her push me through the door and out of her space, my dragon protesting the distance the entire way.

"It's not that I don't want you, Abigail." I don't get another word out. A powerful flash of anger eclipses her pupils, the newly awakened dragon spirit giving Abi a strength I've never seen before. Strength enough to slam the bathroom door in my face.

I'm torn. Proud to see that inner light defend herself. But pissed as hell that Abigail could think I didn't want her. *What the fuck!*

And she thinks a two-inch hollow door can keep us apart... really. I could shred this thing in five seconds... with one talon.

Instead, I bite my tongue and pace the faded wood floor outside that tiny-assed bathroom. *I'm such a fuckin' idiot!* Why didn't I lay her down when she asked and show her exactly why she's mine to begin with? It seemed like the worst idea half an hour ago. When I thought we only needed time. "I just want you to see me as a real mate." I whisper at the door.

I'm not a heat-of-the-moment fling. It's too important, and with so much up in the air, I can't mess this up. So, I chicken out. *A goddamn dragon enforcer chickened out!*

That itself shows I need out of this business before I end up clipped. Worse, death by distraction isn't my biggest worry. It's the possibility of losing my chance with Abigail.

Frustrated, I bang a fist on the door, tempering the anger with myself so she doesn't think it's aimed at her. "Abigail, let me back in."

Drawers inside the bathroom open and close, cabinets slamming right behind them. *What the hell is she doing in there?* There's only one cabinet in that bathroom. What is she looking for? "Abigail." Knock, knock. "Come on! I can help." My woman needs me, and my own stupidity got me kicked out.

This sucks! Getting her wings is a momentous time. I should be in there!

I plant my hand on the wood casing. *Should I just bust the henges?* Just as I think it, the door jerks open, a red-faced Abi huffing irritation and panic in front of me. A bead of sweat slicks her hairline.

"How the hell do I get rid of these things?" she asks, yelping when her wings involuntarily slap the door. The sound causes her to jump—either from the sting of the wood or annoyance at her lack of control—either way, I can't hold the laugh that bubbles up. It's the worst thing to do, but that doesn't make the put-out look on her face any less entertaining.

Chapter Twenty

Abigail

UGH! SCREW HIM!

No, fuck him! Fuck him. You are a big, bad-ass dragon now. You need to learn how to swear. I hit Kris with the strongest glare I can muster. How dare he laugh at me when I need his help?

"Okay, excuse me for not being a skilled dragon yet." Anger balls my fists on my hips, the bite of fingernails into my palm working just enough so I don't smack that grin right off that too-gorgeous-for-his-own-good face. "I've never done this before, jackass." Kris's chuckle rings through the small room behind me, but he coughs, trying to contain what is basically laughing in my face.

All right, I'm second guessing my urge to restrain the violence.

The squeal of frustration surprises me—and Kris—but the burn in my throat says it came from my lungs. Kris eyes me like a live wire dancing in the wind. His back straightens, looking partially worried and partially chagrined. "I'm sorry, Abigail. Really."

I'm having a hard time believing a word Kris says, considering he hasn't lost that infuriatingly sexy grin. Plus, it pisses me off that the little smile lines crinkling the corner of his eyes are one more notch on his attractive list. He shouldn't turn me on so much when I'm this annoyed with him.

I grit my teeth, muffling my wail of exasperation, and step back, reaching to slam the door. "I'm done with this conversation," I huff, except Kris's meaty hand slaps the surface, which bounces the door right back in my face.

He coughs. "I didn't mean to laugh, Abi. You're just too damn cute for your own good."

"Great... cute." I cross my arms, irritated that even with my wings, I'm stuck in the 'adorable' category. "Always the flippin' cute one... always." Grumbling, I duck my head, aiming to scoot below the tan arm blocking my exit.

Kris has other ideas. Those thick muscles drop lower on the door frame, brushing across my breasts and immediately hardening my nipples at the contact. Like Kris needs another clue that I'm hopelessly attracted to him. Scowling, I open my mouth to argue, only to have Kris talk over me while I question if it's humanly—or dragonly—possible to murder someone from the sheer wrath of my eyes alone.

Of course, Kris doesn't show the least bit of fear in the face of my anger. "Abigail, you are cute and adorable *because* of your personality... your sweetness. You gotta understand, little one... I'm surrounded with people every day who'd stab me in the back as quick as they shoot a glass of whisky." Those brooding eyes dim with unsaid thoughts, yet the fingers pinching my chin are gentle. They lift my gaze, dragging his thumb across my lower lip in a way that tortures my wet panties. "So yes, I like your sweetness. And I love that you're mine to savor, too."

Uhm...

Moving slowly, Kris dips his head to prove his point, my chin held still for his pleasure while he leisurely explores. His tongue whisks my lower lip before retreating. His possessive gaze nails me to the floor while he waits for my reaction.

Instinctively, my tongue darts out, relieving the tingles left behind by his soft caress. Kris's eyes track the path and despite his high-handed talk, my excitement reaches a boiling point, impossible to hide behind my shyness in this situation.

"Then why'd you stop? Why do you *always* stop?"

Kris grows serious. "Because you deserve more. You're perfect. Beautiful, smart, caring." His voice drops, the smooth baritone melting my panties with its verbal seduction. Kris looks anxious at his confession, but that small vulnerability is sexy as hell. "Abigail, you're sinfully sexy... but you've always been untouchable."

"Until I'm not," I challenge, matching the burn from those jeweled eyes boring into mine. *I've had enough.* Reaching up, I climb that mountain of muscle myself, gripping Kris's rock-hard shoulders to get to those lips again.

He's ours. Startled, I pull up before getting to my goal.

Oh, my God! My dragon.

"What's wrong?" Concern glows deep in those golden eyes and Kris jerks my weight against his beast of a body, protecting me. Making sure I'm safe and comfortable, even with my cumbersome wings in the way.

"I hear my dragon."

A warm smile lights his face. "That's great, baby!" His hand goes to stroke the tender spot where leathery wing meets soft human skin. "Just think about what you look like without your wings, and they'll disappear. Imagine your smooth skin. Focus."

I do just that. Closing my eyes and resting my forehead against his, I imagine the heavy force not pulling at my back. Kris breathes with me, grounding my concentration. I'm almost sad when the weight lessens, but I open my eyes to find Kris grinning.

"Kiss me! Please." I press into Kris, fired up from the whirlpool of emotions, the highs, the lows. But I'm tired of all this chatter. We need to get back to listening to our lips.

"Since you asked nicely." His smirk mirrors my own as I jump in full force, attacking those sinful lips with an overwhelming frenzy.

His growl encourages my aggression, the sound vibrating deep in my core considering my legs wrap his torso like a vine strangling a tree. Our tongues battle, my hands caressing any body part within reach. I love the freedom to explore Kris's muscled frame. He steadies my weight, but before long it becomes too much and Kris turns for the tiny bed in the corner, carrying us both along to seal our fate.

With one knee on the bed, Kris leans over, effortlessly guiding my smaller frame to the center while I cling to his neck to bring him with me. Gravity wins. But with Kris's hand splayed between my shoulder blades, he softens my fall to the mattress, his body following me down. His hard length nestles against my middle, against my warmth while I drown in his heat. A perfect match.

My senses bombard with everything Kris, and I love it.

That pale blond stubble scratches my tongue when I lean up to lick. The light dusting of hair is kept trim but soft across his chest. The puff of panting breaths in my ear as his rigid body hovers, his elbows preventing that massive bulk from crushing me. And oh my God... that rich scent of leather that follows Kris everywhere. His chest heaves by the time he pulls up. We're locked in a battle of wills... Kris trying to go slow and me pleading for more. I tighten my legs around that trim waist every time he tries to pull back, needing him to let go.

I need Kris to feel. But every time I think he's going to, he holds back.

"Stop thinking," I whisper, squeezing my thighs to rub my wetness against those rough jeans, desperately needing friction for some much-needed relief.

Thankfully, a rolling pulse of Kris's hips rewards my brazenness, bringing the steel rod in the front of his pants to rub against my swollen clit. Even through our clothes, it's exactly what I need. So is that low, sensuous rumble in his throat.

I love being able to affect him this way.

"Abi..." My name sounds like a prayer on his lips, unlocking a small piece of Kris's carefully held control.

Within a few grinds against my heat, I can't think of anything else but him. Kris has shut off all functional thought in my head until I'm practically crawling out of my skin. I want this man something desperate. His tempo is torture. Slow, forceful strokes light me up from the inside. My mouth falling open with noises I can't believe come from me.

Kris's heady grunts beside my ear excite me even more. In a frenzy, my fingernails and lips mark everything they reach, except Kris won't let me move far. His hand circles under me, cupping my neck, and holding me in place for this delicious torture. With a look of awe, his free hand strokes the wild hair from my face like he can't bear for anything to block his view.

I feel seen, but completely open... vulnerable.

Our mate! My dragon's volume startles me, louder each time she pushes through. My entire life, she's been silent until now.

With Kris this close, my beast is scratching for release, but I don't have time to dwell on that long before Kris begins a slow, tantalizing trail of kisses down my neck. My head lifts automatically, giving him access to anything he wants. Right until one flick of his tongue hits the sore spot Red bit earlier and I tense, involuntarily.

He jerks up, his fiery green eyes searing mine before his head dips again, softly licking my wound with the slightest nuzzle. Steadily, the ache lessens, leaving me speechless with the power Kris has over me.

"I'm so sorry, baby. I'm sorry I didn't get there in time." His voice cracks, barely audible over the pounding in my ears.

"You did." I don't want his guilt. Doesn't he get it? "You saved me." I draw Kris's mouth to mine. I can't think about any of that. Not right now.

"I wasn't fast enough." He shakes his head.

"Don't," I say, clutching his head. I kiss his mouth hard, tasting and shushing at the same time. I'm reluctant for any conversation that'll break our spell of lust. Not when I finally have the one man I've longed for most of my life wrapped in my arms.

As if on fire, my lips try to recapture our moment, tasting up Kris's sharp jawline toward his ear. Groaning, he pulls back, those swimmable eyes searching mine for what feels like an eternity, until finally satisfied that I'm not thinking about tonight's trauma. I know when his head dips a fraction that he's caved.

Nothing else can stand in our way.

Fortunately, a switch flips in Kris with my reassurances. His demeanor changing instantly as he peers into my soul. Now he moves purposefully, eyes flaring as he nibbles along my jaw, stopping when he closes in on my ear. "You're mine now, Abigail. No going back." His heated promise, the sensuousness of his voice sends a rush of excitement below. My body writhes with pent-up passion. It's everything I've ever wanted to hear, and to prove it, my center rubs against the firm muscle that heats me up so easily.

My fingers grip Kris's rock-hard biceps, hovering just inches from my head. The problem is, I've got no words because I damn well can't concentrate. And it doesn't get any better when Kris sucks at the soft spot below my ear. Every flick of his tongue steals another breath and stupefies another brain cell.

"Did you hear me, Princess? You. Are. Mine." I smile at the possessiveness in his growl.

But the light energy falls away when his hand spreads over the lower curve of my back, forcibly coercing my hips against his bulging zipper. It creates a wicked friction, and I can't be quiet anymore.

"Yes!"

It's impossible to hold still now. Impossible to think coherently while Kris explores the fevered skin on my neck. This time, he doesn't stop. His teeth nip down, reaching my collar bone where his nose edges my strappy tank out of the way so his kisses can trace the curve of my shoulder. My body goes wild, instinctively wiggling to help get rid of the barrier standing between us.

"So soft," he says, laying a reverent kiss on my shoulder before sitting back with a smile. I'm about to argue that he stopped again, but Kris is rearranging himself, moving his knees to straddle my thighs. The position keeps me trapped.

Oh!

And of course, that bastard smirks at having the upper hand. Which he proves by lifting the hem of my shirt, only exposing my stomach to his hungry gaze and torturing me by not stripping me further.

"Kris... come on," I whine, wiggling under his legs.

A soft purr under his breath is his only response. As if he has all the time in the world, he stays back on his knees, watching those callused fingers stroke up my sides and the goosebumps they raise in their wake. The two of us couldn't look more different. Kris's face shines with victory, biting his tongue between his teeth to keep from smiling, while I moan at his touch like a wanton hussy, shimmy under his weight, panting, fighting the tickling sensation zinging my skin.

About the time I can't take any more of his sensory torture, Kris slides his ass farther down my legs. It gives him enough room to bend and drop nibbling kisses along my rib cage and sides before his fingers drive me to the brink of crazy.

My lungs catch.

"Kris, please," I beg, wishing I could wrap my legs around that trim waist for leverage. Nothing that needs to be rubbed is getting any action. "Come on," I pant. "This is torture." The tickle drives me absolutely crazy. But then again, it's the thrill of Kris's mouth on my skin that truly lurches my hips. My hips fight his heavy weight, becoming frenzied with every drag of those soft lips along bare skin.

Finally, I grip the inch of blond hair on Kris's head, determined to pull Kris's hulking frame closer if he won't listen to reason. Except, instead of moving closer, Kris gets a wicked glint in his eye, watching me watch his hand stroke inch by inch toward my loose pajama shorts.

Chapter Twenty-One

Abigail

*HOLY HELL! I'M GONNA **die on the spot!***

The feeling intensifies with Kris's lips—and that five o'clock shadow—tracing a wet path down my stomach, across my belly button, but stopping when he gets to the waistband of my shorts. My fingertips twitch, tangling the sheets while Kris works his way down, the anticipation sending a gush of arousal into the air that any sensitive nose could pick up.

"Holy fuck, Abigail!" He moans and my neck flames, suddenly overheated with embarrassment from not hiding my attraction from another shifter.

Pushing Kris's shoulders, I aim for a little breathing room between his head and my crotch, but his hands have my hip bones on lock down, the tips of his fingers pressing divots guaranteed to bruise my pale skin.

Do it.

As soon as the thought rolls through my mind, I thank every star in the sky that Kris can't hear it. Although, I'm almost past caring. Hormones have elevated my heart rate until I'm too far gone. Kris shakes his head. On a harsh exhale, his forehead hits my lower stomach, and he pauses, sucking in air like he's seeking the very gravity that keeps us on the ground.

I know the feeling, big guy.

My stomach quivers. Shaking. My dragon screams for the one she wants, the one she's waited for. With that man sitting on my legs, frustrating the hell out of me, her whimpers grow inside my head, hungering for the man driving her crazy.

"Kris, please. What are you waiting for?" I don't mean the question to sound bitchy, but it does. *Sorry, not sorry. My dragon's impatient... surprise, surprise.*

Thankfully, when his head lifts, it's not anger I see, it's a grin. A full-toothed, cheek splitting grin that brings out his rare boyish charm. Charm that's lethal to my heart.

"What do you want, my love?" Sincerity radiates behind those deep green pools, but he doesn't give me more than his rough fingertips curling under my waistband, teasing them down an inch just to make me squirm.

And I do.

"Mean," I hiss, loving his boom of laughter.

"I'm trying really hard to go slow, woman. If I get you naked, I may never let you leave this bed." I tilt my hips, earning the sexiest growl I've ever heard vibrate in Kris's chest. The move challenges him to continue, but Kris clearly wants to torture me.

He waits, and I bite my lip in a silent plea.

"What if I don't want to go slow?" I ask, going hot, but trying to be brave.

Gah! How do you seduce a six-foot something hulk of steel? I've practically—oh, who's kidding, I have literally—thrown myself at the man... for weeks now. Returned kisses, started kisses, got pissed when he *ended* kisses.

What kind of signal does he need? Green light... Go, man!

Is he waiting for me to do something? *Oh my god! He's been doing all the work.* What if he thinks I'm one of those 'dead fish' girls? I'm not a stranger to frat-boy chatter. I spent all four years of college in a dorm with a bunch of drunk numbskulls. I know what they talk about over video games in their scummy rooms, slapping each other's back like they won MVP in the World Series of hook ups.

"Oh, uh Kris, you... you don't have to do that," I say, wanting to give him the out. My smile feels forced, but I'm trying, dammit.

"What do you mean?" he asks, sounding truly perplexed. "What don't I have to do?"

Exasperated, I tilt my head at my shorts. "Y-you know." Immediately, my ears warm and I bury my face in Kris's neck to cover the embarrassment, kissing a line along that pulsing vein and enjoying a lungful of Kris. Until his grip on my arms tugs me back sharply, giving no room to hide from his intense gaze.

"You think I don't want to, woman?" His snarl surprises me. I've never seen that look aimed at me. It sends a shiver down my spine, and I close my eyes, not able to handle this tension on top of all the other emotions in my head. "Abigail..." He clears his throat, his voice softening.

When his hand comes to cup my chin, I lift to pull away. But Kris doesn't give me the freedom. "Woman, listen to me... carefully." He waits patiently until I open my eyes. When I do, a swirling storm stares back at me.

The man is testosterone personified. He expects me to think clearly?

I'm still gawking when his back straightens, towering over me even on his knees. "Baby, you need to understand, I have a much larger problem than not wanting you." He glances down, chuckling under his breath when my eyes widen. The proof of his arousal stares me in the face. *Literally.*

"See, this problem here wants you too much." He grins. "And I'm having the damndest time controlling him when you're around." As if it knows we're talking about it, his freaking penis jerks right in front of my eyes, and I crack up.

"It's proving your point. Huh?"

He chuckles, pressing a hand against his hard length, and groaning with the sexiest, sinful sound I've ever heard. "Don't you see, Abi? Your hands haven't touched him yet, and he's ready to blow a load in my pants." Shocked, I giggle at his crass words, but when a naughty challenge darkens Kris's eyes, I quiet.

Before I can say anything else, Kris grabs the back of my knees and yanks, those herculean muscles pulling me flat to my back. I squeal, surprised to end up underneath those powerful hips again. At least this time I get to wrap my legs around his hips, giving me the perfect leverage to press that impressive erection exactly where I want it.

Our rhythm settles into one as old as time, the sensations blasting fireworks with each pulse against his bulky frame. Inside, my dragon purrs, loving the catch in Kris's breath with every collision of our bodies. I drop nibbling kisses to the curve of his shoulder, peeking from that tattered shirt and my inner vixen soars.

"You should take this off." Grinning, I try to hurry things along, but my vixen isn't smooth. Still, Kris helps me lift the hem of his shirt and tosses it somewhere in the distance, so it worked somehow. *Holy mother of God!*

That biteable torso is on display right in front of my face, the ridges of his chest dusted with the perfect amount of pale blond hair. The curve of muscle shows the power this man holds, the scars his strength. My fingers itch to touch, so I do, trailing them across the tattoos that paint the story of his life, down the ripped lines of his waist. His stomach quivers when my nails score the skin, but Kris holds still, letting me look my fill.

I pray I'm not drooling, but in what world do I get to touch my living, breathing fantasy? The surrealness doesn't stop my hands from roaming the dips and valleys of that sexy mass of man-muscle. My mouth waters to taste. *Is his skin salty? Would it be rough?* My core clenches, and before I'm ready, Kris moves away, taking my toy with him.

His knowing smile teases me as he slips farther down the bed, dragging his fingers in his wake with the same slow torture I did until he settles between my knees. "Tell me, my sweet Abigail. How am I supposed to stop myself from taking you like this? When I know the moment I touch you, I'm never letting go."

Why does his threat sound like heaven to me?

Those chameleon eyes pierce me, as pained as they are turned on. I wait. But I don't have to wait long.

Slowly, the pads of his thumbs slide along my knee, stroking my inner thighs until simultaneously, they drag the leg of my soft pajama shorts higher, until the scent of lust fills the air. Kris pauses. My reaction to his torture is obvious... and embarrassing. I wiggle, lost in the spell of those devious little thumbs until I no longer care about hiding my moans and whimpers. The pressure at my hip removes my filter.

A sheen of sweat breaks out at my temples and I squirm to get closer. "I-I don't see the problem here." My words cut off when Kris rubs circles to my sensitive pressure points, his groan mimicking mine, going primal, before that wheat-colored head bobs down and grazes those sharp teeth where inner thigh meets hip. It's not where I need him most and the sounds falling from my lips tell him that. They grow louder the longer he tortures. My body remembers the pleasure Kris's wicked tongue can bring. It wants more.

Wordlessly, my hips plead, tilting involuntarily as both our scents fill the air. "Are you determined to torture me?"

Kris chuckles. "Only pleasure, my love. Only pleasure." His earnest emerald eyes shine as those strong hands tug my waistband, taking everything—including my panties—down with one fell swoop.

My world freezes. Kris bends, his skilled mouth covering the sensitive skin with licks, teeth nipping along the fleshy part of my hip. His slow exploration across my lower half vaporizes the oxygen in my lungs, flinging my knees closed despite the oversized body blocking the way. The promise Kris is writing with his lips is too much.

It doesn't help that I've never been naked in front of anyone, either... except my doctor. And the woman did not stare at my center like she wanted to devour me, not like Kris. And I wasn't as wet as

Niagara Falls from having her bony, overly studious body between my legs. Now, with every second I'm exposed to those devilish eyes, my insides melt. None of my attempts to move Kris's buzzed head toward my mouth and away from my vulnerability below have worked. That hulking frame stays perched over my middle, refusing to move anywhere except where he wants.

Hell, the tremor in my hands makes it damn impossible to do anything other than follow Kris's lead. But if there's a God in heaven, he won't notice.

"Kris... please," I beg, my throat dry from the sounds of anticipation I've panted for the last eon under this beautiful beast.

There's a well-deserved smugness rolling off Kris when he removes my hands from his head. He kisses inside each wrist before pinning them to the bed beside my hips.

"Stay." His command is as firm as his hold, but that growly nature doesn't scare me. If anything, I feel cherished, almost protected by the way his hold goes possessive. More so, when that scowl morphs into a knowing grin, his body lowering flat between my thighs and looking every bit like a man setting up at the dinner table, waiting for his meal.

My dragon purrs, delighting in her mate's pleasure like it's the key to utopia.

With a playful warning glance, Kris releases my wrists, propping himself on his elbows with a naughty Cheshire cat grin, making me painfully aware of his location as another gush of wetness betrays exactly how much my body wants to hurry. I growl at his unflappable patience and squeeze the sheets to stop from covering myself. The mortification of being so exposed and made to stay that way... *ugh!*

Kris all but licks his chops. "Good girl," he hums, slow and seductive, torturing me on purpose. One enormous hand drags across my belly, fingers splayed wide where it stops, holding my lower half to the mattress, completely at his mercy.

A whimper slips out. But I don't know if the sound draws from me or my dragon.

I can't care anymore when Kris drops his nose to the small strip of blonde hair on top of my mound. The noises filling the room are beyond me. All embarrassment evaporating with every nuzzle along my sex. The way Kris drags in breaths with a content smile, like I'm everything he needs, his sun and moon, food and water. Like our bodies connecting is his heaven on earth, as it is mine.

His orchestra of pleasure increases with a single—almost chaste—kiss placed on the tip of my clit. If anything can be chaste with his head buried between my legs.

"Kris!" I hiss, my legs shaking underneath his grip. It's all I can do not to come immediately, like all my years of shyness have turned into downright gluttony for the man giving me pleasure.

When his lips puff a soft blow of air over my curls, my entire body shudders. "Please," I beg, tilting my hips as much as his hand allows. My hips have a mind of their own, needing his mouth. I feel myself gushing... wanton.

My dragon claws, howling to rub herself against Kris and mark him in return. She knows he's her alpha, and she wants to experience every bit of his possession.

Kris's soft chuckle fills the room when I prop up to watch his sinfulness below. Those glowing yellow eyes lock with mine, casting an erotic spell over us both until his tongue flattens, smoothing across my crease, back to front.

My mouth falls open.

He does it again. Licking, suctioning at the top. Driving me abso-fuckin' crazy the way he laps at the moisture, like it's honey. The way his moan vibrates that tiny nub until my knees shake and my back crashes to the bed. There's no strength left to hold upright.

"Yes, baby girl," Kris rumbles into my middle when my legs fall open, laying myself bare for him. And, holy cow, he doesn't disappoint. He devours.

I pant Kris's name to the ceiling like a prayer, the muscles tensing low in my belly, a pulsing rhythm that pulls my body like an overstrung bow. My fists tangle in Kris's short hair, the whiny mewl slipping out, making me cringe with its neediness.

Kris's rumble of laughter muffles against my wetness before he attaches that talented mouth with enthusiasm. He licks deep, working me into a frenzy before sliding back to suck my clit, alternating his pattern. The flicks to my sensitive nub tease, but that soft suction is driving me completely wild. Over the top. My back arches off the bed with each swipe of rough tongue until I'm on a razor's edge of pleasure.

I'm not sure if the animalistic sounds screaming from this bed come from me, but I couldn't care less either way. Not when Kris has sliced my last brain cell with that wicked tongue.

"Oh my God! Kris!" I choke, sobs cracking my voice as my body shakes. I can't take it anymore. I need relief.

I need Kris.

Unfortunately, the man has limitless patience for torture, because by the time Kris glides the back of his finger across my slick heat, I squeal for release.

"That's it, baby. Let me hear you," Kris says, rubbing our combined juices across my swollen lips. He grins, laying painfully sweet bites at the bend of each thigh, his fingers slide everywhere except where I need him.

"Kris, please..." My hips tilt mid-whine, begging Kris's mouth for more delicious torture. I can't even care about the embarrassment anymore. Finally, Kris gives in, slipping a wet finger inside my channel and curling it along the front wall in smooth, knowing strokes. In a flash, I detonate. Kris's name sings to the heavens like he ripped the sound from my lungs. My heart feels like it's going to explode, the view behind my eyelids going white hot.

He moves over top, continuing to stroke while he guides me through the most significant moment of my life. After the pulses ease, I land on a cloud of bliss, completely boneless. My body trembles, and I'm content to bask in this new connection between me and the man who blew the top off my mind. The visual of the cartoon Grinch standing on that snowy mountain with his heart growing three sizes sticks in my head.

I get it now.

Chapter Twenty-Two

Abigail

MY HEART FEELS STRONGER, larger. I'm downright woozy by the time Kris kisses his way up my heated skin. "Wow." The sigh isn't enough, but Kris's lips cut off anything else I'd say, his tongue lazily caressing. He stays elevated, hovering his weight over me as he nibbles on my lower lip. My fingers dig in, going rougher on those biceps the longer Kris's mouth teases. He swipes again and my cheeks burn when I taste myself coating Kris's stubble.

His cocky smile is back, but I don't dare argue because the man deserves it. Still, those kisses go a long way to reignite my energy, and I wrap my thighs around Kris's hips, bringing his stiff rod against my center. I need him closer.

A frenzy of feelings flash behind my eyes. Only a few seconds ago, my body floated down from heaven like a feather. Now I want more. *How can someone feel horny and content, excited and at ease?*

Kris exhales, dropping the softest kiss to my temple. I get a bad feeling when he lingers there for a few breaths, without responding to my attempts to move forward. "Abigail, you feel this, don't you?" he asks quietly, his face sober.

For the first time—probably ever—I see Kris's cheeks pink under that tanned skin. It's ridiculously adorable and the first sign of vulnerability I've seen in Kris since childhood. It brings up old memories of Kris as a moody teen.

An overwhelming compulsion to make him smile again takes over. I angle my hips, pressing against the hard ridge in his pants. "I feel this," I tease, dying to lighten the shadows flickering across Kris's face. He freezes, brows furrowed into valleys, and locks my hips to the bed.

"I can't give you that, Abigail. Not until I know."

I want to scream. If Kris didn't exasperate me with this back-and-forth game he keeps playing, I might feel guilty about the flash of pain in those turbulent eyes. The vulnerability shuts down instantly, that gruff voice bricking the wall between us higher. How do I respond to that, considering his current position of importance between my legs?

"What do you need to know, Kris? I'm clean? We're exclusive? Not exclusive? What do you need to finally go through with this?"

My patience is nil.

I sit up, remembering I'm naked from the waist down. When Kris's eyes fall, he looks pained for a whole different reason now. I pull a deflated pillow from the old headboard to cover my lap, not at all comfortable having a nude conversation. Especially when attempting a 'don't give a fuck' glare for a man who's gone hot and cold more times than I have fingers.

He's one wrong sentence from having an angry blond thunderstorm on his hands.

The moment Kris lifts to his knees, I immediately miss his warmth. His eyes widen in shock, his mouth gaping for a split-second before snapping shut so hard I hear his teeth clank. "Abigail... come on. You can't be serious," he says incredulously. The bed creaks, its springs bouncing when he hops off in one leap.

A frown mars his handsome face. His boots, that I hadn't realized were still on, stamping out a worn path on the wood floor in front of the bed. Rough calluses scratch the back of his head. The colorful curses flying in an agitated whisper under his breath.

"What, Kris? What is the big problem?"

Part of me feels guilty for getting my pleasure when Kris immediately jumped into stress mode. I mean… It's his own fault. The man should be rocking us both to heaven, not questioning our relationship status. I'm about to remind him of that when he jerks around and I screech, whatever pity I felt evaporating the second I see the anger boiling in his eyes. Kris's hands flex by his side, looking like he's frustrated enough to shake me.

I'm glad I got off and left him hanging.

Kris's hands fly in the air, exasperated. *With me? I'm exasperated with him!* "Abigail… you're my mate, goddammit!"

My breath catches, not expecting a confirmation of what I've wished all these years. His declaration takes the wind right out of my sails. A tenacious dragon like Kris deserves a strong mate. My dragon only started talking to me this week. Plus, I just got out of one man's controlling grasp. Can I really jump into life with another?

"Kris…" I shake my head, contemplating an argument that won't piss him off. I never get the chance.

In a blink, Kris darts across the bed, his lips bruising mine, cutting off my excuses, quieting my jumbled thoughts. Tension fuels the kiss entirely, anger taking over Kris's passionate possession. I never had a chance for a level playing field.

My hands mold against the valleys of muscle in Kris's chest, reveling in the vibrating moan there when I scrape my fingernails across his back. I hold his body like a lifeline, not wanting a sliver of light able to pass between us.

A shuddering breath warms my ear where Kris nibbles, diving his hands into my hair and pulling it to the side for better access. I feel cradled. The gentleness in Kris's hold is at complete odds with the sting of kisses across my jaw, both tender and possessive, comforting and exciting. He supports my body like breakable porcelain, the whole time letting his teeth break my defenses.

Kris's lips grow rougher… tasting, teasing. Driving me absolutely batshit-level crazy with the heat of his kisses. A tornado of chaotic emotion flutters inside my heart. My hands grow manic as I open everything to Mr. Sexy Sin himself, pulling the mountain of male-perfection into me. His body flattens mine, no longer hovering, no longer torturing. His warmth stretches over me, our craving for each other reigniting our connection.

Live in the moment, Abigail.

It's as if fate unleashed everything we held back. Now our hands and lips roam anywhere within reach, ratcheting up my pleasure until I'm ready to throw caution to the wind and agree to whatever Kris wants, whatever he needs. Kris doesn't even hide his enthusiasm for my touch, his masculine moans and grunts making me wonder how delicious he would sound in the throes of passion. The thought of Kris emptying himself inside me liquifies my core.

Our mate, my dragon exhales, happily accepting Kris's claim of my neck as he moves down. She uses me to grind against his excitement, marking him as ours by coating his lower half in our juices.

"How can you not feel this, woman?" he whispers, pumping his thickness against my slit with pained, stunted movements. I reach shaking fingers to his zipper, desperate to feel skin on skin. "You have to." That gravelly voice sends shivers down my spine with its vulnerability, making me feel safe for my own honestly.

I suck in a breath. "Kris... I feel it. I do." It's hard to think clearly with my dragon panting, pushing her own needs as Kris licks the sweet spot behind my ear. But my human-half needs Kris to understand the fear. Every ounce of courage goes into admitting decade-old feelings. Although now Kris holds us back, not giving in unless I commit to everything.

Can I do that? With how different our lives are.

"You have to understand. I've wanted this for so long... dreamed of it, Kris. B-but this is all so new to me." I pause, wishing I were the vixen who throws emotions out the window to say my piece. "I just don't know... the way things are..." I stop when Kris smiles, his eyes morphing into golden orbs, his dragon spirit melting my resolve to think with my head, not my heart.

Why am I fighting so hard when we're perfect together?

So many unknowns hang in the air. What would life be like with Kris? Would he want what I want in a mate? Can I handle worrying every time he leaves home?

Patience is neither of our strong suits. So, it means even more when Kris waits for me to collect my thoughts. No pressure. After years of my opinion meaning nothing, I appreciate the restraint more than he knows. To thank him, I plant a soft kiss over his heart, marveling at the swirl of tattoos giving Kris his trademark bad-boy vibe.

With a deep whoosh of air, Kris's shoulders relax a fraction. "It's okay, little one. I'll wait," he says with a soft smile. It doesn't reach his eyes, but he's trying. Although, I know the moment that colossal body sinks to the bed beside me that my big mouth ruined our frisky activities from going any further. My stomach sinks, an involuntary whine slipping out.

Kris's smile shines brighter.

"It's a big night for you, baby. You should rest." He guides my head to his chest, dropping a chaste kiss to the top of my hair with a sigh. "It's why I didn't push earlier, Abigail. Not because I'm not dying to get in your heat. Believe me." A deep chuckle rumbles low in Kris's chest as he tucks me into his warmth. It lessens the sting of disappointment at our night ending, but only a little. Part of me still wants to cry, as silly as that is. I just never imagined—in all my wildest dreams—that a night with Kris would be so sweet, that he'd be so understanding. Not from a man with his job.

Even now, Kris distractedly sifts my hair through his fingers, letting it fall piece by piece to my shoulders. The rhythm slows his heartbeat under my ear, making me smile through the burn in my eyes. I like that touching me calms him.

Taking a deep breath, I let some of the stress go, focusing instead on my fingers grazing that soft line of hair running down the center of Kris's belly. I've never had this freedom to touch, and I want to enjoy it.

Please don't let this be the last time.

Just in case, I close my eyes, relishing the comfort in Kris's protective arms. Tonight could have shattered me. It only didn't because of Kris. A surge of relief has me squeezing Kris's waist tighter, trying to focus on the here and now, comforted in the feel of the hard, masculine chest rising and falling under my head.

We have so many things to work out. But not tonight. Tonight, I'm resigned to being stuck in limbo. I tilt up, dropping a kiss to the sharp underside of Kris's jaw. "I don't know if I've said it yet, but thank you, Kris." He glances down, finding my eyes, but I don't want to explain anything else. I doubt I need to. Kris hums, pressing those warm lips against my hair.

Not exactly a kiss... he inhales. "You will be mine, Abigail. I'm not losing you now." His whispered promise carries me into dreamland, Kris's lips resting against my head as we fall under the exhaustion of the day.

This time, in my dreams, I let myself believe.

Chapter Twenty-Three

Kris

BEFORE I OPEN MY eyes, I already know something's different. My stiff back feels like I slept in the woods, but that scent... the milk and honey perfection are not normal forest smells.

Dragging my brain from a dead sleep, I sniff for the heavenly smell. When my head turns, I lay still for a minute, knowing the source immediately. With a smile, I breathe lungfuls of that scent into my soul.

My mate.

I've known for so long she was mine. But I never dared say it out loud.

This morning, she's cocooned in my arms like a warm kitten in a blanket and I don't give one single fuck that my arm's gone numb. I'd sacrifice them both for the sheer peace making my body go slack in this bed.

Even with Abigail asleep, memories bombard of the night before. Especially with her body using me as her personal pillow. I'd laugh at the soft little snore falling from her lips, but I don't want to wake her. I might lose this torturesome visual of silky blonde hair blanketing my chest. Not yet. My fingertips graze the soft strands, moving those long curls out of the way to stroke the soft skin on Abi's upper arm.

I just can't resist the smallest touch, but already the brief connection engorges my swollen morning wood.

I need to be careful, keep my baser instincts under control so I don't get ahead of myself.

Make her breakfast. My dragon pushes into my brain. *Show her we make a suitable mate.*

Grinning, I get on board with that plan; for once he and I are thinking in sync.

Plus, I need a distraction from Abigail's soft curves under my hand. As much as I'd like my breakfast to include tasting every inch of her delectable body, Abi needs time. I hate it. But those lithe muscles are kryptonite to my willpower. And I am nowhere as good as the man-of-steel. That boy scout wouldn't think twice about doing the right thing, solely because it's the damn right thing to do.

Shit! Maybe channeling Cavill is the way to go.

Until Abigail accepts our connection, our mating bond won't take.

With her essence still on my lips from last night, I carefully peel myself from her koala grip and slide out of bed. She doesn't budge an inch, her breathing steady with that sweet little snore letting me know she's out like a light.

I use the opportunity to take care of my morning business and brush my teeth with my finger and a travel size mouthwash sitting on the countertop. Not the best, but it'll work in a pinch. One less detail to figure out today. The bigger goal is feeding my woman.

In the kitchen, I scour the stacks of ransacked food for anything edible. The littered countertop is a hunter's wet dream, but all those dry goods and cans of expired crap won't impress my mate. Sadly, the unopened box of pancake mix is about the only thing useful. If the previous owner had a deep freezer, we'd chance into some bacon or sausage for our protein, but no such luck. Problem is, Abi's gonna wake up starved. Shifting burns a lot of calories... especially early on. During my teenage years, I was a walking food pit while my body adjusted to transitioning between species.

This isn't good enough!

I know that. I push aside the ridicule of my dragon and head outside, scouring the wild berry bushes around the cabin. I manage a few handfuls of fruit that I drop on the back steps to clean later. Then, glancing at the tall pines around us, I release my wings to hunt for a nest. Eggs would serve for our protein. It'll be a better breakfast than the bare bones I'm currently offering.

The freedom of flying, of stretching my wings, releases my sore muscles after a night of cramped sleeping.

Most of the skittish birds took flight at the first pump of my wings, leaving their nests abandoned and easy to raid. Scouring them puts the 'Rockin' Robin' song my mom sang when I was a kid in my head, and I whistle the chorus as I fly. Mostly for a distraction from thinking about an almost naked Abigail sleeping in the cabin.

Once I find a Finch nest, I take only the eggs we need for a satisfying breakfast. I don't feel guilty. Dragons could cause a lot more damage in the circle of life than stealing a few bird eggs. And by the time I land, my head is relatively clear.

I set out making a stack of pancakes with the dry mix from the cabinet, grab a fork and whip our eggs for a good scramble, laughing at myself. "Because that's the only way you can cook 'em," I murmur to the quiet kitchen, feeling like a dolt.

A throat clears behind me, startling my hands into nearly tumbling the berries I'm washing into the sink. Abigail grins from the tiny table in the corner. She probably snuck in while I flipped that last pancake.

I stop. People rarely sneak up on me, even with my back to the room. But it's happened multiple times now since Abi came home. She's got me way off my game.

Look at her, my dragon snorts.

Yeah... I don't care if she's laughing at me. Abigail's wearing the hell out of an oversized flannel shirt she must have packed last night. It looks... familiar. I squint my eyes. "Is that my shirt?"

"Oh, uh..." Color splashes Abi's cheeks, and she looks down, tugging at the lower hem. "Yeah, uh, I guess. It was left in the room you used to sleep in." She shrugs. "I assumed you didn't want it. And it was comfortable. And…" She trails off, but my cock is already hard, my eyes scanning those long, pale legs sticking out the bottom of *my* shirt. Every man loves for his woman to wear his shirt. Thinking about her doing it for years now sends me into overdrive.

I don't miss the uptick in her heartbeat as I look my fill, taking in the smooth stretch of skin, those perfect pink toes digging into the floor. Finally, the flow of blood south becomes too much and I have to adjust. Abigail chokes on a laugh, her eyes darting away as she coughs with the widest eyes at my lack of modesty. I grin. I've got no shame if Abi sees her effect on me. That girl has no idea how stunning she is, and I have no problem proving it.

Finally, Abi notices the dishes laid out beside her. "What's all this?" she asks.

And now, it's my turn to blush.

"I made breakfast." Walking over, I divide the serving of eggs between our two seats and Abigail stands quick.

"Let me help," she says, but I cut her off with a kiss, tasting the mint of toothpaste she must have grabbed from her travel pack. "You didn't have to do this, Kris."

"I wanted to," I say against her lips, pressing gently on her shoulder to urge her bottom back into the chair. She flops without argument and smiles warmly at me.

"What's on tap for today?" I expect the question, but I'm not ready to think about it. I'm too focused on watching Abigail slice into her thick stack of pancakes before taking a big bite and moaning.

We made that.

After that first sample, it becomes hard to concentrate on my own breakfast. The sounds of pleasure from that side of the table excite my animal side.

Lay her across the table. We don't need breakfast. We can lick her until she feeds us her sweetness.

Swallowing, I force myself to ignore those urges and focus on Abigail, whose lips are already moving. I shake my head. "Huh?"

"I asked if you heard anything from my father?" That brings my excitement to a screeching halt.

"Nothin' yet." I glance at where my phone's charging on the counter. It didn't buzz all night. Curiosity and concern war in my brain. *Was Red still passed out when the boss got home? Did they find Abigail missing? Is he pissed?*

Abigail's shoulders relax a touch, enough that she eats the rest of the meal with a slight smile on her beautiful face. When we're both done, she carries our plates to the sink. This entire morning feels extremely domestic, something I've never experienced before.

From the sink, Abigail washes a pan, her back facing me like she's nervous for her next sentence. "So, uh, I need to get to school this morning," she says, her voice shaking. I cock my head, taking in the defensive fold of her arms, the way her body leans away from me once she turns. That hip propped against the countertop when she straightens her back for a power play.

"I didn't think you'd wanna go in."

"I didn't exactly plan for a leave of absence, Kris." Her voice rises, getting more agitated with every word, though she fights to hide it.

"You don't have to go in, you know."

I don't want her to go.

Solemn eyes lock onto mine as I walk into her space, cupping Abigail's smaller hands in mine. They're shaking. Finally, she drags in a deep breath, summoning her strength. "I need to be there. For the kids." Her voice stops, her shoulders growing tight. "For Max, Kris."

"You don't have to convince me, baby."

A lone tear slides down her cheek, but I catch it. Her voice shakes. "What if Red gets pissed about last night and hurts Max?" I catch that wobbling chin while she dries her hands, bringing her eyes to mine.

God, that big heart.

My heart clenches and I lift Abigail's waist, bringing her butt to sit on the counter so I can step between her spread knees. "Still, Abi... you don't have to go." I'm dead serious, but her head tilts, mouth falling open like I'm the biggest idiot on the planet.

Patiently, she scoots forward, ignoring my response and instead, pressing her sweet scent close to my chest. "I have to go, Kris. What else am I gonna do?" Even annoyed, Abigail knows the best way to get to me, those tears swimming in her baby blues.

"We, Abi. What are *we* going to do?" My arms circle her waist, offering support. "I'm with you, whatever it is."

A smile teases those perfect lips, easing the sadness as she exhales. "Okay. Well, then... *we* need a plan." I roll my eyes, but she continues without calling me a child. "Look, you beat up Red last night. That's going to have consequences. And I ran away from my dad. I still don't know what to do about him. He's never going to see me as an adult, and... and I just can't live this life anymore. I'm tired of the stress, the drama. I hate hating who I came from."

My heart constricts. "I vote we fly away. We can go tropical, Alaska, Paris... I don't care. We won't tell a soul where we went."

That earns a laugh. "Okay, call that Plan B. But I can't live with all this on my conscience. We need to go back long enough to fix this." I cringe, realizing I will not like her version of a plan. Guaranteed. "Kris, Dad planned a kidnapping! Can you tell me without a shadow of a doubt the girl's okay?" I don't say a thing. "Can you tell me they won't hunt down an innocent woman, the same way Dad's afraid of humans hunting us."

I wince. Abi overheard my original orders. She knows I can't confirm the girl's safety. It doesn't matter if I took part in her kidnapping or not. I've done my own wicked deeds. After all, it's my mess that started this shitstorm.

"Honey, last night was chaos. The mission went sideways. Nothing went right... at least in your dad's mind. Of course, we know why Red went AWOL now." Abigail's eyes flicker to the door, like she expects Red to pop in any minute. Anger simmers in my veins at seeing the fear living in the recesses of those innocent, wide eyes.

I will get rid of that, no matter the cost. But there's no way around it, so I resign myself to an awkward, risk-my-life conversation with Dixon.

For Abigail, I put on my most convincing smile. "Looks like we're going back. We'll fix this drama Red caused, tell your dad what he almost did, and that we're out. I'll be there the whole time to protect you. Sound good?"

"Don't kid yourself. We're on the outs, Kris."

I meet Abi's incredulous stare with one of my own, stubborn fighting stubborn. From her perch on the counter, Abigail glares at me like I'm missing a few brain cells and with that I crack up, not able to hold in my laughter at her face. Plus, her thinking she knows the ins and outs of Dixon when she's always seen him from a daughter's point-of-view.

Smiling, I remind her, "Baby, you'll never be on the outs. He's your father." Abi's face softens. "As bad as Dixon is, he will always protect you. He just goes about it the wrong way."

She scoffs. "But what about you?"

See, she loves us. You should have taken her when we had the chance.

I exhale. Abigail's concern touches my soul, given her other problems. But I wouldn't change a thing about last night. I've never lived up to the callousness of our species. *Why would I change that with my mate?*

Relieved, I twirl a few golden strands around my fingers. My lips plant soft kisses to her temple before moving south. I focus on distracting those worrisome thoughts. Abigail squirms when I trail behind her ear, her legs pulling me closer. The baby soft skin just below her hairline seems to be a trigger spot. And while I try to be an honorable hoodlum, I'm damn sure gonna use my most powerful tools to get what I want. Like squeezing this tiny body against mine cools my nerves, too. It prepares me for whatever comes today.

"I'm gonna be fine, baby." My heartbeat slows a bit with Abigail snuggling into my neck, breathing in my scent like it matters to her as well. "So, I'm flying you to school?"

"You're flying me to school," she says with a smile. "But wait... why can't I fly myself to school?"

"Because I wanna take care of you." That seems like the simplest explanation. I don't want to question her new wings or her abilities. That's guaranteed to piss off the woman I want to impress. And that would be disastrous when I have her delectable body pressed against my morning wood. "I'll drop you off and then go talk to your dad about Red."

"Do you think he'll be pissed?"

"Pissed that Red was attacking you… yes. Pissed that I kicked his ass… no." She looks uncertain. "What?" I laugh, bending to nibble her neck as a distraction.

"We need a plan, Kris. I won't stay in that house."

"That's on my list, little one. I'll get supplies at the store. We'll use the cabin temporarily. After that, I'll talk to your dad. He's already suspicious of Red, so that works in my favor. I just need to prove…" I clear my throat. "Prove I'm good enough to be your mate. Then, I'll get out of there. After school, we'll figure out the next steps."

A deep cherry-red creeps up her neck, but she tries to duck her head and hide that bashful smile. "Your mate," she repeats, awed. Her shyness is at odds with her increased heart rate, but she should know by now… even if she's not ready for it.

She's ours.

Lifting Abigail's chin, I force her eyes to mine. "I know you feel it, Abi." I growl, bolstering the confidence she loves, the one that floods the air with her arousal. To pretend for her, I'll shove down every negative thought about not being good enough.

Good or not, fate gave her to me and I'm tired of fighting it.

Bending, I crush my lips against Abi's, devouring the lingering taste of berry. I hope my kiss will erase thoughts of our other stresses, or the weight of talking to her father about our mating.

"Don't worry so much, baby girl. It's all gonna be okay."

She opens her mouth to argue—or maybe confirm—but I don't wait. I cut her off with another crush of lips, our tongues clashing with excitement for our future. I take the strength I need from the kiss, matching Abigail's tease of a smile when we finally pull away.

Chapter Twenty-Four

Kris

AFTER DROPPING ABIGAIL AT school, I head for Dixon's house, tackling her dad before any of the more domestic tasks I need to set up our cabin. My energy is on a blissful high after this morning. Waking up beside my mate, feeding her, kissing her glorious lips, it was...

Heavenly, my dragon purrs, cracking a laugh from me as I hike away from the school and discreetly take to the air. It's a pain in the ass to hide all the time. Society couldn't handle our truth, though. And I won't be an additional danger to Abi at work either. Especially after our amazing morning.

By the time my feet drop to the grounds in front of Dixon's estate, I know something's wrong. People scour the forest edge, more stand guard at the front door with ARs strapped across their chest. The strain in the air is palpable, but I force as much confidence as possible when I climb the porch steps.

Mikey nods from his patrol, and I note the new youngling standing at his side. "What's up, fellas?"

My best friend smirks, correctly reading my concerned expression before I even ask. "Yeah, man. Boss is in a snit. He can't find Abigail."

"Yeah?"

"Yeah," the kid pipes in. "The boys are combing the woods. But man, *no shit!* Dixon's office was *jacked up!*" He's practically salivating, enunciating every syllable.

Mikey's put out from the greenie's energy gives me the energy to move forward.

"Boss thinks something's up."

My grunt brings Mikey's questioning gaze. My best friend knows my quirks after twenty years together, but I ignore them both and glide past, mind set on finding Dixon.

Inside his house, it doesn't take long. His office is the first place I search, and I find him on his hands and knees behind his desk, digging through drawers and grumbling expletives. "Goddamn traitor!" he yells, a file flying past my head.

Deac's stationed down the hall from the boss's office. He pokes his head around the corner to check for trouble, but backs away when he sees the thud was only from a tantrum.

"Boss..." The accusatory glare he fires my way makes me cringe, but I hide it as best I can. Dixon snorts, his eyes glazing before he goes back to his search. "We need to talk."

"Not in the mood, Kris. Where've you been?"

"I've been with your daughter." That sounded better in my head until Dixon reached for the gun strapped under his desk for emergencies. If Abi would have known about that, Red would be walking a lot funnier today. The thought shuts down when my eyes meet the barrel of Dixon's Colt 1911.

"Whoa, whoa, whoa." I hold my hands up, showing I'm unarmed, and walk closer to his desk. This conversation is the rip-the-Band-Aid-off sort. No time for pussy-footin'. "Boss, Red was here. He attacked Abigail." I pause when Dixon jerks to his feet so fast I worry he'll fall over and that gun will go off, meaning to or not.

For the first time in ages, he's Abigail's father, not one of the highest ranking crime bosses in the south. His face is ashen, fists clenching the sides of his snowy puffs of hair he used to dye but let go in the years since his wife passed.

To discover Dixon's panic, much like my own, reassures me of his love. "It's okay. I got here in time and took her somewhere safe." The venom slowly falls from his face, replaced with relief when it registers that his daughter is safe.

"Where is she?"

"Somewhere safe," I repeat, noting the renewed anger shot in my direction. Dixon presses his hands to his desk, finally, leaning over it with the gun precisely placed by his right fist.

"Where. Is. My. Daughter. Kristopher." His growl is as threatening as the flash of murder in Dixon's eyes. They turn menacing red in an instant and before I have time to react, Dixon's dragon takes over, his skin breaking out in prickled flesh as he leaps across the desk.

"Sir..." I croak when his weight presses my chest into the wingback chair behind me. From the recesses of my mind, my dragon fights to the front, pissed at Dixon's hand restricting our air supply.

I should have thought this through a little better.

As bad as I want to, I can't fight my mentor. He's my mate's father and I need his help if I'm going to get out of this mess with my head intact and Abigail by my side... safe. Dixon's hand tenses, but my hold on his fingers prevents them from squeezing my windpipe. *Thank fuck I'm stronger than the old man.*

"Don't make me regret saving you, boy." Dixon's spittle hits my face as he reminds me of my life debt. His teeth have sharpened into fangs. I know, without a doubt, he'd rip my throat out to get to his daughter.

"She is... my mate." The words struggle under Dixon's grip, but he needs to know the truth. I came to talk honorably, but Abigail is—and always will be—my top priority.

Slowly, his fist loosens, allowing much needed oxygen back into my fuzzy brain. With his dragon eye fading, the boss looks a decade older. His hide returns to its pastier version of aging skin and sunken eyes. "Where's Red?" he asks, climbing off my chest begrudgingly.

I don't argue about the change of subject because I need Red's location as well. But I keep a careful eye on Dixon, not trusting his calm acceptance of Abi as my mate.

"Red is why I came here." My back stiffens at repeating his disgusting betrayal, but if Red has flipped, Dixon and I need to work together. Plus, Abigail and I could never live in peace if we're next on his hunt.

"Last night, Red attacked Abigail after suspecting she and I were together." I pause when Dixon's fist tightens at his side. "I stopped it. She was hurt, and scared. But when Abigail and I left, Red was alive on the floor." I signal to the spot Red hit the wall, smirking at the scuff mark where he made impact with the paint. "Bastard passed out, but I didn't kill him."

Dixon's face contorts. "Why not? Traitor deserved it." Quietly, he walks back to sit behind his desk, completely ignoring the files thrown around the room. He grabs the leather-bound ledger we've all seen before and sits it between us. "What do you know about this?"

It's my understanding that Abigail is the one who found his ledger, but I'm not about to throw my mate under the bus.

"That's your book, sir." I keep my answer simple, hoping we can move on and discuss a plan for Red, or at least give me the opportunity to talk to Dixon about my exit strategy.

People don't leave this organization and you know it.

A growl rumbles from his throat. "I know it's my book, Baldy. How did it get out of my desk and on my floor?" I look to my lap, having experienced the boss's skills as a human lie detector before. "Why were you in my stuff, Kristopher?" My eyes dart up, blood heating my veins, prepping for his attack. It doesn't come.

Dixon's head turns sideways, eyeing me. But eventually, his breath stalls as recognition dawns on his face. "Abigail?" He chokes on the words. It's heartbreaking to watch such power crumble. Dixon's head crashes to his hands when it sinks in that his daughter is fully aware of the dirty deeds he fought so hard to hide.

I stay silent, knowing nothing I say makes this better.

Peter Dixon, the mountain of a man I idolized as a child, just shattered. His fingers press his temples with slow circles, sucking fortifying air into his lungs. In dragon form, I'd fear a fiery exhale. As it is, the air only strengthens his role as head dick-in-charge of our mangy pack. Panic catapults his intensity to the level of a desperate man.

"Find Red. Now!" Dixon's fist slams the desk, anger firing rockets from eyes so close to my mate's. "I can't take what he did here last night. His recent disrespect I could overlook for years of service. But... not this." In the next instant, his eyes track to the wall where I found Abigail, like he can sense her unease.

Who knows? Maybe he can.

I nod, hard up to get out of here. I can't take the visual of my mate's slumped body anymore, either. *That shit's burned in my mind with 4K details.*

"Do you have a lead?"

"Doc's at the warehouse until we get a lock on Red. One way or the other, those backhanded fuckers are gonna pay. I need your skills, Kris. Break 'em." The knots in my back tense, knowing what that entails. *That was before Abi.*

She'll understand, my dragon promises, confident in his mate.

"Boss, Red has the Doc by the short hairs, it's—"

Dixon waves his hand to stop me. "He has to be in on the plan... or at least know more than we do. Red is completely out of reach now. He's gotta know the roof's about to cave in on him." He sneers. "We're gonna head him off at the pass."

"One thing..." My hands clench the arm rest, not leaving without getting what I came for. "We need to talk about Abigail."

"She's your mate."

It's not a question, but it gets my attention. "You knew?"

He nods his head.

"Why?" My voice cracks under the importance of this conversation, which is downright embarrassing.

Dixon's fatherly gaze throws me. I thought he'd forbid me from courting Abigail. Or at minimum, I'd have to fight for respect as his daughter's mate. Instead, Dixon's face is expectant, almost at peace with the resignation.

"Kristopher, I've known you were mates since you were a young teen. It's why I kept you away from her. Nothing was going to mess up her education, her chance to be something better than what we are."

Floored, my chin drops. "But we didn't know!" Inside, anger roils in my stomach, my dragon pressing to fight at being denied his mate. And Dixon's answering chuckle doesn't make it any better.

"I know you didn't know. I made sure of that."

"What!" My roughened voice barely hides my roar as rage bubbles over. The wood edge cuts into my palm where I grip the chair. It's the only thing stopping me from flying across this desk and ripping his throat out the way he tried to do to me. "How!" I yell, watching a flash of guilt pass through his eyes before he turns away.

"With Patchouli. A witch came on Abigail's thirteenth birthday and performed a ritual to tamper her dragon spirit." He pauses. "I had no idea it would prevent her ability to shift."

Outraged, I bolt to my feet. "Do you have any idea what she suffered? The ridicule?" *If she knew!* My rage on Abigail's behalf outweighs Dixon playing puppet master and denying my mate. The sad shake of his head tells me he knows exactly the pain he caused. "What about now? *Why is she changing now?*" I'm practically screaming in the room, my anger taking over my common sense from the shock of his betrayal. The betrayal I know Abi would feel to hear her father's role in her pain.

Dixon shakes his head, looking shocked that his plan failed. "She went to college, Kristopher. And at some yank school in the north, dammit."

"And…"

"What do you mean… and?" Dixon shakes his head, knowing there's no fighting mates' connection once they're aware. "When she went away, there was no way to dose her with any regularity." He laughs, a self-deprecating mock that pisses me off even more. "The shit wore off, Kris."

"How could you do it? Once you realized, how could you still poison her?"

"I made a mistake, son. I know I did, but I did it for Abigail. She should have the best future. She deserves the best."

My dragon balks at the insinuation, his roar distorting every thought in my head.

"She will," I bellow. "She will have the best, goddammit. With me." Goosebumps roughen my skin, my dragon scratching to come out. His talons screech in my head like nails on a chalkboard, inflicting the same pain to me he suffers inside.

"We'll deal with that later. Today we focus on Red. He's gotta go."

"Yeah, and he could be anywhere."

"Is this your first rodeo, boy?" Dixon's tone spikes my irritation, that he talks at me like an errant child, not a grown man. "We have the doc... do what you do." His face says the answer is obvious. And it is. My stomach twists, knowing the brutality involved in getting information out of people. It's a skill I hate that I'm good at. Especially now that I have Abigail.

Dixon sees my indecision. "Do this and I'll let you out."

Mic drop.

I'll do anything for my woman. If this is my last job for Dixon, it won't matter. I'm finding Red. He must die, no matter what. I nod my acceptance but level the man with a look I hope conveys my sincerity in the next statement.

"Boss, you know I appreciate everything you've done for me, but I need your word. This is it." The corner of his eye twitches, and I wait a few torturous seconds for a response. "Abigail and I both." I need to clarify, so there's no doubt about my intentions. "And no one's coming after us. Promise me."

Dixon scoffs, standing to pace, but I push through, keeping him in my sights in case he comes at me.

"I'll get you the answers to finish Red, sir. I just want the chance to live my life with Abigail. She deserves peace, not this world. We'll never have peace with all this hanging over our heads." I wave my hand the same way he had earlier, encompassing all the luxuries in his house. He knows I mean the path it took for him to get it all.

"And what else are you qualified to do, son?" He comes around the desk, resting a hip on the edge, arms crossed over his thick chest with a look of disdain. I know he sees me as just another thug, but fuck that... he's the one who trained me.

"Look, I know I don't deserve Abigail, but that's beside the point. She's mine. I won't let her go."

"Yes. But what will you do?"

"I've got savings," I answer defensively. "I sack money away with every job." My brain searches for a viable plan, something that won't make me look like a muscle-head with a pair of fists. Finally, I shake my head. "We'll figure it out. Abigail and I."

I cringe at his bark of laughter, my ego taking enough of a beating in this conversation. I'm ready to tell him to fuck off when Dixon stands from his perch and walks to the door, effectively ending our little meeting.

Did I end up on top, or did he?

"Just do your job, Kris. Then we'll talk."

God! I hate when he does that. It's like the man can read my goddamn mind.

That he's dismissing me when there's so much left to say rankles. But since we both have the same end goal, and I have one despicable piece of shit to find, I don't argue. I stride right past Dixon, determined to find Red before the sun sets.

Chapter Twenty-Five

Red

THAT RAT BASTARD THINKS he's all big shit now. Kid gets a little pussy and loses his goddamn mind.

"He got the fuckin' drop on me. That's all he did." I step up one bitch of a hill, wondering how that happened.

We got a taste of that hot piece. That's how.

Maybe. But that son of a bitch forgot his place. I'm second in line, dammit. Although, after this mission goes to plan, I'm taking over. Dixon's a chicken-shit just like his daughter. It won't be hard. Earl already promised me control of Dixon's territory. *I just gotta take him out.*

There's just one last chore to finish in that house.

I *will* have a piece of Dixon's daughter. I might just let her watch me put a bullet in dear ole daddy's head. Although, if I take 'em all out, I might as well have Boss's fancy house. It's only fair. Dixon ain't the only one deserving to walk in tall cotton.

Huffing in a breath, I pat my cigarettes in my chest pocket, wishing I could puff a smoke instead of tracking a damn bear shifter up the side of a mountain. *Who the hell likes this shit, anyway?*

I don't have a lot of experience with bears, but this seems like the mud-coated, sweat covered hobby they'd eat up. I just need this one out of my way. The fat, fury ass almost makes it too easy for me, stopping a few hundred yards away to rear up a tree. His snarling growl makes me think he treed some prey, but then the dumbass prances out in the clearing, playing with whatever vermin he skittered away.

Goddamn! I should have just waited for him at his truck and off'd him there.

After coming to last night, I got the fuck out of Dixon's office and put a call into Earl. Dixon hadn't said a word about our little dilemma with the nosy vet and her big bad bear. Big shock. Earl's orders were pretty clear. *Take 'em out.*

So that's why I'm staying down wind, sacrificing my cigarettes, and hauling my ass over boulders with this Winchester propped on my shoulder.

The sun breaks through the forest canopy at the perfect spot, blasting a spotlight on Grizzly Adams there just as he plops on his haunches to munch on whatever he tracked out of that tree. That massive head aimed at the ground doesn't see me coming, a large pine keeping me hidden with the Winchester .375 pressed to my shoulder. Squaring up sights, the little boyfriend enters the crosshairs and I squeeze the sensitive trigger.

Crack!

My ears ring with the bang, gunpowder filling both my sinuses and the open clearing as I let the gun drop to my side.

Fuck, yeah!

I only glance over my shoulder once, unable to fight the grin when shifter boy hits the ground with a howl of pain. *Hah! One down.* Now the girl's open season.

Hitting send on my phone, I dial up Earl. "All done, Boss."

"That's my boy. Now meet me in Asheville. We're going after our snitch."

Chapter Twenty-Six

Abigail

I HAVEN'T HEARD FROM Kris all day.

I know I shouldn't message at school, but I had to know how his meeting with my dad went. So, I held off until lunchtime and then texted for an update. *Nothing.* I texted after school. *Nothing.* Called... *same.*

My stomach channels a decade's worth of Olympic gymnasts for inspiration on flipping over itself. *What the hell happened when Kris talked to my dad?*

Without my car, and without Kris answering his phone, my options are limited for after-school transportation.

We could fly, my dragon pushes.

No, shut up.

I am nowhere near ready for that. Plus, I'm too chicken to transition close to school, which is like ten levels of cowardly.

"I don't even know how to get back," I say to my empty classroom.

"You talking to yourself again?" I chuckle at the sweet voice I hear in my doorway. It's the only person in this school who's made me feel at home, not like a pariah. Granted, Lexi is new to town, and we started teaching the same year, so she's a newbie too. She is a year older and a complete pussy cat. Unless you piss her off or mess with her family or friends, then the girl will claw your eyes out. She's a personified SweetTart, and I love that about her.

Heck, I've fantasized about channeling Lexi into my personality, so I can tell everyone in my life exactly what I think of them. Of course, I never do. Which is why I'm sitting here like a good little girl again, waiting for someone else to decide my life.

The more time passes without hearing from Kris, the more my little fantasy of running into Kris's arms and him flying us back to the cabin vaporizes. All day, I've daydreamed about how to go about seducing him tonight... something I'm not proud of when I teach a rambunctious bunch of ten-year-olds who don't need their teacher distracted by hormones. Throughout lessons and lunch, recess and carpool, I've worried our whirlwind romance will crash and burn before it ever gets off the ground.

My new life is not starting this way!

I glance at Lexi and give her my most convincing 'I'm a badass' smile. "Can you give me a ride home?" New Abigail takes the bull by the horns. And Lexi's furrowed brow doesn't even deter me. I might have said I'd never go back there, but if Kris is brave enough to face my dad, then I can, too. He basically had to quit his job and ask for my hand—at least the shifter version—at the same time. I refuse to begin this new phase in my life as the same pushover as before.

"Absolutely, baby girl. Let me get my purse. Meet me outside."

Thirty minutes later, her tiny blue sedan is sputtering up my front driveway while Lexi babbles to her heart's content. I say nothing when her mouth falls open a bit in awe. I've seen that look before. I'm more nervous about bringing an outsider to my front door. Lexi pops the gear into park, looking prepared for an extended visit or teatime.

"Thanks for the ride, Lex." I grab the handle, attempting to head off any attempt to hang out, or girly bond, when I've got a giant conversation waiting with the pit of dread in my stomach.

"Oh, that's not happening. You've been holding out sugar mama. This is where you grew up?"

I feel my cheeks flame at her squeal. "Umm... yeah." I know I shouldn't, but polite society requires I invite Lexi in, though I have no idea how I'm going to work that. However, before the question is out, Lexi is out of the car and rounding the porch with an excited skip in her step.

Shit!

Flustered, I follow hot on her tail, only to have her skid to a stop when she sets sights on the back door.

"*Good God!* Who are they?"

I glance around her and see Mikey and Deacon parked in their standard patrol. My good friend has no idea what she's walking into, but the grin on her face says she appreciates the man-candy, nonetheless.

Mikey jerks to his feet from the chair he was lazing in, looking a mix of relieved and wary when he sees me walking up. That is, until his eyes land on Lexi and all bets are off. His heated eyes strip her bare, his face falling until it lights up again with a boyish charm that could probably melt the panties off any girl.

"Watch out," I whisper to her from the corner of my mouth.

"Abigail." Mikey nods, giving me about a half second of attention before turning it on my friend. "Who do we have here?"

Lexi's surprised squeak draws my attention—and Deacon's. But she quickly coughs, clearing her throat like it never happened. Mike smiles, watching her cheeks color to a ripe strawberry. Deac stands stock still at his twin's side, going pale when Lexi's standard megawatt smile returns.

"This is my friend, Lexi," I say, trying not to stammer under the nerves of confronting my father. "She gave me a ride, but she's gotta go now. Right, Lexi?" Her eyebrows crinkle, flashing confusion and a touch of hurt as I try to convey that I need her gone without hurting my one friend's feelings.

"Oh, um... yeah," she stammers, and another nail goes in the coffin of a friendship. My weird life steals it before it has a chance to grow... every time. "I'll catch you at school, Abs."

I'm not confident enough in front of these two, six-foot something dragons to turn and watch my friend leave. But judging by the set of their clenched jaws and those piercing blue eyes following her every step, I probably could two-step in a clown suit right in front of them and these guys wouldn't notice.

Using their distraction to my advantage, I slide around Mikey, aiming for the door he was guarding. I will find Kris... whatever that takes. Plus, I'd like to sneak off with my car even if Dad did buy it. It would make hunting Kris a lot easier.

Unfortunately, the movement catches Mike's eye, breaking him out of his Lexi stupor. Within a few steps, his oversized hand wraps my arm from the back, although much gentler than I would have imagined, his voice panicked. "Abi, wait!" he hisses. "Your dad knows."

I freeze. "About what?" I ask, the back of my neck tingling, already knowing the answer.

"About you and Kris." He glances at Deacon over his shoulder, concern sketched in the secrets on their face. "He knows about Red, the attack... all of it." I gasp, assuming Mike only meant about my snooping, not that I'm walking into a whole new world of understanding if I step foot in that house.

No more burying your head in the sand, my dragon bitches needlessly.

I know my shortfalls, ok?

Huffing, I take my irritation out on the boys. Hanging around this mess is my own damn fault. And now, I'm stuck in it for good if Kris can't find a way out. Because I'm not leaving Kris, and this life never lets go without a world of pain. For the first time in my twenty-four years, I feel powerful enough to protect my mate. First, I have to find him.

"Where's Kris?" I eye them both, arching my brow the same way I do my fourth graders when I try to catch them in a lie.

The brothers smirk at each other before turning to me. "You like him, huh?" Mike asks, taking me back. Deacon grins over his brother's shoulder.

"I don't know if that's any of your business." I cross my arms, aiming for a tough Miss Dixon vibe but failing miserably, because the two men in front of me crack up with laughter.

"About damn time," Deac mutters quietly, getting an elbow in the rib from Mikey. He coughs. "What? He's our best friend, dammit. We gotta make sure she's worth this trouble."

I bristle, and Mikey turns to me with sympathy, apologizing for his brother. "He has a way with women," he jokes, flipping a thumb at his brother like we're in on a private joke with a long history instead of this *literally* being the first words we've spoken in five years.

He sobers when I don't join their playful bickering. "Boss sent Kris out."

My stomach drops. He said he'd stay with me. Talk to my dad about Red but come back to that tiny little cabin so I could practice my non-existent seduction skills on him tonight.

"Where'd he go?" Mike eyes me with pity, while Deacon's emotions completely lock down behind him. Neither open their mouths. "Where'd he go, dammit?" I know my shriek will bring my father's attention, but my gut says this is bad. Kris is in trouble, or will be. I don't know. I've just never felt such an overwhelming urge to strangle, break, or kill anything in sight standing between me and my mate.

Told you, my dragon chuffs, lighting a match to my already boiling temper.

Chapter Twenty-Seven

Abigail

INSIDE MY FATHER'S HOME, an eerie silence blankets the atmosphere. It matches the desolate rains outside that drenched me on the way in. This place will never be home anymore, not after last night, but how my father reacts is going to make the largest difference if I even set foot in here again.

I glance around the empty foyer and notice the complete lack of life. There's no laughter, no raucous men treating our basement like a frat house. No fist slamming things. Normally, I'd run to the blissful peace of my bedroom at the first hint of violence. No matter how much Dad warned his men to be discreet, there's only so much a person can unhear. Conducting this kind of business from our house comes with pitfalls.

I guess I won't have to worry about that anymore.

Still, the ominous vibe in the air chills my spine, given that my own footsteps are the only sound as I stride toward Dad's office.

My confidence is in short supply as I open the door, my feet faltering when a flashback of last night punches me in the gut. The fear. The vile memory of Red's hands grabbing me. Utter weakness and failure on my part. And then the pain when his attack turned violent.

"Abigail." My name breaks through the haze clouding my mind and brings me back to the room. "Abi," Dad cries, his lined face coming into focus right beside me. "Baby girl, I thought…" Dad's tearful voice fades the panic of Red's attack, and I blink. "I thought you left."

When did he move across the room?

"Dad?" I almost reach for one of his massive bear hugs before I remember how pissed I am and straighten my shoulders. With my arms crossed over my chest, I attempt to look menacing. I don't know how great that works with sweat trickling down my back, but what my father doesn't know won't hurt me. "Dad, where is Kris?"

Ugh! I sound like a broken record.

Dad sighs, his shoulders crumpling as he trudges back to his desk. "He's out, Abigail."

What the hell?

"No shit, Dad."

"Abi!" he hisses, shocked.

Okay, this may be the first time I've cursed at my dad—or in front of him at all—but I'm sick and tired of everyone believing I'm useless. I know Kris is my mate. Dad can't tell me otherwise.

I know what they do is dangerous. And for God's sake… Red, without a doubt, is the most dangerous of all. But he will not hurt my mate if I have to comb the entire east coast to stop it.

"Dad, if Kris is going after Red, I deserve to know." Dad's shocked expression doesn't surprise me. "Look, I know that was the plan. I'm not stupid. But I-I also know he was coming to talk to you." I pause, my cheeks burning.

Dad's eyes soften and he goes to his desk, pulling out the file I flipped through last night. "He visited. We talked." His stare drifts to the spot Red attacked me last night, burning hellfire through the heat of my father's anger.

On some level, I feel better knowing my dad loves me more than the precious *boys* he spends all his time with. Not that I thought he didn't. Just after Mom's death, Dad shut down when I needed him most. I guess a man who worked in the bowels of Hell didn't know how to be soft for a daughter. He did what he did best... provided financially and distanced emotionally.

"Dad!" I call, snapping my fingers in his direction. He turns, but his stare hard, reminding me of where I got my stubbornness. "Where is he, Dad?" I hate that my voice cracks, the hot tears prickling behind my eyes.

Worse is the tingling of my skin. It's odd, like a rash of electricity that feels just shy of losing my mind.

Dad straightens in his chair, clasping his hands in front of him in the rigid stance of a man set in his ways. "You know, Abigail, that's not something I'm gonna tell you. I don't care how much you hate me for it, bug. It's in your best—"

Howling, I cut off my dad's sentence, clashing my teeth in the air. Dad jolts upright, his eyes sharp, nervous. But there's a small amount of pride shining through from seeing my animal side.

"You found her," he whispers, already knowing the truth.

My dragon snarls at my father, wondering how we can pull his help to save Kris. That's her sole concern.

Dad stops, his lips thinning in the same stern expression I met my entire childhood. "This is for your own good, Abigail."

I jerk back as if slapped. I'm used to his dismissal, but it's not stopping me this time.

"Kris needs us, Dad." I move for the exit, only turning back when I've opened the door and am on the way out. Dad's mouth hangs open. "You know... I'm gonna find him with or without you. It would be easier if you helped. But what else is new?" I leave my parting words in the air and slam the door.

My dragon releases a maniacal cackle inside my mind. The perfect motivation as I stomp down the hall. *Hide in the woods until the boys take off. Then we follow.*

With a new purpose, I snatch my keys off the kitchen hook and hop into the car. I'll park down the road to get myself straight. There's a section of thicker trees I used to get lost in as a child. They'll cover me while I make a few phone calls... get my shifts covered, arrange lesson plans with a substitute. I'll hit the ATM for bribe money, just in case. And drop by the market to stock up for a stakeout. I've never done one before, but how hard could it be?

I have a plan... even if it's only half-cocked in my head.

I will find my mate.

Dad's gonna learn. And if he thinks I won't hunt down Kris the old-fashioned way—hell, by any way possible—he has another thing coming.

Chapter Twenty-Eight

Kris

Almost a week after talking with Dixon.

A brigade of cop cars, vans, and lifted pickup trucks parade away from the Asheville warehouses. The surprising part is there's not a siren in sight across the dead of the night. Everything has gone silent. Even birds and crickets are quiet, like all of animal kingdom knows something went down here tonight, or is about to.

I've been here many times. I know the exits, the alternatives, the pigeon-holes, dead ends. Plus, the response time for the Asheville police if they get triggered.

The only thing that pisses me off is taking six goddamn days to track Red. It's not like I don't have that god awful stench of his Marlboro Reds seared in my nose. The freaking dude was all over the place, from Knoxville to the state line, all over the hills of Tennessee and Georgia. But I knew shit was up when I smelled him in the chick's hometown.

I couldn't get to the girl in time because she had her guard up the past week, never alone, always looking over her shoulder and staying in public. Something changed. Boss has the vet, so I know the doc hasn't talked to her. But she's with these bears nonstop now. The one who didn't leave her side for more than an hour until yesterday.

Everything happened at once... too fast to stop it.

A storm rolled in, grounding me to car level. Red's trail was hot, yet I always showed up steps behind. *That fucker.*

When I met with Dixon earlier today, we locked down a plan to bring him in and figure out how far this had gone. Is Red the only boil we have to cut off? Has Earl turned any of the other men? How long has he worked against Dixon? He must be the mastermind, because I've worked with Red for years. That guy's as confused as a fart in a fan factory... and just as toxic.

At least the facility where we stashed the doc is completely unknown to Red—and Earl. We snatched the place when old man Nash welched on a bet. He got to live with Dixon off his back, and we got the defunct gambling house.

Yesterday, while we interrogated Doc, Dixon warned me that Abi had been at his house every day this week, checking up. She's pissed... rightfully so.

A few days ago, I finally got to check in, making it to a safe landing spot with decent service. I didn't exactly take flight with a bag full of supplies—including my charger—so I've had the phone off, except for check-ins. Still, I fired off a few texts, but every time we'd try to call or video chat, our hope would fall victim to spotty signals and low batteries.

It's frustrating, being apart from Abi, knowing she's my mate, my body craving her touch. I should be wooing her. Instead, we both suffer, sacrificing temporarily so we can be together later.

Saying I've flown until my wings are about to fall off doesn't feel like an exaggeration. Between tracking Red and setting the doc up in an off-the-map location, I've exhausted my mind and my body. And without Abigail here... my soul.

With my heart heavy, I watch the parade of cars leave the warehouse district from the roof of a neighboring building. I know Slim and Red are in different cars, but I'm not here to hurt Slim. I wish I could help him out of the jail cell he's headed for, but that's not my priority tonight. Red, however, I would have taken out on the ground if those bulky shifters didn't outnumber us. And they kept coming in droves. I can't complain, though. Those shifters made tracking Red a hell of a lot easier. The anger blasting off the biggest one stank up the air worse than the fumes off a paper mill.

And that shit stinks!

There's less chaos in the air now. Whatever went down inside that warehouse was over faster than I could find a way in. A few gunshots and snarls, shifters storming the building, followed by a lot of shouts and screams. Then, it was all over, and the big bear calmed.

Probably because more backup arrived moments later.

I glance down at the phone and the photos I snapped. The memory card is almost full. *Figures.*

Logically, I know I'm supposed to call the boss. Too bad my head and my pissed off dragon disagree on loyalties right now. Not that my head would oppose Abigail. I just usually follow Dixon's letter of the law, and this time I have my own agenda that benefits us both. Hell, it benefits Dixon too.

This time I watch from my rooftop surveillance and decide quickly, this one's going down my way. Especially when most of those shifter-scented vehicles stayed behind. Makes sense. If bears are as paranoid as dragons, they're in there cleaning up evidence. Though, I can't tell from this distance if any of that earthy scent left with the police cars. My battle to recover Red could be over in minutes, or the battle of my life.

Quickly, before I lose the cars on these dark-ass country roads, I kick my dragon into high gear because I'm going to need full strength on this one. Rushing, I strip my pants and boots, not wasting a second folding my already dusty, wrinkly clothes. They land on my cargo pack just in time. My skin already tingles, ready to morph into my protective, leathery dragon hide.

Hurry!

The urgency in my dragon speeds through my movements. In the distance, the sound of tires kicking up loose gravel as they hit the two-lane main road show he's right. I toss my cell phone to the top of the pile and brace for the painful transition.

If I've ever been jealous in my life, it was watching those damn bears shift within seconds of hitting the ground. *Fuckin' bears!*

My head ducks, my jaw snapping shut to bite through the agony of bones elongating into dragon form. It strains every muscle in my body until shakes take over, processing the pain. I'm able to muffle all but a few grunts and panting breaths as human thigh reforms into powerful haunches able to launch my much heavier beast into the air.

A whip-like tail extends behind me, topped with spines that penetrate an enemy in battle better than a handheld knife. The appendage's spade tip stabs wood and metal like they're butter, but my favorite use is as a Flintstone-like club. That hard tip will knock any large prey out cold.

In my mind, my dragon snickers close to the surface with the fun of it. Under full shift, his consciousness—his voice and mine—sound one and the same.

Bowed over my clothing, my jaw unclenches, allowing my skull to expand into its Draconian shape. Wider nostrils flare, dragging in more of the night air that acts as a coolant to my volcanic blood. My beast's eyes merge with my own, using the ambient lighting of the parking lot to illuminate the dark sky into glowing golds and reds. The world glows in vivid technicolor clarity, making it easier to see for a nighttime hunt.

My phone lighting up catches my attention. The vibration is quiet enough on top of my stack of clothes that I don't rush to answer. Either it's Dixon checking in on my status, which I won't update until I have Red or a resolution, or it's Abigail, who I can't talk to in this state of mind. It's never been more important to keep her out of harm's way, knowing any of these fuckers could use her against me if they sensed our connection.

We won't let that happen.

My dragon takes over, his razor-sharp teeth snapping ready to tear Red limb from limb once I get a hold of him. That's why I can't involve either of the Dixons. Both would try to stop me, for distinct reasons, of course. But I won't stop until I'm certain Abigail and I are safe to live our life in peace.

A rolling growl fills my head, agreeing with that idea as I peek from my hunched position. It's unlikely anyone saw a grown man transform into a mythical beast, but with the taillights fading about a mile down the road, I know I have no choice but to go now, whether someone sees a fully formed dragon take off around them or not.

In the air, I glide in the opposite direction from the melee of bears. My wings whip, gaining speed toward the cusp of a tree-lined road where the last brake light disappeared. At least the trees hide my approach. One thing in my favor, since I have no idea how many shifters I'm fighting against, or the condition of Red and Slim. Red *will not* go willingly if he's conscious. And Slim's loyalty is in the air.

After only a few miles, I catch a glow of brakes in the distance. I've bailed out a few comrades in the past... that cop car is not driving to the local precinct. I bet that's why he hasn't triggered the siren. Odds are at least one of those cars contains a shifter, smart about keeping secrets. Or we're talking corrupt freaking cops. If that's the case, the chance of Red already having loyalties with them is high and that I'm going to wish I brought in backup, instead of working this alone.

Stealthy, I hover above the caravan, realizing it's only three cars, not the four I originally thought. Which do I go for, though? Would they use the pickup for transporting a suspected shifter or the smaller cop car? Usually, they're reinforced for stronger confinement. The wrong choice takes away my advantage with the surprise attack.

"Which car are you in, you jackass?"

With the squad car in the lead, that's the one I'll ram. There's a slim chance the other two are unarmed, or that they'll be too distracted avoiding the crash to help their buddy.

"Here goes nothing," I think in my head, circling out front in a wide arch. I gain momentum and speed before streamlining my body, nimbly swooping into a dive pattern toward the windshield of the lead car. The forest canopy offers a perfect cover until the cop's headlights light me up, setting off a chorus of horns and tire screeches that cut through the silence. I've got sights set on one thing, a masterful game of chicken between myself and the wide-eyed driver aimed at what I assume is a surprising sight for his part.

Stop, you idiot!

He heeds my thoughts, but the sudden slam of brakes comes too late, and with the jerk of the wheel to keep from hitting the large dragon flying at his face, Mr. Cop Car takes a careening slide off the road's embankment, slamming nose-first into a ditch. My mind shuts down to prevent guilt from distracting my mission. I swerve to the right before car number two takes a swipe at my backside, but not before I catch a slack-jawed Slim gawking in the backseat.

Chaos crashes all around me as car number two locks his breaks, heading into a tailspin across the road. The tailing truck sounds his horn, narrowly avoiding the demolition derby in front of him and sliding off the road himself. This one only topples to its side, luckily missing the trees and the barrel roll it could have taken off the steep drop-off.

There're only a few seconds to play with here.

My feet hit the ground, powered by the haste to move in and out before the other drivers right themselves and come to help. Thankfully, Red's nasty mop slumps against the back window with a smear of blood, so he's one obstacle I don't have to deal with... yet.

Seeing no movement from the front seat, I try the handle. Of course, the locks are engaged. *Fuck!*

Steam snorts from my snout, frustration pulling the last thread on my temper to whip my tail against the backdoor and not giving one shit if I hit Red or not. The spade pierces near the hinge and I grab the handle, using both to rip the metal barrier right off the car. Red's body crumples to the ground like a sack of flour and I have to hold in a chuckle, not wanting to rouse the knocked-out cop.

Is he dead?

Sniffing the air, I smell that earthy scent of shifter on him, so he should be tougher, but I have no idea how hard his head connected to the steering wheel.

A drawn moan sounds in the front seat. "Ungh..." I glance just in time to see a dark head lift and immediately fall back to the headrest.

Shouts sound behind me. *Time to go!*

The sadistic laugh in my head when I snatch the back of Red's shirt in my teeth is full of victory. Piss and vinegar sour my veins, daring me to throw caution to the wind and rip the throat right out of this nasty fucker.

Let the bears catch up. We're stronger together.

I'm smart enough to take to the air, prey hanging limp from my mouth. But the grin is hard to fight, knowing I'm only thirty minutes from the revenge we both crave.

Chapter Twenty-Nine

Kris

I GRIN WITH A sick satisfaction, tossing Red's body unceremoniously on the dead grass behind Nick's old gambling house. The place doesn't look like it's had a single visitor since we took over. I'm surprised no one complained about the stairs practically falling off the back door, rotted and sagging into the overgrown bushes on either side. The house looks one strong wind from falling on its ass.

Dixon eventually wants to reopen the backdoor gaming den. But for now, it sits deserted on his books, which makes this dump perfect for my needs. The only drawback is losing my dragon to fit through the narrow doorways. A warehouse would be easier. "But a lot quicker for Dixon to find," I grumble out loud.

Eventually, I'll bring the boss in for the answers he wants. But Red's going to give me names first. Whoever he's been working with that could track us down. Plus, any of the corrupt bastards stabbing us in the back from our side of the state line.

My dragon grumbles unhappily but recedes to the back of my mind without arguing, which makes transitioning back to human form a lot easier.

Quickly, my hide smooths to its softer tattooed skin, bones and muscles refit to their normal physique. My tail recedes just as the darkness gets more pronounced from my eyes returning to their usual—albeit elevated—shifter sight.

Red's prone body is still visible a few feet away, but I always miss seeing every blade of grass, bug, or threatening movement from a hundred yards away.

Once my bare feet are back under me, I snag Red up by the collar, getting a sick satisfaction from how wet his shirt is from my saliva. His limp body drags across the ground, slapping the steps on the way to the backdoor. Without a credit card to pick the lock, or a key which would have required informing Dixon of my plan, I take it on myself to create a little extra ventilation in the kitchen door.

Elbow, meet six-by-six tiny window.

The best part, Red doesn't budge when the glass shatters, though my ears perk, listening for any rustle on the street, any sign that someone might come check out the ruckus.

Hearing nothing, I twist my elbow through the new access window, reaching for a deadbolt I remember near the top of the door. The loose shards along the edge scrape my bicep at the cocked angle, but I barely feel it. What I feel is antsy to get inside, as a warm trickle of blood slides down my arm. My blood can't scent the air too much or any shifter in the vicinity could track us here. Red's already adding enough of the stench to the air—*snick*.

Thank fuck!

The lock opens and I bend to wrap Red under the pits, hiking his crumpled ass up to cart through the door. A combination of mildew and dust hit my nose making it hard not to cough. With the house dead quiet, I hold that shit in, dealing with the watery eyes and twitchy nose on the way to the basement.

Once inside the door, I flick the switch and only two dangling bulbs flicker to life. I'm not surprised. It is creepy how they cast an eerie, Friday the 13th glow over the space. *God! How ridiculous is my life!* I swear to anyone listening in Heaven or Hell that this is the last time I'll welcome blood on my hands.

Only for Abigail.

Though there is a sick satisfaction in tossing Red's body to the middle of the room, letting him flop whichever way he lands. That man doesn't even need to be awake for his torture to be fun.

Quickly, I take stock of the basement. It's stripped of the card tables, which leaves only trash and litter, and a few rickety folding chairs stacked against the wall. This place barely classifies as a man cave in the lowest form.

I eyeball Red while I set up, moving one chair to the center of the room, before going to hunt down supplies. I need something to secure the man that he can't easily break. Not setting up the hideaway ahead of time was not the best idea. If I hadn't been chasing my tail all over the state, tracking this scumbag, I might have. I just couldn't risk falling off Red's scent.

At least he's out cold.

Who knows if it's from the accident or an injury from the bears? I know he's breathing; I could smell the tobacco stink our whole flight. That clump of matted blood on the side of his head hides any actual damage. He's pale, either from the pain or loss of blood. I don't care which, but that pasty, freckled face is definitely more ashen than usual. Outside of those new bluish bruises, at least.

Hell, I'm shocked the man is still alive after he abducted one of their mates.

He wouldn't be if he stole our Abigail.

Damn straight! I'm in full fucking agreement with my dragon on that.

I get lucky and find a set of wire shelves in the corner that've seen better days. Half of them don't sit straight, tools litter all over the place. The mess is a complete cluster-fuck. Oil residue sticks to the supports, the goo adding its stink to the vile basement. Scouring the clutter, I luck out with a roll of duct tape. That'll be useful with the hammer and pliers I snatch up, too.

Yes... hisses inside my mind.

I keep scrounging, clearing away useless trash. The stack of rags and mineral spirits will be useful if this little shit isn't cooperative. I haul those, and a section of chain that looks too short for anything except binding, over to Red's throne before yanking his weight up by the arm and plopping him in it. His head falls forward.

Damn. Dude's out hard!

I make quick work of linking his wrists with the chain behind the chair, anyway. Without a padlock, I twist the duct tape into a secure, twisting knot between the links. Then, reinforce the hold with tape encasing the length of loose cargo chain around Red's wrists, and all the way up his elbow to his upper bicep. I make sure the angle tugs hard enough to cause an aching annoyance when my sleepy prisoner joins the land of the living.

Speaking of...

On my next circle of Red, I backhanded a knuckle across his cheek, rocking Red's body nearly off the chair before lifting him back in place. "Nuh, uh uh, asshole. You aren't getting off with one hit." I chuckle at how much better Red's company is when he's lights out.

Slap... other cheek. Nothing.

"Wake up, you fucker! Time to play." I jerk the back of his greasy mullet, noting the slackness in his facial features.

Shit! At this rate, I have time to scrounge Nick's old bedroom for something to wear, so Red's ugly mug isn't so close to my junk. *Uck!* That idea puts a nasty taste in my mouth.

I leave Red tied to the chair to wait out his unconscious state and rush the stairs.

Old man Nick lived on the second floor of this house after the bank took his farm during the downturn. He's what I'd picture if a lumberjack bought a farm and spent the last twenty years drinking and working the land all day. Two things that don't go hand-in-hand. It aged him before his time, until the man I met in his late sixties looked early eighties. By then, the only thing that put a smile on his face was a bottle of whiskey or winning a large pot on a Saturday night.

Since Dixon owns his house now, I know which he enjoyed more.

Sighing, I open one of the three doors upstairs, lucking out on the first shot that Nick was lazy enough to claim the first bedroom at the top. It's just as stagnant and disorganized as the rest of the house. Looks like Nick only packed up a few boxes and left everything else untouched. The whole room is an odd diorama to his old life. Just walking in feels like disturbing a ghost.

God! I sound like a sympathetic dolt.

Shaking my head, I stride to the closet and try to channel my ass-holery to deal with Red downstairs. I feel like loving Abigail has made me soft, but I can't let myself give in yet. There's still one obnoxious task downstairs that's going to test my patience like a fucking toddler hyped up on cotton candy.

Unfortunately, Nick's closet is almost bare. Probably things he didn't care about anymore. For clothing, that's an old pair of coveralls from his farming days and a few flannels. Since those would bind the hell out of my reach, I'll skip the shirt. There's not a chance on Earth I'll let anything hinder my swing if it gets Red talking.

Anything less than full power isn't good enough.

With that in mind, I pull on the coveralls and thank the universe for Nick's extra height. The legs are only an inch or two shy once I adjust the straps, but it's comfortable enough to give my crotch some much appreciated breathing room.

I catch sight of myself in the scratched-up dresser mirror and finally do laugh out loud. These things will keep Red's blood away from my skin, but damn if I don't look like a hillbilly who lost his shirt gambling. Although the lower half of me busts the seams like I'm wearing my non-existent little brother's clothes.

I'm still laughing in my head when I walk back down to the base-ment, but quickly sober when I notice Red has come to. Part of me liked the idea of torturing his heart rate into waking up, but I appreciate that this way is faster.

"Rise and shine, you lazy shit!" Red startles at my growl. *You better be scared, old man.* He's in the same position I left him. Only now, his head scans his surroundings, I bet wondering where the hell he is and how he got here.

From this angle, I can see Red, but he can't see me. He's blinking to clear his eyes but has nothing to go on but my voice. Last he knew, he was with a group of bears. And I have no idea what went down before they knocked him unconscious, but I do hope they worked him over good.

"Kris?" His hushed voice sounds confused. Exactly how I want it.

"Ding, ding, ding. What's the man win?" My laughter booms dark and sinister through the room. It's needed to throw him, even if I don't find a lick of humor being on the same planet with this pond scum. However, playing this role is the only thing preventing my anger from ripping Red's freaking head off, so that's what I'll do.

"What the fuck, man? Never thought he'd send you to help me. Whatever. Bros stick together right. Untie me," he says in a panic, tugging at the restraints behind him. "Those bears got the jump."

I just chuckle darkly, letting him hear how truly and wholly fucked he is, because I'm not here to save him.

"You're going to wish the bears had you by the time I'm done, asshole." I can't hide the venom in my voice and Red freezes. From the stiffness in his shoulders, he knows I'm walking up behind his chair. He knows the angle is on purpose, too.

"The fuck?" A quick jab to the lower rib cuts off the rest of his sentence, pleasing my dragon when Red folds in on himself with a painful groan.

"You aren't in a position to ask questions, Red... in case that wasn't obvious." I walk around in front, taking in the bloodshot eyes of my former comrade. I don't care if we hated each other; he's not supposed to betray the brotherhood. "Let's start with an easy one. What happened in that warehouse?"

Red cackles. Not the response I was expecting.

"Let me go and I'll tell you everything," he says, knowing damn well I don't believe a word.

It's my turn to laugh. "You think I'm stupid all of a sudden?"

His snicker pisses me off more. "I don't know, Baldy. With that outfit... maybe."

I growl. "You think you got the upper hand here, Red? Does it look like we're gonna have a cold brew and shoot the shit?" My hand dusts down the front of my borrowed coveralls, pretending to pretty them up. "I kinda thought these styled," I say, shrugging like I couldn't care less. "Thick, durable... waterproof, so your filthy blood won't dirty up my sexiness." My laughter echoes, but it seems Red doesn't find my shit-eating grin all that funny. His face turns a cranberry shade of red, diffusing the color of his bruises. *Figures.*

Red's face contorts with disdain. The same disgust he's aimed our way these past months. "Whatever, you little shit. What do you want?"

I shake my head, picking the hammer off the ground and squaring to Red. With arms crossed, my biceps look like they'd pop his head like a pimple, add in my tactical advantage and the threat of torture devices, and Red should be more than willing to talk if it saves his ass anymore pain.

"You deaf? Or did you not hear me the first time?"

"Fuckin' warehouse? Goddamn, man, I was takin' care of business. Dixon's too chicken, so I got Earl. He got no problem getting' shit done." Red's chest rumbles in a growl, his eyes narrowing into slits before he continues. "You know this is all your goddamn fault, too, Baldy."

"How you figure?"

Red's shoulders jerk in the chair, struggling to attack where I stand a few feet away, but a yelp of pain stops his forward movement when the chain pulls at his wrists. "You know damn well, Kris. If that little bitch hadn't heard you roughin' the doc, we wouldn't have looked twice at her. She started this wild goose chase... which means you fuckin' did, too. Your laziness and always thinkin' you're better than us." He battles the chains again. "You're the goddamn reason Earl's dead. *Grrl!*"

His impotent roar cracks me up, but I hold a straight face, snapping the flat side of the hammer against my thigh a few times. Can I trust anything coming from this loser's mouth? It's almost too perfect.

Chapter Thirty

Kris

DID THE BEARS TAKE out my biggest problem? Well, next to this jackass.

"Explain," I growl, stalking closer, flipping the hammer in my hand, biding time. Red snaps his lips shut, going stock still in the chair. "Oh, tongue get tied?" He glowers from his lower position, eyes transforming to their raging ruby hue.

That fucker thinks I'm dumb enough to allow a shift.

"Hah!" I smack the flat side across his shoulder before tossing the hammer to the side. "Don't even try it, Red." My fists itch to get in the game, but Red's still talking. I can't mess that up.

Slowly, his eyes lighten closer to normal. "You piece of shit," he snarls, saliva dribbling down his chin, making him look rabid. "Earl's dead. So is JB." His teeth snap in my direction. I wouldn't put it past him to bite me with those nasty tobacco-stained teeth if he could. I keep up my psycho charade, even though part of me feels bad about the kid. He was too young and stupid for this life.

"So, Jon was riding your twisted arrangement, too?"

"Me and the kid got the girl." Red looks twistedly proud. "He was on the fast track, Baldy. Unlike your ass. Lost all your damn nerve. JB would have been a good enforcer after I take over Dixon's territory." He must catch my surprise because that maniacal laughter bounces through the basement. "What? You think we gonna to let you two keep bringing us down when you couldn't find your ass end if your skinny little girlfriend had her nose stuck up it."

Pop. Pop. Pop.

My fist connects with Red's jaw, knocking his head back and the chair almost going with it. "Watch it," I bark, the venom pushed through it, scratching my voice. My death grip on Red's shirt gets rougher, giving me leverage to hold him still for extra blows to his already bruised eye socket. "Don't you fuckin' say her name, Red."

The groans from Red get louder with every hit, and he battles to free himself from my hold without use of his hands. It's all clumsy feet kicking and jerking. Although one of his small combat boots connects with my knee, it's not enough to temper my anger. I regret not bolting them to the chair now, but with two strategic blows to Red's quad and one very satisfying howl of pain, his reflexes lock up and I pull myself away, panting.

Red turns, spitting a mouthful of blood on the floor. His grin through that cracked lip never reaches those swollen, dead eyes. *He's a fuckin' sociopath!*

Needing Red's focus, I back off the beating. Seeing the perfect tool, I jerk one of the loose iron pipes from the old sprinkler system falling off the ceiling. I prop my back against the wall, giving the illusion to Red as if I have all the time in the world. I like him stewing over my next move. The black pipe rests at my side, waiting for its call to action.

"Who else's helping you?" Red's jaw locks. "Come on, dumbass. This'll hurt a lot less if you give up details before I call in Dixon."

Seconds tick by.

Red has shut down. With no jokes, those smiles and cackles go quiet. That bitter, sarcastic tone is out the window. What's left is the psychotic mobster and his hard-earned reputation.

His scowl turns nasty. "I shoulda fuckin' killed you when I had the chance."

"Like you could." I laugh, watching the corner of Red's eye twitch when I step off the wall, loose pipe in my hand.

"You were a sitting duck back then, kid." Red's sneer shocks me as I go to stand in front of Red—out of his foot's reach—and wonder if I'm hearing what I think I am.

"I knew you didn't like when Dixon brought me in the ranks. I wasn't a threat to you, dumbass." I shake my head. "I was barely holding my shit together. *You* were the number two until you fucked it all up."

Kill him, my dragon growls, his temper barely hanging by a thread. His cylinders are firing, telling me to kill now, question later.

Red's maniacal laughter chills my spine. "Oh, kid. Oh, God! It's too good. You don't know, do you?" His cackle spreads through the room, body lurching forward in a fit of laughter. He doesn't go far with his arms tied behind him, but it strikes me as odd that Red doesn't have a clue for how fucked he is here.

"You don't have the upper hand, idiot."

His loud cackle of a laugh surprises me... and cringes my eardrums. "Oh, I think I do," he says cagily.

Abandoning the shelves, I walk toward Red, whacking the metal rod I still hold to the back of his chair. The slaps are strong enough to splinter the wood backing, tottering Red forward as he grunts from the battered vibrations. Somehow, it makes him giddier, until years of smoking catches up and those tar covered lungs break into hacking coughs.

This fucker's gone crazy.

I search for something better to tie Red's ass down. He's too injured to shift, but I don't play with crazy. My jerry-rigging of those restraints won't hold indefinitely.

Wheezing, Red lifts his head, a morbid glee crinkling his eyes. "I didn't lay a hand on you that day. Dixon wouldn't let me." That oily mane shakes across his ears. "We were both under orders and Dixon chickened out." Red shakes his head, his unintelligible murmurs ramping up his internal temper better than I could.

My mind feels like a cat in a bathtub: pissed, confused, and frantic to get this shit over with. "What the fuck you talking about? What orders?"

His smirk freaks me out more than a loose pile of fire ants. "I could've had you, dummy. You should kiss my boots, not trap me in this shit-hole." Red's head cocks back, licking his tongue across the open gash in his lip before a brazen smile cracks his face. "Baldy, you wouldn't be breathing if Dixon would've followed orders that day."

Like Red could kick my ass.

"What day?" A niggling feeling in my mind says shut him up while I have the chance. Is he talking about when Dixon brought me in? I was a kid when they found me. That's not useless, it's goddamn nature. Anger boils my blood, but Red's surprisingly pleased with himself. His eyes dance, obviously enjoying stringing me along.

I've had enough. "Spit it out, fucker!"

Red laughs and shakes his head. "I can't believe you're this stupid," he spits, his shoulders straightening like he's proud of whatever odd memory rolls through that demented head of his. "The day we found you in the streets, dummy. You never wondered why Dixon was out front when he was? What did you think once you found out what work he did?" That sketchy cackle fills the basement, muffled under the roar in my ears.

Sharpened nails dig into my clenched fist, the pain of those memories hardening my already murderous heart.

"Shit! You didn't!"

My dragon zeros in on the expanse of vulnerable neck on display as Red's head falls back in hysterical laughter.

He continues stupidly digging his grave between bouts of breathlessness. "Dixon wouldn't let me touch you. Fucker said you were too close to his runt's age. Don't know why he gave a shit, but I followed orders back then like a good little boy. Back 'fore I knew what kinda pansy Dixon really was."

"What are you saying?" I growl, my hands shaking as I lose my grip on reality. He can't mean what I think he does. All these years... Dixon knew who killed my parents.

I worked with Red side-by-side... *was I working with...*

His snarl curls his lips. "I do whatever needs to get done, you cocky little shit. Your pops was late on his payments to Earl. *Loser was late all the time,*" Red mumbles under his breath. "He showed no respect to the people who helped him get that pretty little house. Turned his back on us the *second* he got in your poser neighborhood." Red's face darkens. Does it mirror my own at hearing this despicable man spew garbage about my father? "Your pops thought he was better than the rest of us, kid. Just 'cause he went straight when you were born. But I knew... it was your ma that forced his hand." He cackles again, laughing like we're bonding over old war stories and not the worst day of my life. His sadistic voice chills my bones, freezing my feet to the concrete.

In the recesses of my mind, I hear floorboards croak overhead, but it doesn't register fully. Especially when Red shivers, his face twisting in a disgusting, orgasmic face, like a wave of pleasure washed through him. "*God!* It was stupid fun watching her get hers that morning. *Hah!* When she realized what was happening... you should've seen her face, man! She knew what was next, but I was quick. Couldn't have that bitch get a scream off and warn you—."

Argh!

A wail echoes through the room, but I can't tell if it's out loud or in my head. Either way, Red's last word never sees the light of day. Rage sends me flying across the room in an instant. The dank air breezes past my head with the speed as I descend on that piece of shit.

Red grunts as his body hits the floor, sandwiched between myself and the chair when the sheer force of my weight carries him over. Laughter barks from this psycho on impact, dirtying me with his sick enjoyment of getting his ass kicked. Even with my fist pounding his face, swing after swing, adding bruises and welts, stacking across the others.

My dragon roars, barreling to the surface for a spontaneous shift as his strength surges into my punches. *Get down!* I scowl. *I'm not taking that fucking chance.* Shifting would give Red too big of an opening to gain the upper hand. My dragon fights me with every step, not listening to reason as little prickles tingle across my skin. It's a struggle to keep him at bay as he prepares for transition, shortening my breath.

Still, I work a rapid succession of hits into Red's ribs, his kidneys. I upper cut his chin, nailing whatever body part rocks closest. His face flings to the side, spitting a mouthful of blood on the floor, but still cackling wildly.

"You... you just sat there the whole time." Gasp, spit. "You and your stupid video games." Wheeze, spit.

"Kris! *Oh my God!*" The warbled version of my name cried into the room flips me around. I'm slapped by the shock on Abigail's horrified face at the top of the stairs.

"Abi?" *What's she doing here? How did she find me?*

My mate blanches and I feel like I do the same, my skin going cold just having her here.

She can't be in the same room with this monster! I agree with my dragon on this one.

In a flash, I fly off Red, stopping Abi at the bottom of the stairs before her mad dash makes it any farther into the room. "Abigail, what are you doing here?" I ask, my voice harder than I intend.

She stares, open-mouthed. Her eyes flash anger briefly before slicking with tears, those amethyst jewels taking in my disheveled state. I'm embarrassed for her to see my worst, not only these hideous clothes, but the blood and bruising on my hands... the dirtiness. I didn't want my darkness to tarnish Abigail's light, yet here we are. And I can't stop yet. I will complete what I started. I don't care how low that makes me.

Her hands tangle in my overalls, tugging me toward the door. "You were in pain. I felt it." My body doesn't move, even with that beautiful face pleading. "Let's get out of here, Kris. Fly away. We can go... tonight."

"I can't, Abi. Not yet."

The hope on Abigail's face falls at my denial, her arms crossing stubbornly like a good pout will get her way. For anything else, it could. Not when I need her away from the devil incarnate.

I glance behind her at those gorgeous wings shimmering in this grungy basement, like the grime can't touch her pure heart. Don't know why that surprises me. It shouldn't. It's another reason I don't deserve this woman for my mate. I feel bad that I'm the one fate gave her. Deserved or not, this woman is mine to protect.

It's why I'll say anything to make her listen. "Abigail, I need you out of here," I whisper.

"You need me, Kristopher."

"I really don't, Abigail." I shake my head. "I need you out of here." Shock registers in those beautiful eyes before they harden, the sharp tilt of her chin daring me to repeat my stupidity. Even with my heart torn to shreds over my parents, pushing Abigail away cracks the tiny pieces stitched together. She soothes my soul. I know it.

But I can't have smooth. I need rough to push me through the pain. I'll finish tonight or die trying.

The fire raging in my blood is hard to control, but I shake my head, pulling from her love long enough to be gentle with my mate. I grab her hands, pleading. "Abigail, please. I need you away from Red. No arguing. I need to take care of a few things that you can't witness."

Abigail opens her mouth, the fight nowhere gone in her eyes, but a jarring pain explodes through my shoulder, seizing the air in my lungs. The intensity steals the scream from my lungs, but no sound registers. The agony cuts off the link from my ears to my brain. I see Abi's lips move, but she's mute. Nothing registers.

In a daze, I turn, my steps faltering, stumbling back as my hand slaps at the source of agony in my arm. Wetness coats my fingertips when they draw back. Numbness takes over, dropping my arm by my side with Abigail's muted voice yelling in my face. *Why does she sound so far away?*

Abigail grips my other arm, pulling, but my eyes lock on the mangled, warped view of Red's face and my vision tunnels in a surge of anger. With my one good arm, I shove Red, distancing his threat from my mate, and pounce.

Useless shoulder or not, that man is going to die tonight.

Chapter Thirty-One

Abigail

"Kris!" My shout falls on deaf ears as Kris flings Red halfway across the basement, pouncing on top of him with fists flying at his already bloodied face.

What the hell did I walk in on?

After my dad tracked Kris's phone to that rooftop—which took an act of congress for him to agree to—I had to rely solely on my newly awakened dragon to find our mate.

I don't know how long after Kris left that I landed on that pebbly roof, but his scent was still strong where my virgin wings dropped me like a rock. I was too nervous to drive closer with the sirens lighting up the warehouse district like a summer afternoon. I drove as close as I could, but it wasn't fast enough to catch him.

It took longer and a lot more effort to stay hidden when you're tracking someone I found out. Like parking behind a boarded-up pawn shop instead of the more convenient warehouse parking. The privacy of the vacant lot helped hide the release of my wings, though, with much less panting and pain than the first time.

Because of the craziness of hunting down Kris, I haven't practiced shifting. He took all my mental energy, and honestly, the possibility of pain without his calming touch held me back. Not that my dragon has been easy to live with. From the second he disappeared—*thanks, Dad*—my dragon's rampage inside my head has driven me absolutely mad.

Hence tonight's urgency.

Our mate! my dragon screeches, worsening the headache. She's scratching and clawing her way to the surface, frenzied to save her mate after being denied all week. Especially after I took my head out of the sand and learned my father's role in it all.

I still have a lot of questions, but my first focus is Kris. And after so many years of biting my tongue, I didn't hide my irritation at Dad interfering in my life, nor how stupid he was for allowing Kris to go off half-cocked without backup. It helped some of the built-up rage, but not much. Now, watching my injured mate fight for us both brings all that anger back.

Despite having a metal pipe sticking out of his shoulder, the man's pounding his healthy arm into Red with sloppy swings, his head wobbling. Kris's left fist connects with the ribcage it aims for sending a wild laughter into the room. *What the actual hell has happened to Red? He's off his rocker!*

"Ahh... little girl." Punch. "You see your man?" Grunt. *Ungh!* "How easy he is to take down?" Red mocks, swinging his legs wildly until one sucker punch connects with my mate's jaw.

I scream, "Kris!" But Red already has him flipped to his back, his face going ashen as his stabbed shoulder impacts the floor. Red is on him before my voice stops echoing off the wall, taking advantage of Kris's pain. "Kris, watch out!" I step forward, not knowing what to do with Red's skin prickling. A shift is imminent. I've never been in a fight. And the last time I went against Red, I lost.

But the more they struggle on the ground, Kris trying to right himself, the larger the pool of blood grows under his body. *No!* My hands twitch as Red slams fist after fist into Kris's vulnerable ribcage. I'm screaming, I know, a dark rage churning my stomach, tainting my thoughts. *How dare that sicko hurt him?*

Protect our mate!

My fists clench, vengeance taking over my thoughts as a gut-wrenching howl wails through the room. It draws both sets of eyes my way, their surprise halting the fight as both men watch me double over and gasp for air.

"What the hell?" Red leaps to his feet and darts in my direction.

I can't do anything more than track his motion as my dragon forcefully pushes to the surface. But Kris—always my protector—snatches the back of Red's overgrown mullet and jerks, flinging Red backwards to the concrete floor where Kris laid moments before. The quick motion tilts Kris, and he stumbles, his eyes glazed over with pain. Unfortunately, he's woozy from the loss of blood and Red capitalizes, working the advantage to sweep Kris's legs and knock him to the floor.

And there's nothing I can do about it. My body rebels at the helpless feeling as another round of their wrestling begins. A symphony of cracking bones silences my ears, so I don't hear the slap of fists, the painful moans, the grunts of impact as partially shifted males battle for dominance mere feet away.

That would have terrified me weeks ago. Now, whatever change affects my body clears my mind from the anxiety and fear.

Gradually, my entire being snaps and reshapes into a whole new design… longer, leaner… more powerful. To quiet the pain of the shift, my lungs breath heavily, sucking in an astonishing amount of oxygen needed to build a body I long ago lost hope for. *How? After all this time?*

We will protect our mate, rumbles in my fully formed dragon head. *How did this happen?*

I glance down to where Red and Kris roll on the floor. Details pop clear as day, my vision focused, crisp and sharp, intensifying the colors around me. Even in the dim light, the grain of wood on the rickety stairs, the stains on the concrete, stand out.

Both men shimmer, partially covered with dragon skin. Red's tarnished yellow hide is scarred, discolored from years of battle. However, Kris's masculine hide practically glows to my dragon. It protects his exterior despite the injury to his shoulder, since it's impossible to fully transform without causing more damage. Not to mention the energy and time required to do so.

At least neither man has the ability, but with Red's cheap shot to wound Kris, he gained the upper hand. Normal circumstance would result in Kris's much larger human self as the obvious superior, but Red fights dirty.

"Go... now," Kris says, panting. My dragon's keen hearing picks up the staccato of his heartbeat, syncing it with my own.

No! I scream in my head, becoming ecstatic when Kris's eyes fly to mine, the fated connection linking our emotions as well.

The room deafens with my shout of pain, and Kris's of anger. I spring closer to the rumble on the basement floor, growling when Red has the audacity to hoot his disdain at my smaller dragon. He doesn't show a lick of fear in her presence, pissing her spirit off even more. She snaps our newly pointed teeth in Red's direction with a snarl. Saliva builds in my muzzle. Her craving for Red's blood grows stronger with his belittlement.

My narrowed tongue flicks out, tasting a tinge of Red's blood in the air. Razor-sharp spikes lift along my spine, resembling a pissed-off canine ready for battle.

Abigail, go now! booms a frantic bass in my head.

I'm startled until I realize it's Kris. His eyes zero in on my fully formed dragon for the first time. Even from his vulnerable position, my mate smiles his appreciation at the compact, blinding white stack of supernatural muscle. I feel Kris's confidence, that he feigned weakness during my shift to steal Red's attention. Now with his shoulder limitations, and Red shifting his nastiness back to Kris after dismissing me, a renewed panic sours the air.

His prone position isn't an act anymore.

Mate, leave me. I open my mouth to roar in defiance but hesitate hearing Kris's plea inside my head. *Please, baby. I need to know you're safe.*

I glance at my newly formed claws, nervous to risk a battle with Red again. But I don't know how much longer Kris can last. He grows paler by the second.

What are you waiting for? My spirit growls her frustration, clearly trying to overpower my human hesitancy.

Red's evil eyes turn their sneer on me. "You're next, bitch."

In a flash, Kris's non-injured hand flies up, latching onto Red's Adam's apple. He tugs but can't pull his neck free. The maroon color of his face deepens, his hands gripping at Kris's wrist for release. I notice too late that Red is within reach of the thick length of chain that tied his wrists when I entered the room. Snatching it, his arm lifts high over Kris's head, preparing to swing.

No damn way.

Instinct takes over, whipping my tail through the air in an arc that nails a vibrating shot against Red's ear. It knocks him off Kris, his surprised screech ringing my ears. "You bitch!" Red lands on his ass, his hand pressing against the blood oozing from his head.

I flinch, but stand my ground against Red's vile eyes long enough for Kris to right himself. He staggers to his feet, coming to a defensive stance beside me. His face hardens as he jerks the metal rod protruding from his shoulder with only a grunt, readying for battle. He's a lot calmer than I could ever be. "Two against one, Red. Your ass feeling luc—"

Red lunges, cutting Kris off mid-sentence. He flies into action, throwing himself in the way to save me from the brunt of Red's attack. Their two battered bodies slam mid-way with a thunderous clap. My dragon rushes to the surface, ripping a banshee wail from my lungs that startles even me. I wasn't fast enough. The momentum of Kris's much larger body tumbled him over Red's head, leaving my mate sprawled on his back again.

Before he can recover, the slimeball gets his bearings and pounces.

This time, I'm there.

I stalk closer, feeling optimistic as Kris pummels Red's ribcage from below. "You goddamn." *Slam. Grunt.* "Son-of-a—" *Jab. Groan.* Every swing from Kris meets with a howl of pain. *How is Red holding on?*

Blow after blow glances off Kris's hard muscle between the pain. Until one lands against his temple with a sickening crack. My protective spikes stand on end.

Stop! I shriek, forgetting that it's in my head.

My dragon acts fast, springing to Red's back with her impressive hind legs, digging our sharp teeth into his scruff and biting down until the nasty man yelps and loses focus. I barely hold on to my gag reflex. Red's taste is god-awful, a mix of oily dander, noxious musk, and coppery blood sourness.

Sucking air through my sensitive nostrils doesn't help, either. It only brings more of Red's filth into my lungs. Still, my jaws maintain their lock, not giving in, even as Red flings and tosses his body, desperate to knock me off.

"Get off me, you witch!" Red's curse cuts off when my entire—granted smaller—dragon body wraps across his back, sinking my talons into the meat of his arms and ripping back.

Get off my mate!

"God da—!"

Even with lesser strength, I dislodge Red from Kris with a battle of snarls and growls echoing off the cinderblock walls. His attention is on me now. I lock eyes with a blinking Kris, noticing he's not as injured as I assumed, but Red's shifty ass takes advantage of my distraction. A bony elbow connects with the underside of my jaw, sending my dragon skidding across the floor with a yelp.

She groans in my head, skittering to right herself over the deafening vibration of Kris's roar shaking the basement walls. Red pounces before I have my feet under me, his weight knocking me back with a bruising intensity. His arm cocks, preparing for a swing that will probably knock me out. I brace, squeezing my eyes shut against the pain, but... nothing.

Instead, a hollow thud startles them open just as the blood explodes from Red's head, splattering my face. His dented skull is the most horrifying thing I've ever seen. Now it's burned into my memory. My stomach rolls as I shove his crumpled body to the floor beside me. The vision above, of my battle worn, protective hero standing guard over me sends a wave of relief through my system. His fist holds the bloodied pipe he tore from his shoulder, the one he obviously used to end this for good.

With one boot, Kris slides Red's limp body farther away, his eyes lit red with the fire of hatred. "Abi, are you ok?" he asks, his breathing taxed as he turns back. He tosses the bloody pipe to the other side of the room so he can reach for me.

I spare one more glance to Red's vacant eyes and say thanks that I'll never see them again. The ones above me, staring down with so much concern, are my sole focus now. I nod at Kris, trying hard to look tougher than what I feel inside. It may be wrong, but I don't feel a lick of guilt over that man. He caused so many people so much pain. His death is a gift to the world, nothing else.

Chapter Thirty-Two

Abigail

Red is gone.

I don't know what to do if I don't have to fear this scumbag. It's monumental. Even Kris's aura is lighter, the toxic torch of vengeance he normally carries finding its mark in the dead body a few feet away.

I do know, I want my human form back. I want Kris's thick arms wrapped around me. After a week of missing Kris, and then almost losing him multiple times tonight, I'm itching to return to a new normal, whatever that is. Slowly, the transformation takes over. A calm peace washing over me that reins my dragon in a lot easier than the first time. Concentrating on my mate lessens the pain until she fades completely. My face softens to its human shape. The protective hide disappears, becoming my normal pale skin.

Kris's eyes melt, love shining from the emerald depths with the brightest smile splitting his face even with the busted lip. I don't miss the way his gaze stays above my lips, respectfully avoiding my nudity. *Dammit! Why couldn't we have this somewhere I had a change of clothes post-shift?*

"Abi?"

I smile. "I'm pretty good... considering." Except.. my eyes fall to Red's corpse. "Are we going to be in trouble?"

Kris smiles, extending his hand to lift my weight off the grimy floor. His thumb traces the soft skin along my jaw, keeping my face angled to stare deep into my soul. My smile widens when Kris is the only vision I see. *I'll take it.*

"Never, baby," he says, his voice raspy. "This was always the end goal. Your dad might be pissed he didn't get his own jabs in, but there was no way around it."

I sigh, knowing he's right.

Thankfully, the most beautifully intense eyes distract me from worrying any further. Kris folds me in his warmth, one large hand tangling in my hair and tugging back. His nose runs along my temple, nuzzling softly with a shaky breath. The light touch is at odds with his all-consuming hold, squeezing me until I can barely breathe. I don't care that the rough fabric of his coveralls scratches my naked skin, or that I'm on display in the first place. Kris's touch is a balm, nothing else matters.

When he finally pulls back, searing me with the heat in his eyes, I'm gone. "Abigail, you know I got you. Nothing like this will ever touch you again." His voice is hard, adamant in his vow, and the confidence seals my fate.

It's then I remember the significant blood loss Kris suffered in the last thirty minutes and I gasp, ashamed that I'm wallowing in his comfort instead of caring for my mate. "Kris, your shoulder!" I press his arm, aiming to turn the giant hulk, but his grimace churns the guilt already roiling my stomach.

"It's fine," he says, but for once, Kris gives in to my manipulation without a fight. That alone tells me his wound is serious.

Carefully, I guide Kris by the elbow to the chair Red knocked over, righting it before Kris flops his weight onto the rickety wood. The grossness of the flayed skin on his back must show on my face because Kris chuckles loudly when I pull my hand back, not wanting to injure his shoulder anymore.

"It's not as bad as it looks," he promises. I cross my arms and stare down the stubborn idiot... waiting. His laughter soothes my worry a bit, so does the color returning to his annoyingly handsome face.

"Kristopher, you were about to fall over a few minutes ago. I have to bandage you somehow."

He smirks. "That would be a first, princess. You know how many times I've been injured on the job?"

"Too many, judging by all the scars."

"Hah! You're damn right there. With how fast our species heals, I'd be a pussy to worry about every little gash and broken rib. We go to Doc for the big stuff... that's where the scars come from, otherwise I just wait out the pain until I can shift again."

I glower at that, but head to the shelves along the wall, mumbling under my breath. The pile of rags there look moderately clean. I pray they don't cause an infection because I know the chance of getting Kris to the doctor is slim to none.

"What was that? I couldn't hear you." The man has the nerve to laugh again, even knowing I'm worried.

To say playful Kris is frustrating is a colossal understatement. "Do you not remember that you were two steps from passing out earlier?"

His eyes narrow. "I was fine."

I bite back a squeal of irritation. "Ugh! Men!" I groan, but like a dutiful nurse, I huff back to his side with my handful of the least dusty towels I could find. "You know, after almost dying tonight, I'd think you'd be more grateful that I'm here to take care of you."

At that, Kris's expression shutters. "You shouldn't have been here in the first place, Abigail. Red is dangerous." He glances over at the immobile lump on the floor. "Was."

A dark cloud of what could have been hangs in the air.

"Yeah, well... you were hurt, so bend over, you big lug." I close the distance, adding a little extra sway for Kris's distraction. He chuckles, but props his elbows on his knees, dutifully giving me access.

"All right, pit bull, do your worst."

I growl playfully and set out to wipe the dried blood from his back. Thankfully, the sink in the corner helps and before long, I'm able to see the two-inch hole in Kris's skin a lot clearer.

"At least you've stopped bleeding." That must be why Mr. Tough Guy's snark is back. Seems like Kris's macho-man routine is directly proportional to the color returning to his face. "But what's the deal back here?"

His head twists over his shoulder to see what I'm pointing at. "I told you. We heal fast."

"Yeah, but Kristopher, this is ridiculous." I tie two ends of fabric together, creating a make-shift sling... not that it's needed. "How is your flesh that was pouring blood ten minutes ago, already mending?" At this point, the only need for a bandage is to decrease scarring.

Kris lifts his brow. "You sound annoyed that I'm not about to fall over."

"No, no... ugh! Stop it! You know what I mean. I've never seen this type of thing up close. My experience so far has been with rapidly healing razor cuts and scraped knees as a kid." I pause. "I was always slower than all you guys, anyway." Kris hears my low grumble and nods, his eyes falling to his hands as I finish tying off his bandage. I want to ask what the forlorn look is about, but he straightens up before I can.

"Will this interfere with my wings?" he asks, wiggling his injured shoulder.

I glance at the spot where Kris's wings usually extend. "I don't think so. But it's gonna hurt."

"Don't worry about that. I've had worse." With lightning flaring in his eye, Kris grasps my chin between his fingers, lightly tilting my head to look up at him. "You ready to go deal with your dad?" My eyes close against the tears threatening. Whenever I think about Dad, anger burns inside; all the stress and pain he's caused in the name of money and power.

"No." Adamantly, I shake my head and Kris loosens his grip. His fingers slide into the tangled hair at the back of my neck and scouring my face for hidden meaning. I'm more determined than ever, though. "After how Dad handled this past week, I think he deserves a little payback. Don't you?" I hold Kris's gaze, burying the morose feelings that pop up thinking of Dad's lies.

I interlock our fingers, digging deep for the strength to get through these next steps. I only hope Kris doesn't fight me on it. We have to extract ourselves from under Dad's thumb. We have to stay in charge from here on out if we're starting our new lives, no matter what hell we have to pay.

Even if I'm freaking out inside, my heartbeat thundering in my chest.

On the outside, however—and to Kris—I hide behind the proudest, most shit-eating grin I've ever used in my life. I'm going to take what I want for once.

"What do you mean?" Kris asks, tightening his fingers in mine.

"I mean—making me wait for you." The more I think about it, the angrier I get. "It's horseshit, Kris."

"We have to deal with him, Abi."

"We do. But we don't have to do anything tonight." I try to hide the plea in my voice and hold a stiff upper lip. Just in case Kris wants to argue, I smash my lips against his in a rough kiss and shush any further attempts to argue a moot point. I don't even care that our teeth clank or how clumsy I am. This heat is the only thing I need, not some tête-à-tête with dear ole dad.

"Stop thinking," I whisper, licking at Kris's lower lip as a distraction. His laugh vibrates against my mouth, but he doesn't pull away far.

"As you wish, my princess." Smoothly, Kris lifts under my hips and I circle my legs around his tight waist with a surprised giggle, excited to my very core that he's giving in to my way of thinking. On the way to the stairs, Kris drops soft kisses along my shoulder while somehow managing the steep incline without tumbling us both.

"Kris, you're gonna hurt yourself," I argue. Kris shouldn't be carting me around like a sack of groceries, not with his injury.

"Oh, yeah?" He scoffs indignantly, scratching that five-day-old scruff along the line of my neck, just to make me squirm. My hands grip those massive shoulders for dear life, trying desperately to avoid his injury and keep myself upright as Kris hoists my weight higher with his good arm. The problem is, the more Kris licks and moans his pleasure along my ultra-sensitive neck, the less I care about any fallout, like actually... falling.

This, I've wanted all along.

At the top of the stairs, Kris pulls back, his chest pumping heavily between every kiss, between every breath. "So... what's next?" He smirks, but I appreciate the give by Kris even asking that question.

Still, I can't stop myself from poking the dragon, just a little bit. I wiggle my increasingly wet center against the front of those god-awful coveralls and turn the tables on his tease. My fingers find the latches at his shoulders and make quick work of undoing them while I nibble a line of kisses up Kris's sharp jaw.

"You know, since I made all this effort to come up here and save you." Kris coughs to cover his laugh but I ignore the interruption completely, smiling when every little lick I give Kris ramps his heartbeat. "I thought... we could find something to entertain ourselves. Somewhere we won't breathe ten pounds of dust like this hellhole."

The cocky grin that spreads his face tells me I succeeded; I broke through Kris's tight coil of control. "My place then?" His growl is low, thick with need, rough enough that my dragon hums her agreement inside my head.

Is he finally ready to take that final step? To solidify our connection.

"God, yes!" I twist my body so his last piece of clothing drops to the floor, the last piece separating my heat from his wall of muscle.

He grins. "And why do I have to be naked? All I need are my wings."

I giggle at my sudden brazenness, my heart soaring as Kris heads for the door. "S'only fair." I shrug, smiling so wide, I fear it will crack my face. I love this playfulness, seeing Kris's joy lighten the darkness he usually carries.

Outside, under the cover of heavy oak trees, Kris unleashes those powerful wings and takes to the air. Neither of us says a word. It's not needed. One day we'll fly hand in hand into the sky, but for tonight, my mate's protective arms are absolutely perfect.

Chapter Thirty-Three

Abigail

BY THE TIME KRIS lands outside his two-story, slightly dilapidated complex, my fingers and toes have frozen through. In fact, every inch of my skin is sheer ice. Or it feels that way with winter nipping in the air, like the first snow will be any day now.

I glance around the quiet parking lot, noticing that Kris dropped us in a darkened corner in the back, right under a busted street light that I'd bet my favorite tea set on Kris having knocked out himself to give better cover. That extra cover means the only light that could give us away is the impending sunrise. Which, judging by the silvery hue washing through the sky, it could be anytime now.

"Kris, I'm naked," I whisper, wondering if there's anyone awake at this early hour.

"Woman, you'd think I'd bring you in public naked if there was a single scent of male in the air?"

"Male? It's not just men," I say, annoyed. "I don't want you naked in front of any females, either!" My mate playfully nips at the tip of my ear, chuckling darkly as he squeezes my—very visible—rear still sitting in his hands from our flight. I screech at the grope, smacking Kris's uninjured shoulder. He doesn't even flinch. *Damn steel core muscles! "Kris! Stop it!* It's got to be four a.m."

He laughs louder this time, my body shaking as he nearly doubles over. "You're the one that quacked like a duck!" I pull back, mouth hanging open as Kris tries to sober himself. "Besides, if someone sees us landing, I don't think their first thought is that we're naked."

"Uh." I pause. He's right, but I don't know what to do with a new, lighthearted Kris. Smartass, yes. But a content smile stretching those perfect lips is... well, it's something I've never seen before. "All right, who are you and what have you done with Kristopher?"

He smirks, the dark promise in his eyes reminding me of who I'm dealing with here. "I'm still me, Abigail," he says, striding through rows of parked cars for the closest section of apartments like a man on a mission.

I grin. "Thank God for that!"

Kris grunts, shaking his head as we approach the light pink façade of his building. His side-eye would be hilarious if not for the vulnerability hidden in those green jewels of his as he takes the concrete stairs at the end of the corridor two at a time.

Clearing my throat, I laugh when Kris rushes up the stairs with faster than human speed. I'm thankful for the darkened corridor, considering our current state of dress and the fact that our bodies slap together like dry-humping teenagers. Just my hips bouncing against his rock-hard abdomen sends a surge of volcanic level of hormones through my system.

I swear, if Kris doesn't let me down soon, I foresee an embarrassing self-implosion—or seismic orgasm—in the very near future.

"I can walk, you know," I argue.

"Congratulations." His tone says there's no chance I'm getting down and I couldn't care less. Still, my smile widens at his ridiculousness and I scooch closer, involuntarily writhing as my legs tighten around his waist. I catch his eyes in a challenge, sliding my wetness against his naked skin.

He growls, finally reaching the top floor and slowing his speed. "Watch it there, princess. You deserve more than a bang in a dirty hallway. But you're pushing that possibility *really* close." Kris's labored breath adds fire to his words, but it's his vice grip on my hips, locking my warmth against his hard length that does me in.

"Kris," I pant, cringing at the neediness I can't hide.

"A few more feet, baby." This time he brings my body in, pausing in the hallway. Those enormous hands wrap my back, pulling my shoulders in tight and leaving not a lick of air between us. "Abigail, you sure about this?" he asks, drowning me in his soulful eyes. "It will kill me, but I will wait. If my dragon wouldn't stage a protest, I'd say we should wait. Talk to your dad first." My heart catches, but the soft caress of his lips eases my worry. That he lingers, letting our breaths mingle as one, muddles my brain. *How do I word what I want to say?*

"Kris, I have wanted you since the first day I saw your sad heart and wanted to make it better. I've wanted the protective middle schooler who beat up my bullies and bandaged my scrapes. You were my best friend back then, and you didn't even know it." A lone tear slips down my cheek and Kris's face softens as he kisses it away. "You were also the name I drew inside little hearts in my notebook and carved into trees. I prayed to the gods or God that you would see me as the woman for you. I prayed for my dragon to show herself, so I might be worthy of you."

Kris gasps, pulling away to search my face. "Abigail, no, baby. It's not..."

"*Shh.*" I silence him with a quick kiss, hugging the back of his head to mine and continuing before I lose the nerve. "Kris, I'm just saying, you are it for me and you always have been. I'm not waiting to talk to my dad because he doesn't matter. You matter, and we matter. And that's it." I swallow, battling the nerves trying to shake my body. "Kris, I love you."

His head jerks back, choking on his quick intake of air. I feel a blush creep over my skin that I just professed love, naked, in a breezeway of an apartment complex that smells slightly of the neighbor's pizza box sitting a few doors down.

"Abigail."

I think he's going to say more, but Kris shakes his head in disbelief, his lips crashing down hard on mine, not a gentle thought left as his tongue dips past my lips. He tastes freely, our tongues battling in a sensual dance as he strides forward, coming to a stop outside of apartment 324, where he reaches an arm up over the faded forest-green door, not losing his grip on our kiss, nor dropping me to the ground.

Instinctively, my thighs and my arms tighten, having no argument for smushing my breasts against the valley of muscle in Kris's chest. My nipples respond to the close contact until I see what he's pulled down from over the door and I scramble from his hulking arms, putting distance between myself and one of my worst fears.

"What the hell, Kris? A wasp's nest?" My heart thuds in my chest, ready to hightail it away from this thing at the first buzz. Only Kris's chuckle rumbling down the hallway prevents me from scurrying farther than I do. I watch in awe as he casually flips the top of a—apparently fake—mud nest and lifts a tiny gold item from inside.

"Key," he says, grinning.

I shake my head, fighting a smile now that my heart rate's slowly returning to normal. "That's just wrong!" Not wanting to let him off the hook yet, I cross my arms over my still naked chest and raise an eyebrow, seriously doubting my intimidation at this point, but still I argue. "A girl could use some warning, you know."

This time, Kris's brow arches to match mine as he holds his arms out wide. A hulking load of manliness is on display for my perusal. "Where am I supposed to hide a key after a shift?" he asks, challenging.

I don't think he'd appreciate the first suggestion that popped to mind, so I take my time looking Kris up and down like I'm truly debating his options. Really, I'm enjoying an eyeful of man-candy: from the smattering of light blond hair covering his tattooed pecs to the ridges leading my eyes south, the narrowed V highlighting those trim hips, and the sinew of muscle building to an impressive set of thighs. I hum, watching Kris's face beam with pride the longer I stare. His obvious arousal twitches as my scent circles the air between us.

"Abi, you need to get inside."

Without waiting, Kris scoops me into his arms, cradle-style, and I laugh, running my nose along the enticing scent at Kris's neck, licking and nibbling at the thick vein calling to my dragon. She's loving the feel of my nails scratching the back of that buzzed head. The moan that slips from my lips causes Kris to fumble the loose key, taking more than one shot to get the door open. His grumbled curses only make it harder, but all I can focus on is the heat pumping between us, Kris's scent, and the anticipation of what's to come when we cross that threshold.

"Bout fuckin' time," he groans as the door opens and he carries me straight into the living room.

"Where's your room?" I ask, not lifting my head from the heaven of Kris's neck. To say I'm surprised when my feet hit the floor and I'm tossed behind Kris's back is a massive understatement. "What the—?" Kris's warning growl stops me short. The sound rips through the room with so much venom, the hair on my arms stands on end.

What the hell?

"Kris," I hiss, my fingers digging into Kris's sides to move this im-movable force and figure out what the problem is.

He doesn't budge.

"What are you doing in my apartment?" I stop.

The voice that answers tosses a bucket of ice water on my heated hormones. "Dad!" I lean around the brick wall of Kris to find the eyes of the last person I want to face naked. *I thought I'd have more time to prepare for this conversation.*

"*God!* I can't unsee that!" Dad shakes his head, jerking his eyes to the ceiling and away from the picture in front of him. I'd laugh at the stupidity of Dad rubbing his eyes like he's trying to erase his retinas, if I didn't feel like my skin was a roasted tomato from the embarrassment as well. "*Shit!*" Dad jumps from the couch like his pants are on fire, his face crinkled with disgust. This whole situation has *the most awkward moment of my life* written all over it. "What the hell are you doing, Abigail?" he asks, walking to the sliding door on the opposite wall.

"I was invited. What are you doing here?"

Dad's spine goes rigid. His head dips, inspecting an invisible speck on the vertical blinds instead of what he doesn't want to see... Kris snuggling me naked like the most natural thing in the world.

I'm even more thankful for Kris when he widens his stance to hide most of my nudity from my father because... *ick!* Doesn't matter how accustomed dragons are to nakedness post-shift. This is my first time and I appreciate Kris's kid gloves.

Dad's sigh is heavy. "I knew this would happen, eventually." His hushed whisper immediately triggers that horrible old feeling of disappointing my dad. I'm tossed back to when I came of age and couldn't shift, or when I had a friend that he didn't approve of or brought home a *B* which is under the standards for a Dixon. I know that Dad doesn't see me as a competent adult ready to find her mate.

Hell, he's not used to me standing up for myself at all.

Right now, those once immovable shoulders fall heavy, the weight of the world aging Dad right before my eyes. Even his salt and pepper hair stands on end, likely from hours of running his fingers through it since I dropped out of contact. Briefly, that familiar guilt twists my stomach into knots. I'm all Dad has left... since Mom passed.

For that reason, I want to be as gentle as possible, but I'm not willing to give up Kris either. My body and my heart already know Kris is mine; it just took my mind longer to believe.

Finally, Kris breaks our uncomfortable standoff. "Sir, we asked you a question." His gravely rumble is defensive, yet somehow respectful, even with the agitation rolling off his back in waves. He doesn't seem the least bit intimidated. *How?* My knees are shaking, waiting for my dad's reaction. I seriously wish I had found some clothes between the Carolina mountains and here.

"You dropped off, son. I knew you'd come back here eventually, so I waited." Dad peeks his head in our direction, a disturbed mix of shock and resignation playing in his eyes.

With one eye on my dad, I massage the tension out of Kris's corded muscles. My mate looks ready to spring, which would be a horrible start to our future, even if my dad did break into his apartment. Unless we want to go on the run.

Chapter Thirty-Four

Abigail

"How long?" Anger rattles through Kris's voice, but outwardly, he's calm, standing tall and proud, despite Dad catching us in one of the most vulnerable situations a man can face—nude with a mate to protect.

Dad drags in a deep breath and flips to face us, meeting only Kris's eyes and nothing else. "I've been here a few days, off and on. Betty was parked outside, so I knew you'd be back." Dad shrugs, his little poke at Kris's love for his car, cutting enough tension to unclench Kris's fists. Dad clears his throat. "Kristopher, can you get my daughter a covering, for Christ's sake? Then we'll talk."

Kris grumbles but dutifully tucks my body in front of his, shielding my exposure as he guides me left through the only door in the tiny one-bedroom apartment.

To his credit, the beige room is tidy, even with the barebones bachelor style. The gray Berber carpet has faded with age, but it's obvious Kris made the bed before he left on his mission. The navy comforter tucks neatly at the edges without the girly additions of throw pillows I have in my room. An antique dresser sits along one wall, the mirror removed and, in its place, a tv sits facing the bed. Not a stitch of clothing is out of place, neither on the floor nor thrown across any furniture like I'd expect from a guy's apartment.

"Nice." I smile up at Kris, who tucks me into his warmth so I won't see the slight blush on his face.

"It's not much, but I always figured I'd make a home eventually with my mate. I didn't want to waste the money for needless stuff if I'm the only one to enjoy it."

"I think that's sweet." I stand up on my tiptoes and plant a light kiss on Kris's lips. He sighs when I pull back, his hands threading into my hair to keep our heads close.

"It's me and you, Abigail," he says against my lips. "No matter what your dad says." I nod as Kris drops another kiss, marking his words with the promise of more. Slowly, his lips become more demanding, each tease of his tongue heating my blood until I'm more than ready to hop back into his powerful arms and pick right back up where we left off.

A throat clearing from the living room startles us apart with guilty smiles. Well, mine feels guilty. Kris looks like the cat who ate the canary with his grin, and I can't help giggling like one of my fourth graders.

Until Kris bends those sinful lips to my ear. "To be continued." His sexy promise sends a thrill straight to my core, liquifying my insides as he works his sexual torture on my body.

Those gentle nibbles to my earlobe pull a sharp gasp that I can't hold back, even with my father one room over. Kris's hands tighten, pulling my head back to trail bites along the edge of my jaw. By the time he pulls back, I'm panting. My fingers hurt from the grip they have on Kris's shoulders.

His forehead rests on mine, our ragged breaths mingling with pent up passion ready to explode. "Let's get this over with." It's not that I want to leave. The quicker we clear my father out of here, the sooner I can focus on the tattooed temptation in front of me. I'm ready for the more pleasurable part of our evening.

"Where did your brain just go?" Kris cocks an eyebrow, correctly reading my naughty train of thought.

My cheeks heat and I scoff. "Nowhere." That's the problem with dating a shifter; you can't hide a single emotion from them, especially arousal. It pains me to pull away from the arms I've dreamed of for years, but we need to concentrate. I wave a finger up and down my body. "Clothes."

Kris smirks but lets me get away with the change of subject since my dad is crashing around his kitchen, slamming cabinet doors and making all kinds of racket to draw us out of the bedroom. "Subtle," he huffs, heading for his dresser. He collects a pair of boxers for each of us and a plain black t-shirt for me to wear over top.

I hold up the shirt, smiling when the hem reaches mid-thigh. "Guess I won't need pants. You could give me a belt and I'd make this thing into a dress."

Kris grins. "I like seeing you in my clothes. Not my fault you're all itty-bitty."

"*Ugh!* Don't make fun of my size." I smack my palm across Kris's freakishly hard shoulder, stinging my hand. I jerk it back with a pout and shake out the pain.

"Careful there," Kris says, kissing my palm to ease the burn. "Can't have you hurting yourself, now." His smile spreads so wide, I worry for a second his face is going to crack, until his mouth opens, and I want to smack that satisfied look right off his face. "Plus, if you think you'll be interested in spanking, it's going to be the other way around, princess." I jerk my hand away, smacking a few lighter hits to his chest that don't hurt nearly as bad as the others, but it only makes his laughter boom through the room louder than before.

To save my dignity, I snatch the offered shirt over my head and slide on Kris's oversized boxers, so my dad doesn't think we're up to other things in this room with all the noise Kris is making. "Let's go," I growl, pretending to be angry as I roll my waistband over a few times, so I don't have a wardrobe malfunction the moment I step out there.

I turn for the door, but Kris is hot on my heels. In two steps, he catches up, wrapping my waist from behind. His hands splay sensuously across my belly, pulling my hips against his still hard erection. I gasp, fighting my smile as Kris leans over, his height dwarfing my smaller frame, much the way his clothes do.

"Are you mad, princess?" His voice is a purr, his soft breath tickling my ear, sending a shiver down my spine as those soft lips move to caress my neck.

I tilt for better access, and he knows the answer. Kris chuckles, taking advantage of winning this argument, even if it's a fake one. "Not fair." The smallest touch from this man makes me weak, but I don't care. I love the way Kris's wide hands grip my waist, how his tongue licks a firm line up to my ear in the best tease. The delicious pressure tumbles butterflies through my stomach with an eagerness for what's to come.

"I don't play fair, sweetheart. But I do promise to take care of you... every step of the way." I hear the smile in his voice as he drops an almost chaste kiss to my cheek from behind. My feelings right now are in the opposite hemisphere from chaste, but Kris straightens up and slides on his boxers with a self-satisfied fire in his eyes. *Damn him.*

I reach for the handle, holding while Kris heads for the closet and dresses in a pair of basketball shorts that dips tantalizingly close to where I want to explore. My hands twitch. "Eyes up, woman. I need the blood flowing north for this conversation with your father." I try to stifle my laughter at watching Kris straighten himself in his shorts. He stalks forward, and I'm frozen in his sexy trance, desperate for another melting kiss so I can get my hands on those abs. Kris squashes that idea by stopping a few feet away, his finger circling for me to turn toward the door. "That way, Abigail. I can't touch you again or we'll never leave this room."

I let my eyes roam his fine, masculine lines from top to bottom. "Shame." I shrug like it's no skin off my back, knowing very well I'm burning up inside.

"What?" Kris narrows his eyes at my quip, primed to pounce.

My eyes go wide as he lunges playfully, trying to tackle me but missing when I jerk the door open and dart through. I squeal, bouncing and dodging down the hallway with Kris hot on my heels. I'm at the other end before he catches me, wrapping an arm around my waist as we skid into the kitchen laughing like children on a playground. Dad's mouth gapes, his face frozen in comical shock where he paused his search of Kris's fridge.

Gradually, his brows lower from that salt and pepper hairline, his eyes going shiny as he closes the fridge and leans against it. "My God! I have never seen you laugh like that," he says, swallowing thickly.

"Dad, you've heard me laugh." Kris squeezes my middle and I feel the silent promise—we stand together.

"Not you, baby girl." Dad nudges his head to my steadfast protector. "Kristopher... man, you've never laughed." Dad clears his throat. "At least not like that."

He walks to stand in front of us, and I tense. Kris tucks me to his side, offering extra support. Dad smirks. It's not like I think he'd hurt me, but I'm not keen on getting screamed at either.

"I owe you two a load of apologies." He reaches forward and lifts my hands with a tight squeeze. My mouth falls open. I'm sure I look like Dad did earlier when we walked into the kitchen. He glances at Kris again, his face hardening. "But first, I assume our threat is neutralized since y'all are here and looking more playful than I wanna think about."

Kris nods. "It is, sir. We were planning to debrief you tomorrow after resting up."

Dad harrumphs. "Yeah, well. There's plenty for us to talk about, including dropping out of contact when there's a threat on your tail and not telling your old man." I sputter, searching for an explanation he'll accept, but Dad just plows through. "You too, Kristopher. I tell you that you're like my own son and then both of you go off half-cocked and almost give me a heart attack."

My eyes fly to Kris's. He hadn't told me that, not that we've had a lot of time for pillow talk in this past week's drama. "Dad—"

"No, Abigail. I'm not angry... exactly." I feel that tightening in my chest, waiting for the other shoe to drop. But Dad stops suddenly, shaking his head. "This is a pitiful apology. How 'bout some dinner?" He looks at Kris. "No offense, son, but you ain't got jack-shit for food in this place."

That Kris turns pink again is incredibly cute. The man has blushed more in the last twelve hours than I've seen since he hit puberty.

"Yeah, uh... sorry, sir." Kris rubs the back of his neck with the hand not holding me. "I can order pizza."

Nervously, I glance at Dad. We haven't eaten pizza together since we lost Mom. That was our Friday night go-to. We'd chat about our week and make plans for the weekend. Usually, it was an outing for me and Mom with a guard on watch, but sometimes Dad would come along.

Dad nods, looking down at our connected hands. I didn't miss his watery eyes, though. "Sounds like a plan. My treat." Without another word, he turns for the living room, moving to sit on the rustic couch where we found him.

Kris glances down, a look of pure confusion wrinkling his forehead. "I guess we're ordering pizza," he says with a laugh. "Why don't you go keep your dad company and I'll finish getting dressed?"

I nod, but snuggle into his side before he can walk away. "Thank you," I whisper into his chest, loving those strong arms circling my shoulders, making me feel safe and loved. Despite Kris's hard edges, I know he'll always be my safe place to land.

"No need to thank me, Abigail. I'd do anything for you. Don't care what." Kris drops a kiss to the top of my head, inhaling a lungful of my scent, which warms my heart. Until he pops upright and playfully turns my shoulders toward my father. "There you go, now. Scoot." The brute pats my bottom to get me going, laughing sneakily as he darts away from my retaliating swing.

"Grrl," I growl playfully over my shoulder but take off for the living room, wondering what kind of fun a naughty Kris would get up to.

Chapter Thirty-Five

Abigail

THREE HOURS AND A full belly later, Kris and I snuggle together on his couch in shock.

Over a dinner of meat lovers' pizzas and garlic knots, we regurgitated the details of our last week, answering questions here and there. Both overprotective men chastised me for going off with no backup and dropping out of contact. But I flipped the accusation against them, by pointing out their secrecy and keeping me out of the loop are what drove me to find my own solutions.

The hardest part was going over our confrontation with Red. Dad couldn't sit still. He paced the small living room until I feared for the health of Kris's carpet. We explained the entire evening, from our different points of view, Dad's scowl deepening the more we talked. I gasped multiple times during Kris's retelling, worried about his confrontation with the cops, the risky accident. I can't help but worry about the other men in the incident, too. I don't know them, but if they had Red in cuffs, they can't be all bad.

I remind myself to follow up on that later.

What surprised me the most wasn't Dad's reaction to Red's betrayal, it wasn't the risk of exposure. It was Dad's reaction to the fact—shared by Kris—that my long dormant dragon is out and proud. He boasted about how strong she fought to defend her mate, beaming with enough pride that I couldn't help but blush.

Together, we laughed at our species' transitioning woes over pizza.

"How are you feeling, baby girl? First shifts hurt," Dad says, stating the obvious. He glances at Kris, questioning, like he's going to have some magical insight into my feelings. *He might. But he'd never share them.*

"I'm fine, Dad." He looks off-kilter, his eyes swirls of stormy Atlantic, clueless for what to say or what to do.

He tops off my glass of cheap chianti, which was all the restaurant would deliver—for a hefty extra charge, of course. We both watch the liquid fill Kris's plain glass tumbler, silence thick in the air. Dad straightens, dropping the bottle to the table with extra weight behind his frustrations. His hand grips the neck for extra heartbeats, increasing my anxiety. *What's he waiting to say?*

Suddenly, Dad wrenches away from the bottle and I feel the comforting arms from my childhood wrap me in the tightest hug. "Dad," I choke as one larger-than-life hand presses my head to his soft middle.

That sweetness is all it takes for my emotions to explode. Tears spill over, but I squeeze my eyes closed, fighting and losing the battle to not burst into a blubbering idiot just when these two started seeing me as more than a little girl.

Thank God the rest of the night went off with less emotion. To say I was proud of the change in Dad is an understatement. His concern was Kris and I, and our health after the fight, not his business. Of course, we verified what Red told us, that Earl and JB are dead... that the cops invaded Earl's warehouse and rescued the girl—which I was extremely happy to hear.

The only point that almost crashed everything was learning Dad was the root cause of my inability to shift.

He can claim all he wants that he kept me and Kris apart so he could raise us in the same house, but there were a lot of years after Kris moved in with the older crew. Kris and I rigidly processed the information thrown at us in the name of clearing consciences and starting over. Talk about difficult. It's not like Dad altering the course of our lives is easy to forget.

I'll forgive eventually. The speed might depend on how Dad handles things here on out.

I angle my head up at Kris. "Can you believe that's over?"

He shakes his head, smirking. "Not one single bit, actually. I'm waiting for him to bust back in here and change his mind."

"What do you mean?"

His face grows serious. "I mean, come in here and snatch you back to his house. Put you under lock and key, protected from the likes of me and all my dirty thoughts about his baby girl."

I chuckle as I move to straddle Kris's lap, wiggling a little extra to settle myself across those impressive thighs. His shirt hit the floor the second my dad walked out the door. Now the broken shield blazoned across his shoulder and the script lettering twining through the cross on his chest is on full display for my enjoyment.

Kris's eyes glaze, his calloused palms spreading the width of my thighs and slowly sliding upward, revealing more pale skin under the baggy boxers I forgot I was wearing until my shorts bunch high at the crease of my hip. I try not to let those circling thumbs distract me, but it's near impossible.

"I'm not going anywhere, Kris." He gives me a sad smile.

"Baby, do you know how long I've loved you from afar? How I've felt your pain? Every hurt, I hurt. Every tear, I wanted to go to battle." Kris stops, his eyes falling to my chest. It breaks my heart that we lost so much time when we both obviously cared all along.

"I'm not a good man, Abigail. Even if your dad agreed to let me out, I've still done things in my past I'm not proud of."

"*Shh!*" I drag my lips across his to quiet those thoughts, knowing Kris will never see himself the way I do. "Kris, I love you. I told you before, there's no getting rid of me." I swallow. "The past is done. We will figure out the rest... your job, where we'll live. It doesn't matter as long as we're together."

Shifting in his lap, I work myself closer to my tortured mate, letting his stiffness rub against my aching clit through the shorts. I can't deny the pull between us, even with this heavy conversation. It increases my urgency for Kris to understand so we can get to the happily ever after... and I hope that includes the satisfied ending his cock hints at below.

"There's not a thing in this world I wouldn't do for you," he says, working at the hem of his black shirt I'm wearing. His hands peel the fabric to expose more of my hips, and continue until his rough thumbs can trace the ticklish skin along my sides.

I smile, loving his hands roaming, driving me wild. Still, I have to tease my broody mate a little bit. "Pink tutu?" I lift one eyebrow and he snorts, spreading my grin wider. It's a happiness beyond anything I ever imagined.

I breathe the irresistible scent of my mate, circling his neck with an extra wiggle of my bottom against his straining erection, wanting to drive Kris as crazy as he makes me. It's near impossible considering I've got twenty-four years of pent-up hormones here.

I watch as Kris rolls through something in his head, that beautiful brain working while I wiggle in his lap. Eventually, he smooths his hands up the back of my shirt, pressing my chest forward against his until one hand grips the nape of my neck, locking me against his body to keep still.

Like I'd ever try to escape!

The knots in Kris's shoulders are gone. They sag the smallest amount as he spreads his thighs, sinking us deeper into the couch, our bodies lined up perfectly, chest to chest, hip to hip. The rough cotton of Kris's t-shirt teases my overly excited nipples and I moan, loving when Kris adjusts my head closer. His jaw sets with that cocksure doggedness I love as he dips to scrape his teeth along the tendon at my shoulder.

His nose strokes up the vein in my neck, inhaling.

"You know, I didn't fully believe it until you came home again." He pauses, sucking lightly at my exposed neck, making me tremble in the steady hold of his hands. "The moment I saw you again, I knew. You're mine now, Abigail." His voice vibrates against my skin, his tongue licking between each sentence until I'm a moaning mess in his lap.

Mark me! my dragon howls, pleading for her mate.

A fine sheen of sweat breaks out on my skin and I gasp, pulling away enough to rip Kris's t-shirt over my head and expose my burning skin to the cool air in his apartment. Kris's hands fly to my breasts, rewarding my braless nipples with the sweet plucking torture of his fingers.

My head falls back, my hips moving involuntarily as Kris dips to taste at my exposed skin. His mouth nips at the small outer curve of breast, circling his tongue everywhere but where I want it.

"Kris... *please!*" I pant, tugging his immovable head where I need relief.

He chuckles against my skin, kneading my breast as he lifts those sinful eyes to mine with a smirk. "What is it you want, baby? Tell me." His thumbs linger beside each stiff peak, slowly flicking back and forth, making me delirious with his sweet torture.

"Kris... you know what I want." I groan, swallowing down the nerves as my back arches involuntarily, seeking his hands, his mouth... something.

"*Tsk, tsk, tsk...* nuh, uh, baby. I wanna hear it."

My jaw drops, but with his next stroke across my nipple, I scream, "You, dammit! Kris, I want you! Please lick me." I gasp when his mouth falls before the sentence is out. He growls against my breast, sucking hard now as I writhe in his lap, dancing with deep, pulsing strokes along his rigid cock. That wicked tongue alternates between rapid flutters and deep sucking pulls, Kris's other hand mimicking each movement as I grind down on his length. I gasp at the sweet friction, my body flaming until my hips stutter.

I'm so close.

Our arousal taints the room, but I need more. I need Kris.

Grabbing the sides of his face, I maneuver Kris until I can taste his swollen lips, lingering there with our tongues curling against each other's in a passionate battle.

Gasping, Kris jerks back, the yellow gleam in his eyes lighting an inferno like a siren's call to my dragon. "I need you, Abigail," he says roughly, holding my hips in a death grip against his. "Are you sure?" he asks, eyes flashing a moment of vulnerability. "You're stuck with me after this."

I tilt my forehead, that sweetness making it impossible not to smother Kris's lips until he feels my heart. "Kristopher, take me to the bedroom. Now."

That bark of laughter is my favorite reward, but when Kris springs from the couch with me in his arms, I know I'm in for an even better one soon. He walks us to the bedroom, leaning forward to catch my ear between his lips with a sexy growl. "Woman, you better watch what you ask for." One large hand slaps my butt for emphasis, making me squeal even as Kris carries me through the dimly lit room. Even without the light, his eyes shine with joy, and I know they match mine.

With Kris's strength, I feel secure, trusting him to hold me and protect me wherever we go. When we reach the bed, he climbs on and tries to lower us carefully, but my thighs have a different idea. They squeeze his middle to bring his weight crashing into me with a startled grunt.

"Careful. I'm heavy, baby." Kris rests on his elbows with his weight hovering. His lips drop a soft kiss to my temple, almost bringing tears to my eyes. "Abigail, I don't want to hurt you. Go slow."

The last thing I need is slow. I need Kris close. *I need his passion.*

I stroke the side of his jaw, needing him to see me as the woman he can't resist, one that will drive him crazy, not as this fragile creature. I tilt my pelvis against his, hoping he takes the clue as I bite higher up his neck. "I can take it, Kris. I need you."

Kris moans. "God, I hope so, baby. Because you've got me strung so tight, this first time won't last long."

Chapter Thirty-Six

Abigail

A GRIN THREATENS TO split my face, and I reach down, sliding my hands into the back of Kris's shorts to feel the smooth slope of his butt. "Mmm, I've always loved your butt," I purr in his ear, loving his sharp intake of air. He flexes, tightening those firm muscles as he grinds against my center.

"Too many clothes," he says, sitting back on his knees. It breaks my grip, but the hand that he runs down the center of my body makes up for it. His fingertips curl under the waistband of my boxers, rubbing back and forth in a tease. "These look so sexy on you."

My smile widens and I'm about to say something cheesy about them looking better on the floor when Kris reads my mind and slides them down my legs. They fly over his shoulder, neither of us caring where they land.

Kris kneels up, his eyes raking down my nakedness spread beneath him. I'm wet, aching for his touch. "You are so beautiful," he whispers, kneading his hands up my thigh muscles, spreading my legs wider as one thumb parts my crease, releasing the thick scent of my excitement to the air.

I suck in a sharp breath when the cool air hits my middle, but it's Kris masculine purr that has me ready to beg. "Kris, please." I reach for his waistband, needing to touch him, to end this blissful torture.

He rubs the pool of wetness across my lips with a hum. "Baby, you're so ready for me."

I nod, a buzz of awareness tightening my stomach when his eyes meet mine. My dragon is just below the surface, bursting to get out. *"God, yes! Now!"* She's taken over my voice, but it gets me everything I've ever wanted when Kris jerks his own shorts down and tosses them to the floor.

He settles over me with his cock nestled against my core. "Is this what you want?" That arrogant smile makes me wetter. He knows what I want, the ass. I don't have time to respond though, because one of those massive hands curls under my head as he supports his weight on one elbow.

Our lips lock, battling with years of pent-up passion. Kris is everywhere, his masculine scent surrounds me, his stiffness rubs my core, coating himself with my wetness. I lift my hips, tilting with the rhythm he set, but urging Kris closer as electricity lights up every cell in my body with each stroke of those skilled hips.

"Kris... please." My voice shakes, matching the desire trembling through my body. I grip his head to steady myself as he trails a line of kisses to my ear, blanking out any thoughts except Kris's soft lips, those strong fingers stroking the hair from my face, the love and desire shining from his eyes.

I lean up, nibbling the rough edge of Kris's jawline while his hands strum my body like a fiddle. His thumb tweaks my nipple and I jump, digging my teeth into the tendon at his shoulder in a biting kiss. The sexiest moan rumbles under my lips before Kris tugs my head back, his eyes firing as he renews his attack on my lips, building a blinding tension in my core, begging to be satisfied.

That talented tongue distracts my mind from the inevitable until his cock nudges my entry. Kris tugs my legs higher on his waist, opening me, letting his tip tease my clit before sliding forward again. Each glide across my crease drives my desperation higher, makes my legs shake harder.

Kris comes up for air, his chest heaving as his forehead falls to mine. "You're so goddamn beautiful, Abi." That's my Kris. His hard sweetness draws me in and I smile, leaning up for another tender kiss that goes from zero to sixty like Kris pulled the pin and tossed a grenade. Only it's passion, and moans, and chaotic hands that explode between our writhing bodies.

I squeeze my legs around Kris's waist until he takes the hint and rears his beast of a body over me, curling me to his will. He aligns with my center, one hand gripping the fleshy part of my hip, bracing me. Kris's muscles strain to go slow, rippling as he sinks a few inches into my warmth. My breath catches at the intrusion, and he stops, those massive shoulders rigid with the effort to hold himself back.

Instinct locks my hands against those rock-hard abs, keeping his lower half at a controlled distance. Inch by inch he pulls back, until only the tip remains. "Do you want to stop, Abigail?"

My eyes widen. *How could he ask that?*

I suck in a shaky breath. "Don't you dare."

His offer goes against everything I've heard about men. It shouldn't surprise me with my dark knight, but his comfort takes my love to a whole new level. It relaxes my hands to give up control, letting them slide across the lower curve at his back to the taut muscle I've ogled for years. One I can finally touch.

His skin is amazing! How can part of him be so soft skin when the rest of him is so damn hard, so ripped?

Kris's eyes flare, either my words or my exploration convinces him to stop holding back. He dips until his lips trail my temple, my brows, murmuring sweet words against my skin until my body slowly relaxes, letting him in.

I groan, my head tossing back when he slides forward again, his thickness stretching me in the most delicious way. My nails dig into his shoulder, holding on as I writhe to get closer. The burn in my thighs from stretching around his thick middle only increases their shaking. Kris's eyes never leave mine like he's peering into my soul, reading my every reaction to the flex of his hips. His movements stay shallow while I adjust to his size, the muscle ticking in his jaw the only sign of strain in my mate.

"*God, Abi!* You're heaven." He grits his teeth, his fingers tightening in my hair as his tight rein on his control slips. The pain in my scalp is worth it. I dive back in, flicking Kris's lower lip with my tongue, need him to let go. His cock jerks in response, sliding deeper and I gasp, my inner muscles squeezing, sending another gush of arousal through the air. Kris groans into my mouth, pressing deeper still. "Abi. Are you okay?" He pulls back slightly, but I tighten my legs to stop that thought.

Get out of your head, Kris!

I want to scream the roof off, but I can't stop panting and my voice comes out choked. "Don't stop, Kris. Please. Don't stop." My dragon rears up, calling for her mate. Neither of us have patience and this speed is driving us wild. *Just do it!*

I'm about to say that when Kris bends, closing his eyes as he kisses along my jaw, trailing to my ear where he sighs. "I'm sorry, baby."

On the next push, he sheathes himself to the hilt and I scream, the sound catching in the back of my throat. My fingers dig into his back from the sting, from the pressure of being so full. I grip those powerful muscles like a lifeline, willing my body to relax.

Kris drops love bites down the length of my neck, to my shoulder, while his free hand caresses every inch he can reach. The sensation lights my body on fire, quickly washing away any discomfort and replacing it with toe curling pleasure.

Even Kris's hold on the back of my neck excites me. It keeps me still for his lips and fingers to explore. I do the same, running my fingers across the dips and valleys of Kris's shoulders, his chest. When Kris leans up to plump my breasts, my back arches, begging for more. My hands trail the narrow line of hair on his stomach, amazed by the silky texture that leads to where our bodies join.

I glance down, feeling my face turn ten shades of red. But Kris tweaks my nipple, jerking my eyes back to his smiling ones. Kris drops his head to suck one stiff peak in his mouth, leaving it wet and tingling in the cold air when he pulls away. He moves to the other one. "Don't be shy with me, little one."

My dragon purrs as he bites the curve of each breast, moving up to my neck. *Mark me!*

I tug on Kris's head, bringing his lips to mine for a slow, erotic dance. Our tongue swipe to tease, dip to taste, building a sensual tension that's going to explode. "Kris... move... please." I wiggle my bottom, biting back a groan from the fullness. My eyes roll back in my head as Kris pulls his hips back, dragging through my wetness with the same decadent pace as our kiss, like he enjoys every inch of our connection, too. His mouth stays locked to mine, trapping the sounds of our passion inside each kiss. My palms tickle against his short, buzzed hair, but I hold on for dear life, saving myself from the blinding emotion blowing up my heart.

A small tear leaks from the corner of my eye and Kris swipes it away, a deep V creasing his brow. I smile to let him know everything's perfect, I just can't hold back anymore. "I love you, Kris."

His face softens with a bright smile he so rarely uses, and he shifts, leaning on the elbow under my shoulders. His other arm curls my lower half, keeping me locked in a hug against his waist. "I love you, too, Abigail..." He drops his head to mine, keeping our eyes connected. "Always."

Kris begins the steady rhythm of sliding back and forth, drawing out his length with our bodies curled together, before pressing back in. Each motion pulls a moan from my lungs I can't hold back. Each push grows a little stronger, a little deeper, until he's moaning right along with me.

Our passion echoes through the room as we both relish in each other's bodies, the tempo increasing until every clap of skin to skin jolts my nerve endings. His pelvis grinds against my clit, amplifying the tight coil of pleasure settled in my lower stomach.

On instinct, my hips angle, meeting Kris stroke for stroke. He lets me use him however I need, rocking and sliding against his hard length until I can't move through the pleasure. My muscles lock, my back arching in Kris's confined space. A floating sensation takes over my body and I grip Kris's back, my fingers pressing divots into his skin as a dull roar deafens my ears. The room shines, sparkling like the brightest diamond, or like someone set off fireworks inside my mind.

I'm aware of Kris's eyes on me, vibrant... knowing.

My inner muscles squeeze and his eyes change, his mouth dropping open as his cock pulses. I know he's close. His head dips and the last thing I hear is his deep bass moaning my name before his teeth sink into the mating spot where the curve of shoulder meets my neck. A scream rips from my body as my eyes blur with an explosion of color, blinding me as our hearts link, and my body does the same.

He's ours.

Kris's mouth holds through the tide of pulses inside my core, groaning into my flesh when he finds his own release, his shaft throbbing as his warmth fills me up. My chest swells with intimacy, from taking everything my mate has to offer, from his love bite hanging on, sucking up every ounce of pleasure.

My vision returns by the time Kris lets go, though we're both panting, covered in a thin sheen of sweat. Distracted, my thumb strokes the vein in his neck, knowing I'll leave my mark there one day soon.

Kris's chest heaves as he captures my lips in a consuming kiss, carefully sliding his length from my warmth. I grimace, immediately missing the connection until his promise fills me in another way. "It's you and me, Abi, from here on out."

I grin. "Kris, nothing in this world would make me happier!" Our laughter rings to the ceiling, both taking the moment to study the other. The hard edges of Kris have softened, his stress lines smoothed into a man ten years younger. I wink. "Aren't you happy you finally gave in?"

Kris smirks, dropping a kiss to each of my temples. "Baby, I might be sorry fate dealt you shit cards, but there's nobody that could love you more than me. I'll take care of you, protect you..." He grins, sliding his still erect shaft through my wetness. "Protect our babies."

I chuckle, grabbing both sides of his head for another taste of my future. "Kris, *we* will protect each other. *We* will love each other. I hate to tell ya, big guy, but you're mine as much as I'm yours." My arms squeeze his neck. His contented smile completes a missing piece in my heart I didn't realize I lost. "So, what do you say we stop talking and start practicing for those babies?"

"Yes, ma'am." Kris's laughter rings through the room as he drops to capture my lips again. That's a sound I could hear for the rest of my life.

And I damn sure plan to.

The End

PLEASE CONSIDER LEAVING A REVIEW

See the other side...

SHATTERED ILLUSIONS: A BEAR SHIFTER PARANORMAL RO-
MANCE

Evelyn Amos left her Cherokee homeland desperate for independence. She had it... briefly. Until her crooked boss blows up her careful five-year plan, hiding secrets, and money laundering... mafia enforcers. There's only one safe place Evie can run. A place with no surprises... except one.

The last thing Evie needs is a sexy mountain man getting in the way. One whose magnetism overpowers her good sense. Whose stacked muscles and irresistible brown eyes torture her dreams. Whose love of animals matches her own. It doesn't matter if it's the worst time for love... Wyatt kick starts Evie's scared heart, and she's having a heck of a time denying the inevitable.

For Wyatt McAllister, future alpha of the Big Paw Shifters, his basic needs, and those of his bear, have taken a backseat to his responsibilities. He has no time for a mate, but when she shows up in the middle of his adventure tour, Wyatt is powerless to deny fate. She drives his bear crazy! Could a human accept his big secret? He needs to tell her, but Wyatt won't risk scaring her away.

Unfortunately, Evie's trouble hasn't forgotten her. Heartbroken and scared, she's in a fight for her life and all alone. Turns out, her secrets were a lot more dangerous than Wyatt's.

Good thing he won't let anyone hurt his mate. Wyatt's paws to the ground, fighting for his happily ever after, even if he needs to tear through the entire mountain to get it.

First in the *Big Paw Mountain Series* full of protective Alpha shifters, small-town life, and a slow burn of steamy chemistry to drive you crazy. *HEA, No cliffhanger, No cheating. Shattered Illusions* is the mirrored timeline of *Unleashed: Dixon's Dragon Mafia. Unleashed* goes behind the scenes of the crime organization and events in this novel.

Also By Annie

BIG PAW MOUNTAIN SERIES
Shattered Illusions: A Bear Shifter Paranormal
Romance
Beyond Expectations: A Bear Shifter +
Firefighter Paranormal Romance ⧅ Sign up for preview & get notified
on release day!

DIXON DRAGON MAFIA
Unleashed: Dixon's Dragon Mafia

WELCOME TO KISSING SPRINGS
Salty Santa – *Also, available in German.*
Sunshine & Sabotage– *Also, available in German.*
Bourbon Boss

FOLLOW ON **REAM STORIES!**

About the Author

Annie Rae

Annie is a wife and mom, living in Texas with her two amazing kiddos, dogs, bunnies, and the sexiest, suited, mountain-man a girl could dream to be her prince (beard included).

Weekends are for cheering on the kiddos in all their craziness and curling up with a steamy romance book and missing too much sleep because of it. The self-proclaimed sunflower would love nothing more than to be on a beach, writing her day away.

Annie loves escaping into great novels where you ride the ride and feel the emotions of great characters, laughing with them, crying with them, and missing them after "the end." It is a dream come true to be able to write about those protective heroes, fated love, and happy endings.

Follow Annie for more fabulous book boyfriends and playful laughs.

www.AuthorAnnieRae.com